FAKE NEWS

A NOVEL

TROY WILSON

DEFIANCE PRESS
& PUBLISHING

Dedicated to my late mother, who inspired my love of reading, learning and journalism.

ABOUT THE AUTHOR

TROY WILSON IS THE PEN NAME for a former journalist who spent more than thirty years working in television news.

He achieved many professional accomplishments over that time employed mostly as a manager of television newsrooms across the United States. He would tell you that his greatest accomplishment was the recruiting, training and mentoring of hundreds of talented journalists. His achievements in television news have not come from what he did himself but through the efforts of the teams he helped build and mentor.

Under his guidance the television newsrooms he supervised were recognized with hundreds of awards for excellence in journalism. They ranged from several regional Emmy Awards and AP awards for overall excellence in news broadcasting to award-winning investigative reporting, storytelling, breaking news, videography and more. Perhaps not coincidentally that award-winning journalism often also led to higher newscast ratings.

Troy has retired from the news business but remains a 'news junkie' of sorts. With dismay, he has watched the deterioration of electronic journalism when it comes to important issues of trust, balance, accuracy, ethics and fairness. 'Fake News' to him is more than a slogan meant to demean journalism today. It is becoming increasingly a reality in a media world where once high standards of good journalism have significantly eroded.

He believes you the news consumer not only deserve better, but that a functioning democracy depends on far better journalism than is practiced in the United States today.

Fake News, A Novel is a work of fiction. It speaks, however, to a new reality which surveys say has led to an historically high distrust of our news media. This book could not have been credibly written twenty-five years ago. Even as a work of fiction it is unfortunately very relevant today.

INTRO

TOMAS STEIN SAT IN A CHAIR in a dark room. Water had just been splashed on his face from a bucket and the cold liquid dripped from his hair down his cheeks, nose and chin. He was groggy. He knew instinctively that he had been drugged and while he had no idea where he was, Tomas was able to quickly surmise in his semi-conscious state what was to come next. He had been warned after all.

Three shadowy figures in a dark room stood around him. They were not wearing masks, but their large hoodies did enough to obscure their identities, not that he would likely be able to recognize them if the men had removed them. One of the men standing beside him pushed a cold revolver nuzzle against his temple.

Tomas's knees buckled in the chair. He wasn't crying, but his breath rapidly cut in and out uncontrollably as he anticipated what was to come next.

It's been said in moments like these that your life will flash before your eyes. For Tomas his mind conjured images of the past few years of his life. A series of momentous and unpredictable events which had brought the TV journalist national fame, professional praise and scorn, had thrown him unexpectedly into the center of a scandal, and now landed him in this chair with a gun pointed at his head.

In a strange sense he now realized that he was sitting on the precipice of becoming a deadly casualty of 'fake news'.

CHAPTER 1

TOMAS WAS SURPRISED THAT HE HAD landed his new job in Washington, DC in part because he had not been looking for one. The process had started as a seemingly random invitation to connect on a social media website frequented by journalists. The invitation came from someone who had recently looked at his profile. He read the online moniker and remembered seeing it somewhere else before, but could not place it.

He attempted to click on the profile of the person who invited him. It was as blank as it could be. No name. No photo. Only the initials RMM and the vague title 'business investor'. There was no work history and no other connections to anyone else. If this page had a purpose, then it wasn't for the standard self-promotion and exaggerated resume building that plagued most profiles on the website.

One week later, he received a phone call on a Saturday afternoon from a Philadelphia area code. Normally Tomas let numbers he didn't recognize go to voicemail, but he had a strange feeling that he should answer this call and so he did.

"Good morning Tom. May I call you Tom?" said a deep voice with a touch of a New England accent on the other end of the line.

"Sure. How can I help you?" Tomas answered.

"I'm sorry to bother you on a Saturday. I thought it would be better to talk when you were away from your TV station."

"And why is that?" Tomas, the inquisitive reporter asked inquisitively.

"I would like to talk to you about a possible reporter job for a client of mine. Have you given any thought to possibly making a move in your career?"

The conversation went silent for a moment. Of course Tomas had thought about looking for a job in a larger city with more money and more interesting news to cover. He loved living in Boise, Idaho, but it was a small market which didn't pay very well. At this point in his life he felt that he was ready for more.

"I guess it depends on the job, right?" Tomas responded cautiously. "Who is this anyway?"

"My name is Jerry Winston. I'm a consultant who works with some television stations nationwide and I help them recruit talent. One of my clients has an interest in interviewing you for a reporter/anchor position after seeing some of your work there in Idaho."

The terminology Winston was using seemed a bit odd to Tomas. Most industry insiders used the term 'anchor/reporter,' not the other way around. It indicated to him there may be something unique about this position and he wanted to know more about it.

"Which station?" he asked.

"WWDC-3 in Washington, DC," Winston replied.

Tomas let out a slight gasp. Instantly the pieces were starting to fall in place in his mind. *"The Industry Tonight,"* he blurted out.

Tomas could hear something akin to a knowing smile on the other end of the line. "Yes, Tom, *The Industry Tonight*."

WWDC Channel 3 was an independent TV station in Washington, DC which had been bought by a billionaire businessman back in the 1990s. Rumor had it that it was the wife of billionaire Joseph Midas (yes his name was Midas) who wanted him to make the purchase. Marjorie Midas had been a former business reporter for a cable network. The two met during an interview on the floor of the New York Stock Exchange. They would be married a year later, and she left her job to be with him full time when they moved to Washington, DC. She never lost her love for broadcast news and so her husband bought her a TV station right in their own backyard.

DC-3 would become known as Washington, DC's 'Non-stop News' station. As an 'independent' station it had no network programming to fill the airtime, and so it would bet its fate instead on round-the-clock news programming. That did not make it a great ratings success. The station often finished last in most every time slot and reports in trade publications indicated the Midas family lost money on the station every year. As business analysts used to say when it came to broadcasting, the family definitely did not have the 'Midas Touch'.

But *The Industry Tonight* was different. It was a political news program named for the fact that politics was Washington's main industry in much the way the film industry was to Los Angeles. Each night the program's focus was squarely on politics in the DC area, especially the federal government, complete with expert panels and news segments which played off the show's title such as "Industrial Spin," "Industrial Power" and one often humorous fan favorite called "Industrial Waste." The news set for *The Industry Tonight* even included virtual backgrounds which combined industrial images like steel being melted with political ones such as scenes from inside Congress and the White House.

The audience for *The Industry Tonight* was not large but it was influential. Presidents current and past reportedly all either tuned in from time to time or devoured its news content on the web. Members of Congress did too. But the brilliance of *The Industry Tonight* was that it covered DC in a way that was both broad-based and unique. Segments could range from changes to federal land policy to tax subsidies for bizarre museums nationwide.

Viewers tuned in because they learned something every night about the government for which they worked or served or lobbied or had to live with. It made DC-3 a haven for political news tipsters and the station often broke stories about the government as a result. It also made the program nationally renowned, especially in TV news circles.

Owner Marjorie Midas was known to be a politically liberal socialite and philanthropist who gave money generously to left-leaning causes. She was also respected as a fierce advocate that her station's news department maintain its objectivity even as other news channels and networks became more hyper-partisan. Many journalists considered the station a great place to land. Job openings were regularly met with thousands of applications.

Tomas Stein hadn't ever thought of applying there. Why would they hire him? The social media hit he had received two weeks earlier now popped back into his mind.

"RMM," he told Winston.

"Excuse me?"

"RMM. I was being checked out on a social media page by an RMM."

"That's actually Marjorie Midas. RMM stands for the Real Marjorie Midas. She uses the social network page as part of her research. She fashions herself as having an eye for talent. She told me that your work on 'Fast Cash in the Foothills' had caught her attention."

'Fast Cash in the Foothills' was an ongoing story about urban development that somehow had morphed into a political scandal and then a sex scandal. It had begun with a tip to Tomas from a City of Boise employee who had flagged some suspicious emails between two city council members. The more Tomas looked into it, the bigger the story seemed to get.

For decades conservationists had worked hard to protect the foothills overlooking Boise from what they saw as over-development. The foothills were a popular recreational area and also were home to many native animal and plant species. The sight of homes stacked on top of each other on the mountainside that made up Boise's backdrop was not just environmentally harmful but just plain ugly to them. Limiting development would help keep the city looking beautiful while preserving important environmental areas.

Some politicians who were friendly with developers disagreed. As the city grew Boise was getting hemmed in. Other surrounding communities were allowing foothills development so why not Boise too? This was especially true as people from cities like Los Angeles, San Francisco and Seattle moved to Boise with bank accounts flush with cash from homes they had just sold. Houses in Boise would cost them a fraction of what they sold their houses for in California, Arizona, Washington and Oregon. Many craved a beautiful view in the foothills high over what was called the Treasure Valley and they had the money to buy it if they could find it.

Tomas discovered that one developer had found a work-around to the city's restrictive foothills development ordinances. He then reached out to two particular city council members to help him exploit it. Both of them agreed to help him knowing full well the developer would fill their campaign coffers with lots of cash. It was well known that one of the council members had her eye on statewide office next election. Befriending a wealthy campaign contributor would only help her in that effort.

The more Tomas dug for information the stranger the story got. It turned out the other city council member involved had been questioned by police in front of the female council member's house after they spotted him hiding in a rental car there. There were rumors the two, who were both married, were having an extramarital affair.

As Tomas aired more reports, more tips came in that the developer had also paid off other city officials to keep his applications for permits and other foothills dealings quiet and away from other city council members and the mayor. By the time of Winston's call there was a full-fledged state and federal investigation underway all because of a series of news reports Tomas had begun airing months earlier. And it just kept going. More reports led to more tips, which led to more reports, which led to even more tips. It was a virtuous news cycle that even got the attention of a socialite TV station owner in Washington, DC.

"I'm interested," Tomas blurted out to Winston without really knowing much about the job itself.

Winston thought it would be wise to fill in some of the blanks first. "You know the newscast. It's mostly reporting. There would be some anchoring as well. The money is good but you should also know that living in DC is expensive. I will tell you Tom that lots of people want this job. You are one of the few where this job wants you."

"I'm interested," Tomas repeated.

Things happened fast from there. In four weeks' time he would be starting as a news correspondent working on the news program *The Industry Tonight*. At just twenty-eight years of age he would be doing something other far more experienced reporters could only dream about.

And right away he would break a big story in Washington, DC with an odd Boise connection.

CHAPTER 2

THE THIRD DAY ON THE JOB AT DC-3 for Tomas was Christmas Day. He would joke that the real reason they had hired him was because they needed more Jews like him to work religious holidays. He was happy to help out even though he felt like a small fish learning to navigate a very large pond.

His assignment that day was to cover a couple of candidates running for president who were doing the standard photo op of helping out at a local soup kitchen. Most politicians had gone home for the holidays but two of the presidential candidates, one Democrat and one Republican, had come to DC. It was a critical time for them. The Iowa caucuses were just weeks away followed by the New Hampshire primary. There wasn't much going on in Des Moines or Manchester on Christmas Day but candidates could still discuss political strategy with their DC based campaign staffs, then get in a decent photo op on a day when even the national networks were desperate for news content of any kind.

Tomas was thinking about how he would frame his holiday political story as he headed out to their first assignment. Just then his videographer partner's phone rang. It was the station's news assignment desk. They needed to divert to a 'spot news' scene.

Tomas took the job at DC-3 thinking he would mostly work alone and have to shoot his own video. Some old timers called it being a 'one-man band' versus the traditional reporter and videographer setup. The actual job title was Multi-media Journalist or MMJ.

Today Tomas was assigned a videographer however. A guy everyone called Al who was Muslim and who, like Tomas, worked Christian holidays for the double-time pay. Tomas was pretty sure Al was not his real name but they hadn't been in the car long enough for small talk and so he didn't get the chance to ask his real name.

"Okay, we're on it," Al responded and hung up the phone as he sped up the car. "Some Christmas Day polar plungers found a car in the Potomac. They're fishing it out now."

"Is that a big story here?" Tomas asked.

"It is on Christmas Day!" Al responded with a wry smile.

Al knew exactly where to go. He didn't even ask Tomas to plug any addresses into his phone for mapping help. He was driving fast. Videographers instinctively know that every minute away from a spot news scene is one more opportunity to miss a 'money shot'. They all learned to drive just fast enough to keep from getting pulled over. Traffic was light on Christmas and they were on the scene by the banks of the Potomac River within 20 minutes.

Al and Tomas arrived to find several police cars and dive team vehicles parked by the side of the river. Divers were already in the water attempting to attach steel cable to the vehicle so they could winch it out of the water. Tomas noticed something else. "There's a body in that car," he told Al.

"How do you know?"

"The Coroner's Office is out here," Tomas observed.

Al pulled out his camera and tripod and the pair attempted to move closer to the water. Police hadn't taped off any of the area yet with crime scene tape and made no real effort to stop them. Al began shooting video as Tomas snapped a couple of pictures using his cell phone to send back to the station to be posted on DC-3's website. He then walked around the scene to see what he could find out.

A small group of people were huddled by one of the dive team trucks. They were talking to each other, looking out onto the water and pointing. It was obvious to Tomas that these people were the 'polar plungers' just by seeing how they were dressed. "Hey, any of you here see what happened?" Tomas yelled over at them.

"We're the ones who found the car man," said a large, heavyset man wearing a thick jacket over an obviously wet bathing suit.

"My name is Tom Stein with *DC-3 News*. Can I interview you?" Tomas always went by Tom when trying to get interviews. He thought Tomas was too formal sounding. Besides, Tom was also the name he used on-air and so that's what most everyone except his family called him.

"Sure man. I'm the guy who called your station."

Tomas stopped for a second and then looked around. He realized there were no other media to be seen anywhere. Tomas and Al were the only news media there because the station had gotten a news tip from an obvious DC-3 fan.

"Thank you for that," Tomas replied as he reached into his pocket for his wireless earbuds. He didn't want to take Al away from the scene and so he would just shoot the interview on his smartphone. It was a common practice in Boise but he wasn't sure if it was done much in DC. For all he knew he was violating the station's labor union contract rules. He figured he was so new that he could ask for forgiveness later.

The heavyset man put the earbuds in his ears as Tomas held the cell phone horizontally to mimic what viewers would see on a flat screen TV. "Please don't look straight into the phone," Tomas asked. He hated it when people he interviewed with his phone looked straight into it. "Look at my left eye, okay?"

"Sure thing man," came the reply.

"Okay, say your name and spell it for me."

"My name is Carl Brookington. C-a-r-l .. B-r-o-o-k-i-n-g-t-o-n," he spelled out for Tomas.

"And can I call you a 'polar plunger'?"

"Yeah. We're with a local Kiwanis group. We do this for charity every Christmas."

"Okay, Kiwanis Polar Plunger then."

"That'll work," came Carl's reply.

"Tell me what happened?" Tomas asked while checking his cell phone for the framing of his interviewee.

"We were just diving into the water and some friends of mine and me make a bet every year who can swim out the farthest in the cold water. I was wearing this diving mask when I looked down and saw what looked like a car."

"Why were you wearing a diving mask?"

"I don't like getting cold water in my eyes. I wear one every year. Especially this year since we were diving from a new spot."

"This isn't your usual spot?"

"No man," Carl replied. "We had to change locations because of the drought."

Washington, DC had seen a severe drought that summer and fall. People told Tomas they could not recall ever seeing the Potomac water levels lower than they were now. It was pure luck that the polar plungers found a car. Tomas realized it may have been in the river for some time.

"So what did you see out there?"

"No much really," Carl replied. "But it was definitely a car. We called police right away."

"I noticed the Coroner is out here. Did you see any signs of a body?"

"No. He didn't show up until after the divers went out there. I'm guessing they found something inside," Carl said motioning toward where two or three divers were in the water.

"Describe the car. Sedan, minivan, SUV?"

"Definitely a car. A big car. I'm guessing a four-door. Seemed like it might be an older car from what I could see just from the shape of it and,

I dunno, seemed like it had been down there a while."

"So have police taken your statements?"

"Not yet. They want us to go to the station later this week, it being Christmas and all."

"Definitely not what you expect to find on Christmas Day, huh?"

"No, I guess not. I'm just sorry to learn there may be someone in there. That person's got family somewhere. Not the kind of news you want to learn on Christmas Day man."

"And what time again did you spot the car?"

Carl looked around at his friends. "It had to have been around nine this morning, right guys?" The other members of the group nodded. "Yeah, around nine," a woman in the group agreed vocally.

Then a taller man in the back interrupted. "Hey, they're pulling the car out!"

Tomas turned around. The rear of the vehicle was emerging. Tomas rushed over toward Al and took some more video on his smartphone. The car was clearly older and looked like it had been in the water for some time. The license plate was rusted, its edges ragged from the river's abuse. As the car emerged Tomas could make out the raised lettering of a license plate. He zoomed in with his smartphone on the plate to get a photo and also to see if he could make it out. It was almost like he was trying to solve a *Wheel of Fortune* puzzle because it was clearly a personalized license plate with some sort of odd message.

Tomas could make out the first letter M. There appeared to be seven letters in all, the last three spelling out the word MAN. "M ... is that an O?" he asked Al who was viewing the whole scene through his viewfinder screen.

"That or a zero," he replied.

"MO-MAN," Tomas blurted out. And then, like a thunderbolt, the message on the personalized license plate hit him. "Oh My God!"

"What's wrong?" Al asked him looking up briefly from his viewfinder.

"Oh My God, I think I know whose car that is!" Tomas turned away from the scene for a moment staring at the image on his cell phone. "Oh My God, Oh My God!" Tomas then held the phone up to his mouth to make a call. "Call Prudence Young." He put the phone up to his ear hoping the woman would pick up. She did.

"Hello?"

"Ms. Young. I'm so sorry to bother you on Christmas Day but this couldn't wait. This is Tom Stein the TV reporter. Do you remember me?"

"Of course Tom. How are you?"

"I'm good. Look, the reason I'm calling on Christmas—I just felt it couldn't wait."

"Wait for what Tom?"

"Ms. Young, I think they just found your son's car."

"Where? In Boise?"

"No. I work in Washington, DC now and I'm at a search and rescue scene by the Potomac River and a car with your son's license plate on it was just found in the river."

Prudence Young's gasp was audible. She had been waiting to hear that news for such a very long time.

CHAPTER 3

TOMAS STEIN'S MIND FLASHED BACK to a fateful day more than a year ago although he remembered it as if it had been that morning. He was working on a bright fall Sunday and was excited for the day that lay ahead. He was scheduled to be the fill-in anchor for the evening newscasts that night. 6 p.m. and 10 p.m. Mountain Daylight Time. One day Tomas had hoped to take on anchoring on a full-time basis so these occasional opportunities to fill-in anchor were quite valuable to him as a way to expand his TV news skill set.

He had come in a little early that day because he had been assigned to pick up a quick news story shoot before settling in to anchor that night's newscasts. It was assigned as a VO/SOT, short for video and sound over tape. It was typically a 35- to 40-second news blurb somewhere in the middle of the newscast. More filler news material than a "Top Story."

He was assigned to go to an event outside of Boise's main Mormon Temple. A family which had been longtime members and benefactors of the church had asked the media to attend a news conference. It was a typical Sunday ploy to get some media attention. Hold an event in which there wasn't much real media interest but that news crews would attend anyway because they needed the content for their local Sunday night newscasts. Those events were normally pretty thin when it came to actual news content.

When he arrived at the Temple, however, Tomas could see that this news event was different. Four large posters on easels displayed a man's face. A lectern had been brought out so the news crews would have a place to put microphones while they videotaped whoever was speaking. Tomas had glanced at the short press release before he had left. The topic was about some guy who had gone missing many years earlier. What he was now witnessing was looking like an event which was being staged by a public relations professional of some sort. It was not at all what he had anticipated.

Tomas pulled out a microphone and a small mic stand and placed it on the podium. He then set up his tripod, put his small camera on it and began shooting video of the posters.

All the local TV stations were there. Each had sent single person crews with almost identical tripods and camera gear. Tomas knew all the journalists who had assembled there but he was the last one to arrive and so there wasn't any time for the typical pre-news conference small talk with his rivals.

A group of people emerged from the front door of the Temple and headed to the podium. The group was made up of three young men and one older woman, all well dressed in their Sunday best. One of the men surveyed the scene and stepped up to the podium.

"Are you all ready to go?" he asked the two young newsmen and one young newswoman. They were.

"Okay then, let's get started. My name is John Dowd. I work for a local public relations firm, am a member of a local Mormon church, and am here helping the Young family organize this event. I am not here to speak today but should you all need any additional resources or help, I will give you my card after the news conference. Feel free to call me at any time."

Dowd then cleared his throat for a moment.

"Joining us today is Prudence Young and her two sons, Jeremiah and

Ethan. Her third son, Jason, could not be with us today because he has been missing and presumed deceased for nearly twenty-five years. The photos you see around us are family pictures of him. The family is coming forward today because of a special request by the man's father who also could not join us today. Ms. Young."

Dowd gestured toward the older lady to approach the podium. Her light gray hair was pulled back into a bun. Her mouth was barely visible over the microphones with attached mic flags identifying each station. She pulled out a piece of paper from which to read. Tomas sighed. *Nobody does well on television reading off of a piece of paper.*

"My husband Edward cannot be with us today because, because …" She began to choke up. One of her sons stepped forward and put his hand on her shoulder as if to steady her.

"My husband cannot be here today because he is dying from cancer." The word cancer was read with a heart-breaking crack of emotion in her voice, but Prudence kept reading. " My sons and I are here today in hope of fulfilling his last dying wish." Her words were slow and methodical, but every word also clearly came from the heart even though she was reading from a piece of paper. Tomas could tell this whole media event was very difficult for her as she seemed determined to press on.

"For nearly twenty-five years we have lived every day with the pain of not knowing what happened to our beloved son Jason. We did everything we knew how to do to find him. We prayed that one day we would see him again alive. As hope for that faded we prayed for the chance for closure. To bring him home. To let him rest in peace."

Prudence Young was still reading from the piece of paper but her prepared remarks revealed tremendous emotional pain. Tomas could not tell for sure but he thought she might be crying.

"Today I am asking for the public's help in making a dying man's wish come true. I'm asking that anyone with information on the disappearance of our son Jason Young come forward." She looked up from her written remarks for a second to look up and give a stern, emotion-filled ad lib. "Please, tell us what happened to our son!"

Prudence Young then returned to her prepared remarks. "We have no illusions that our son is still alive. We know he is looking down upon us today from heaven as one of God's blessed souls. And we know he wants his father to know what happened to him on this earth before he joins him in heaven. It's been nearly twenty-five years. Whoever out there knows what happened, do not take this secret to your grave. Make your peace with God and do the right thing so that a man's father may leave this earth without the pain he's carried with him for so many years not knowing what happened to his son. Thank you!"

Tomas almost wanted to applaud. It was the most compelling scripted news conference speech he had ever seen or heard. He also realized he had no idea what this woman was talking about. It would seem he was in diapers when this all went down after all.

Prudence Young stepped back and John Dowd walked up to the podium. "Thank you Mrs. Young. I realize that some of you may not even have been born yet when Jason disappeared. I've prepared a packet for each of you with information and I'm also here to take any questions you may have. As you can see it is a difficult topic for the family even after all these years."

"I will take your questions too," Prudence Young said from behind him.

"Yes, Mrs. Young will take your questions too," Dowd confirmed. "She's never spoken publicly about this before and so we wanted to make this as easy on her as possible. Before we take questions though I wanted to show you some other things which you might find helpful for your story. Did you all get video of the posters?" Everyone had. Dowd then walked over to one of the easels and pulled a poster down revealing another behind it. He then removed another and another on the remaining easels revealing four new posters. Tomas marveled at the setup. This guy really knew he stuff. Dowd then walked back to the podium.

"On your far left. No, actually on my far left you'll see a photo of the front of Jason Young's white Chevy Impala with the personalized Virginia license plate 'More-man'. Jason was a devoted member of the LDS church and the plate was a play on words to display that."

"The next poster is a rear photo of the same vehicle with the same license plate. Again, Jason was very devoted and sent these pictures of his new personalized plates to one of his brothers before he disappeared. On your right, ah I mean *my* right we have an artist's rendering of what Jason might look like today were he alive. As Mrs. Young told you we have no illusions that he is alive today, but if he were alive we believe he would look something like this."

It was an odd thing to have a rendering done of a man likely dead for decades and then to include it in a news conference. Tomas surmised that someone in the family had demanded the rendering be included just in case Jason was still alive.

"And over on the end," Dowd concluded. "Something important. Jason always wore a locket around his neck. When he left for Washington, DC to pursue his dream career in government service his mother gave it to him to help protect him. Inside the locket there are two pictures. One is of Brigham Young of whom the Young family is a descendant, and the other is of Our Lord and Savior Jesus Christ. It's a very unique piece of jewelry which if found could hold a clue to Jason Young's disappearance."

Tomas hurriedly got shots of each poster. Another reporter asked a question. "I'm sorry. I'm somewhat new here and not familiar with what happened. Could you give us some background on Jason's disappearance?"

"Sure," Dowd replied. "Jason Young was working as a staffer in a Congressional office in Washington, DC at the time of his disappearance. The family doesn't like to talk about it but he had become embroiled in a bit of a scandal. His wife had filed for divorce after alleging Jason was having an affair with his boss. The family admits that Jason was despondent when he disappeared but does not believe he would have committed suicide."

"He did not commit suicide!" Prudence Young yelled from behind Dowd.

"I'm sorry Ms. Young; what did you say?" Tomas replied. He had heard her the first time but needed a moment to train his camera on her as she said it again. "My son Jason—he would not have committed suicide!" she said even more defiantly this time than the first.

"Mr. Dowd," the female reporter asked, "you said Jason Young had an affair with his boss. Who was his boss?"

Dowd looked stunned for a second as if to ask her with his eyes *You seriously do not know the answer to that question?* He looked around for a moment to see if anyone else was as shocked by the question as he was. He then produced a brief smile and said, "Well I do suppose there was a sex scandal involving the President of the United States at the same time, so I can see why this story may have not gotten more attention. Um. His boss was Marilyn Taylor-Brown."

"Wait," Stein interjected. "Representative Marilyn Taylor-Brown! One of the most powerful women in Congress. That Marilyn Taylor-Brown?"

Dowd nodded. Tomas was dumbfounded. How did he not know about this scandal?

But Dowd was correct. It was a huge story inside the Washington Beltway at the time and also big news in Boise. But the rest of the country was transfixed on a different sex scandal involving the most powerful man in the world and an intern and a blue dress. Back then Rep. Marilyn Taylor was a freshman Congresswoman from a somewhat obscure suburban district in Minnesota, and so media interest in her was not all that great.

After Young's disappearance the Congresswoman resigned her seat and left the Washington press corps behind for her family's large ranch in Minnesota. The story pretty much died after that. It wasn't as if there was no interest at all in the story by the news media after Jason Young had disappeared. It was that no journalist could really get to her and there were other stories to cover.

More than a year later Marilyn Taylor would reappear on the political scene after the death of the man appointed to fill her vacant seat until the next election. He died unexpectedly of an accidental prescription drug overdose. She publicly apologized to her constituents and to the Young family. She said that she and Jason were new to Washington; she was lonely; his marriage was on the rocks and they had found comfort in being together. She conceded that it was a terrible mistake and Jason's presumed suicide would be a burden she would carry for the rest of her life because she truly had deep feelings for him.

Voters would give her a second chance. And then a third and then a fourth. They would re-elect her again and again. Whatever happened to Jason Young—it never really stuck to Rep. Taylor. No one believed for a minute that a woman like her who was so respected, kind, thoughtful and generous could have anything to do with Jason's death.

She would add *Brown* to her name a few years later when she married a political consultant. Once again though love was not kind to her. Her husband was killed when two men tried to carjack his sports car. He had also become immersed in a controversy at the time because he had been implicated in a scheme involving illegal ballot harvesting for another prominent Democrat with whom he did business. The rumor after his death was that in order to save his own skin he had become an informant for the FBI. Marilyn Taylor-Brown kept her late husband's name but remained single from the time of his death to the present day.

As the news conference continued Tomas began to flip through the folder Dowd had handed out. It was an incredible story to fly so far under the radar for so long. Power, sex, mystery, death. He felt that it needed more attention than he could give to it at that moment because he still had to rush back to the station, put his VO/SOT together and then get ready to anchor the news. But Tomas wanted to do something more because of the emotion he could physically feel coming from Prudence Young.

Later that night after he anchored the 6 p.m. news with a lead story about the news conference he decided to upload it to the national news video services. His newsroom used a few news services, all of which in one way or another fed stories to the major news networks, news cable stations, and pretty much every TV station in the nation with a news department.

Normally a producer with one of the services would call to get video of a story after seeing it on the station's website. No one called for this story but Tomas had been around long enough to know how to sell it. His headline for the news service script read, "Family of former lover of powerful Congresswoman seeks answers in his disappearance." On the Monday morning after a slow news Sunday he thought it would definitely capture the attention of at least a few news producers around the country.

Tomas was off on Monday and tired from a late night in the newsroom but he was still up early enough to catch the morning network news. As he watched while making breakfast in his small apartment he heard one of the anchors read a story. "The family of a former lover of a powerful Congresswoman is seeking answers in his disappearance this morning."

Tomas couldn't believe it. Not only had the network decided to run the story but they used his headline practically verbatim. "Crazy!" he said to himself out loud.

And they weren't the only ones. Similar versions of the story ran across the country. One reporter even managed to track down the Congresswoman herself in her home district in Minnesota for reaction which would run that night on TV stations across the country. She replied that she still thinks about Jason today and wonders what happened to him. She then apologized again for any grief she had caused the Young family.

A couple of weeks later one of Jason Young's brothers who had been at the news conference gave him a call at the TV station. His father had passed away and his mother wanted Tomas to attend the funeral—not as a journalist but personally at her request. It was a baffling offer. "You're inviting a Jewish kid to a Mormon funeral?"

"Well, I didn't know that you were Jewish, not that it really matters, but yes, my mother was hoping you would honor her with your presence."

Tomas really did not want to go. He would be the one stranger in a church packed with the Young's family and extended religious family. It would be uncomfortable for him and maybe even for a few of them. He didn't know how he could really say "no" to Prudence Young the grieving widow either. Tomas agreed to go.

The funeral was surreal to him. As he expected Tomas didn't know anyone and when asked why he was there all he could think to say was that he was invited by the family. What more could he say?

Prudence Young would be the second family member to speak after an introduction of sorts by one of her sons. She was elegant in a very modest way, her gray hair pinned up for the occasion in black lace to match the black dress of a woman who was truly in mourning. Her son introduced her as the family "rock" who was not only a loving wife and mother but a staple of the church. "The strongest woman I know," he told the congregation in his introduction, "my mother Prudence Young."

Prudence walked up to the lectern and placed her notes beneath the microphone. "Thank you all for being here. I don't think Edward ever appreciated just how much he was loved by all of you. I have much to tell you about him, our love, and our loss today, but first I have to get something off my chest. There is one special person I've invited today who I would like to personally thank and ask you all to thank as well"

She then peeked out into the audience assembled inside the church. "Tom, Tom Stein, are you out there?"

A sense of panic gripped the chest of Tomas. *What in the world is happening?* he thought silently to himself.

"Tom. Tom! Would you stand up please?"

Tomas could feel the heat building in his face. He wondered if his cheeks looked as red as they felt because at the moment they felt like they were absolutely on fire. He nervously rose slowly from the pew.

Prudence Young continued as Tomas staggered to his feet. "I am about to tell you a story that I have told no one until now. A few weeks ago Edward and I were sitting quietly in his room watching a popular national morning news program when a report came on about my son Jason, who has been missing for twenty-five years. Maybe some of you saw it." Prudence paused as many in the audience murmured in recognition and nodded their heads that they had.

"The story was about a news conference my sons and I had held asking for information to fulfill a father's dying wish to know what had happened to his son." As uncomfortable as Prudence Young had seemed at the news conference she seemed quite at home here even while in mourning. This was her church family after all in a sanctuary filled with friends. She was grieving but was surrounded by love. Her voice was naturally high-pitched but it was also confident. Here in this church she felt supported and protected.

But then her voice began to crack with a hint of emotion. "And I can tell you that seeing a story about his missing son on the network news brought a light to Edward's eye and joy to his face that I had not seen in some time. Seeing that story made him realize that people still cared and that maybe Jason's disappearance would be solved one day. It might not be solved in his lifetime, but we prayed together for answers and that with God's help those answers would come, at least before me and his sons joined Edward and Jason in Heaven."

Prudence was full-on crying now but the words still seemed to flow easily from her mouth as she was determined to finish her story. "So do you know what I did Tom? I got on the phone and called one of the news networks in New York."

"You did what?" Tomas interjected. He didn't mean to say a word. It was as if something or somebody else was in control of his body now. He was just along for the ride.

"I did! I did called them!" Prudence responded somehow managing to chuckle and cry at the same time. The congregation responded with a mild laugh as well. "And I got ahold of a network news producer who told me the story had come from your station and that you were the one who had posted it on a news feed!"

Prudence was both beaming and sobbing at the same time. Tears of joy and sorrow somehow gathered together on the very same face. "And I cannot tell you what that meant to Edward in his final days. A sorrow which had been hanging over him for decades was lifted and in its place was hope and it was a feeling that would stay with him until his very last breath."

Tomas was numb. He like the others in the room was hearing all this for the very first time. He tried to do a body check. Eyes were very tearful. Cheeks were flaming hot. Chest was extremely tight. Hands were shaking uncontrollably. Legs felt loose and wobbly. He looked out toward Prudence but couldn't really see anyone at all. He only knew that every eye in the room was focused intensely on him and it was overwhelming.

Prudence continued, "And so that's why I wanted to publicly thank you for what you had done. Edward wanted me to thank you too. It may have been a little thing to you but it meant so much to him and me. Thank you Tom!"

The room erupted with applause, and some in the crowd began to stand. Others joined in until the entire congregation was in a full-blown standing ovation for what felt like hours to Tomas even if it was only for a half minute or so. Tomas was quietly, softly sobbing now. At one point he thought he was able to raise a hand to acknowledge the crowd. He was pretty sure he mouthed the words "Thank You" in response. It was all a blur.

When the episode finally, mercifully ended and Prudence continued with her eulogy, Tomas was able to somehow sit back down on the church pew. An older man next to him gave a gentle fist bump on his shoulder as Tomas tried to collect himself. The whole thing was just a big surprise.

After the funeral Tomas tried to make his way to Prudence but an onslaught of admirers kept stopping him to shake *his* hand. When he finally made it to her, he discovered that he had no words for her. A smile came to his face. "You could have just called me to tell me you know," Tomas blurted out in an emotionally cracked voice.

She responded with a sort of sob-smile of her own, and with tears in her eyes moved to give him a tight hug. "I wanted these people to know what you had done," Prudence whispered in his ear before relinquishing her grip. "And Tom, if they ever do find Jason, you call me. I will only interview with you!"

Tomas nodded, his Adam's apple feeling as if it had quadrupled in size. "I don't have your number," he replied meekly while making a vain attempt to smile.

Prudence reached her hand out. "Give me your phone." Tomas pulled the smartphone out of his pocket and found that he was so full of emotion that his face would not unlock it. He dialed in his security code and handed it to her.

For a woman in her late 70s, Prudence Young sure knew how to make quick work of a smartphone. In seconds she had put all her contact information on it.

One of her sons came up to Tomas and Prudence and then reached out to shake his hand. "Thank you buddy." He then turned to his mother as if to escort her away. Prudence hugged Tomas one more time and then turned away. He was sure at the time that he would never see her again. He also doubted he would ever be able make that call because Jason had been gone for so long. *Dead bodies do not just show up decades later* he thought.

Now eighteen months later it appeared that Tomas was wrong. Standing on the cold bank of the Potomac River, not even 50 yards from what would appear to be Jason Young's final resting place, the first call he made was to Prudence Young.

CHAPTER 4

THE PHONE CONVERSATION WITH PRUDENCE YOUNG was short. Tomas didn't know much. He promised to call her later when he had time and had learned more. He could tell by the sound of her voice that she was anxious, but she also expressed her gratitude that Tomas would call her to let her know—even on Christmas Day.

Once he got off the phone he began to work on texting a script to the assignment desk to be put on the station's website. They had already put out a cell phone push text alert about the news of the car found in the river and Tomas suspected other news crews would be joining them at the scene soon.

Police had managed to finally get the car out of the river and winched it up to the back of a flatbed tow truck. They were in the process of placing a tarp over it when the second news crew arrived. Soon there was a third and then a fourth. By then police had put up crime scene tape blocking all access to the car on the flatbed trailer.

Al had taken a ton of video—far more than he probably needed—as the other news crews shot away trying to play catch up to the *DC-3 News* crew. Al grabbed Tomas by the shoulder and pointed toward a group of police officers. "You see that man in the blue jacket?" Al pointed out.

"They're all wearing blue jackets," Tomas replied.

"I mean the blue blazer." Sure enough among the officers there was a man wearing a suit and tie. "That's Lt. Manuel Alvarez. He's one of the top PIOs for the DC Metro Police."

PIO stood for Public Information Officer. Lt. Alvarez was a liaison between the public and the police, and his primary responsibility was providing information on police investigations to the news media. Alvarez was standing with a group of officers near the car when one of them wearing gloves appeared to place a piece of jewelry in a plastic bag. *The locket* Tomas thought to himself.

After a few minutes Alvarez walked toward the news crews encamped safely behind the crime scene tape. He would be the one giving them their media briefing. "Hey guys. Is everyone here?" Alvarez looked around at the camera lens all pointed right at him.

"I don't see Channel 4," one of the reporters answered.

"Their loss," Alvarez responded. "Because after this I'm going home to enjoy the rest of my Christmas Day."

Al and some other news videographers converged on Alvarez to attach wireless microphones to his blazer and tie. In half a minute he had four mics on his body and was looking for any pocket where he could place the wireless transmitter boxes to which each microphone was attached.

"Testing 1-2-3. Testing 1-2-3. You got me?" All nodded that they did.

"You all know who I am and so I'll spare the formalities. At approximately 9:30 this morning a group of individuals participating in an annual Christmas Day polar plunge called the police. They had spotted a vehicle in the water. The metro DC fire department and rescue team were called to the scene and upon further investigation determined the car had been in the Potomac River for some time and there was no need for any water rescue. An on-call dive team was dispatched and was able to get the vehicle out of the river. You can see it over there under a tarp. I can tell you that there does appear to be human remains in the car but no actual body. There is also a great deal of silt in the vehicle and so it will be transported to the DC Crime Lab for further analysis. At this point we have no indication of foul play but the car had clearly been in the water for quite some time and so further investigation will be needed. We'll also obviously follow up on what human remains we found to see if this was a fatal event. I will now take your questions."

Tomas faced a dilemma. He didn't want to let his competitors on to what he knew, at least not yet. All the other news reporters there thought this was likely just a random car in the water that was the result of an accident or maybe even a suicide attempt. He didn't want to give them any reason to think it was more than that.

"What type of car is it?" a reporter asked.

"The vehicle appears to be an older model Chevy Impala."

"How long was it in the water?" he followed up.

"Quite some time. We're likely talking at least a few years. The crime lab may be able to better pinpoint how long but we're a ways away from that."

"Did the car have any identifying features like a license plate?" another reporter asked.

Uh-oh Tomas thought to himself. This could give it away.

"The front license plate was not recovered. The rear license plate appeared to be a vanity plate but it deteriorated some while in the water. We are going to take it to the crime lab for positive identification."

Technically what Lt. Alvarez was saying was true. Tomas wasn't able to make out the 'R' or the 'E' on the MORE-MAN vanity plate either, but it seemed like an odd omission by the lieutenant. Police certainly had to have some idea of what they had. He decided to test his luck.

"Any identifying objects found near the human remains?" Tomas asked.

"There were some fragments of clothing and personal items but no wallet or ID if that's what you're referring to."

"I was also wondering if you found any jewelry. Like a ring or a locket?"

Alvarez appeared to freeze for a second while looking straight at Tomas. It was one of those 'How-the-hell-did-you-know-that?' looks. The wheels were clearly turning in the lieutenant's head while he thought through his answer so as not to give too much away. "There was some personal jewelry found at the scene but I'm not prepared to go into details yet about just what was found. It too will be processed at the crime lab and we may have more for you after that."

The news conference lasted for about another 5 minutes. Whatever Lt. Alvarez did know he was not prepared to reveal and in a short time the reporters ran out of questions that he wouldn't answer anyway. As the camera crews were breaking down and heading back to their news cars Alvarez walked over to Tomas and Al.

"Channel 3. Over here," he motioned.

Tomas didn't know what he wanted and Al had a perplexed look on his face as well, but they followed Lt. Alvarez over to the edge of the crime scene tape.

"Hey Al," Alvarez said to the videographer. He then motioned to Tomas. "I know you Al. I don't know him."

"He's new," Al replied.

"My name is Tom Stein," Tomas offered.

Lt. Alvarez gave Tomas a good look as if he were scanning him for his future memory bank. "So rookie, how did you know about the locket?"

"So there was a locket!" Tomas shot back using the lieutenant's question as confirmation.

Alvarez rolled his eyes slightly. "A police source close to the investigation confirms a locket was found at the scene. Now how did you know about the locket?"

"Jason Young's mom gave it to him," Tomas replied. "I was just on the phone with her a few minutes ago."

Lt. Alvarez seemed amazed at all the information Tomas already had from a crime scene barely 2 two hours old. "I see," he said. "So then you think you know whose body was in that car?"

"Yes, I think I do. Do you?"

Manuel Alvarez dealt with the news media virtually every day but he clearly had no idea what to make of Tomas. Alvarez knew more about the scene than he was letting on and yet here was a reporter who maybe even knew more than he did. The lieutenant clearly was not comfortable with that. He reached for a card in his blazer and a pen and started writing on the back of the card. "Merry Christmas rookie. I'll be interested in your report tonight. And here's my cell phone number. Let's meet for drinks one night, okay?"

"Sounds like a plan," Tomas replied. He and Al then shook the lieutenant's hand and headed back toward their car.

"What in the world was that?" Al asked as he opened the back hatch of the car to stow away his gear. He had known Lt. Alvarez for years but had never seen him react the way he had reacted to Tomas, much less to invite one of the station's reporters for drinks while at a crime scene.

"You seem to know him. What's his story?" Tomas asked while helping Al pack up.

"I met him years ago when he was with the capitol police. He had a good job there. Was a supervisor but I think he got bored and so when a job with DC Metro opened up he jumped at it. Eventually became their PIO. Odd thing though."

"What's that?" Tomas asked.

"What is the PIO Supervisor doing out here on Christmas morning?"

"Don't know but pack up because we still have a lot of work to do." Tomas was in a rush to get moving.

"Oh, yeah?" Al replied.

"Oh, yeah!" Tomas responded. "Remember that soup kitchen meal shoot we were supposed to pick up?"

"We're still going?" Al asked. He had figured that they already had their story for the day and so they would skip out on all their other assignments.

"Still going!" Tomas said emphatically.

"How come?"

"Because one of the people carving the turkey and handing out meals is Congresswoman Marilyn Taylor-Brown, and if the body in that car is who I think it is, then she knew him very, very well.

CHAPTER 5

"I KNOW SOMETHING YOU DON'T KNOW." Tomas could remember the singing taunt from his childhood. He was the last of four children, two brothers and a sister. He was the 'accident'. His was an unexpected pregnancy after his parents had decided they didn't want more children but also didn't do enough to prevent a fourth child from being conceived anyway.

His brothers were ten and eight years older. They were too far ahead of him in age to have any real meaningful bonding experiences with him. When Tomas was just starting school they were learning to drive. He was still in elementary school when each of them left for college.

It was his older sister Susan with whom Tomas was closest. They were the two younger children who came after the two boy heirs to the family business.

His mom and dad would dote on their older boys. The younger ones grew up after the couple had become exhausted by being mom and dad. Tomas and Susan were loved but treated differently and perhaps less carefully by their parents.

Being the only girl in the family Susan would become her mom's confidant. She would then eagerly and recklessly share any information she obtained with Tomas. It drove him a bit crazy because no one in the family really confided in him except Susan. He learned to be more inquisitive around his parents once Susan had fed him a few crumbs of this or that information that her mom had told her. It was a relationship which perhaps sowed the seeds of the persistent, probing journalist he was to become in adult life.

Now his adrenaline was pumping as he and Al drove to interview the Congresswoman from Minnesota. He knew a secret no one else did. This was going to get interesting.

The general rule in TV news is to get every piece of information on a breaking news story out as fast as you can on every possible platform. Text, web, social media and on-air all helped to feed the never satiated news beast! Tomas wasn't doing that. He felt he had an advantage on everyone else. A scoop! He was not going to let his competitors in on what he knew about the car that was just fished out of the Potomac River until he was forced to do so.

Washington, DC's roads were still nearly empty on this Christmas morning as Al drove a bit too fast toward their next assignment. Tomas didn't know the city very well but with traffic as light as this he figured they would be early to their next assignment, and so he proposed a detour.

"We have to stop by my apartment," he told Al.

"You're apartment. How come?" Al questioned while looking straight ahead.

"I need to pick something up. We've got plenty of time, right?"

"Maybe. Where to?"

"We need to get on the beltway," Tomas told him. They didn't actually need to get on the beltway. As Tomas barked his home address into his smartphone map app Al's ears perked up. It was an area he knew very well.

"Tomas, you live at the 'Hijab Hilton'?"

"The 'Hijab Hilton'?"

"That's what it is known as, at least in the Arabic community," Al responded.

Stein's apartment, which was really more of a townhouse, was within a large sprawling complex of apartments which housed mostly Muslims. As Al navigated the streets of DC to get to the apartment Tomas explained to him how he had ended up there.

He had not had a lot of time to find a new place to live after the deal to work at DC-3 was finalized, and he wanted to spend Hanukkah with his family in Richmond. There were several high-rise apartments within walking distance of the DC-3 Broadcast Plaza, but they were pretty pricey and he wasn't sure what it would cost to park his car there. Besides, he didn't like heights and every available apartment in the area seemed to be above the tenth floor.

He expanded his search area for living quarters on the web and sorted everything available for rent by price. That's where he found an apartment which seemed ideal. The rent was high but not too steep. It was two floors with two bedrooms upstairs and a kitchen and living room downstairs. The inside wasn't elaborate but it was clean and there was parking right outside his front door. He saw that there was a Mosque nearby but didn't think anything of it.

Move-in day was when Tomas realized exactly where he would be living. The whole area was a Muslim enclave of sorts. Shops, stores, apartments and some homes all had the appearance of some sort of connection to the Muslim faith. It looked like an interesting place to visit. He just wasn't sure this was the best neighborhood for him to be living in.

The very white Jewish kid met a neighbor as he was moving in who seemed nice enough. His name was Omar and he was from Ghana. Omar was about his age, but he had a wife and two kids and was studying pre-med while also working in one of the local food stores part-time. He explained to Tomas that Muslims tended to live around Mosques because their daily prayer schedule made it more practical for them. His wife and kids would also take advantage of social and educational as well as religious programs at the Mosque, all of which were within walking distance.

Tomas knew it was more than that. He had been to the heavily Jewish neighborhoods in New York where his grandparents lived. Being around others like you was also about safety and security and a sense of community with others who thought and acted like you did. *Birds of a feather* Tomas would say. He held no animosity toward Omar or Muslims or anyone else, but he also didn't want to be seen as an invader either. When the cable guy came by to install his cable box and DVR and asked him, "You live *here*?" that's when Tomas told himself he would break his lease and look for somewhere else to live. Some place where he was less out of place. But for now the Hijab Hilton would have to do.

Al pulled into the parking space in front of the apartment and Tomas raced inside. Most of the boxes in his townhome hadn't been unpacked, yet he knew exactly what it was he was looking for and just where to find it. On the kitchen counter was a clear plastic bin. Tomas opened it and grabbed a large box inside. It was a video storage device capable of holding several terabytes of footage including the video he shot at the Young's news conference in Boise more than one year ago, video he needed to help tell his exclusive story.

Tomas now had in his possession video of photographs of Jason Young, pictures of his car and personalized license plate, and of course a photo of the locket a police lieutenant had inadvertently confirmed they had found at the scene. He also had the old interview with Prudence Young. The one last missing piece he needed for the news that night was a soundbite from Jason Young's former lover Representative Marilyn Taylor-Brown reacting to the discovery of Jason's car and—likely—the remains of his body from the Potomac River.

The soup kitchen that the Taylor-Brown for President Campaign had chosen for her photo-op was in a lower income neighborhood not too far from the Capitol building and White House. It was being held in a black church and most all of the volunteers serving as well as those receiving the meals were African-American. Every candidate knew how important securing the votes of blacks would be to winning the Democratic nomination. Obama needed it; Biden too, but it was a demographic in which polls showed Taylor-Brown was struggling to gain support. Democratic pollsters had also emphasized to party leaders how important it was to nail down African-American support since it seemed a possibility at the moment that the Republicans would nominate a black man for president.

When Al and Tomas arrived other news crews were standing by the front door waiting to be escorted inside. The event was open to the public but the crews waited for a guide as a courtesy. They didn't want to upset anyone by just barging in and videotaping those who didn't want to be on camera.

Tomas surveyed the news crews and realized none of them had been at the Potomac River scene. No one but him had drawn the connection. Advantage Tom Stein!

A minister and an aide to Taylor-Brown appeared at the door to escort the news crews inside. The minister introduced himself as Pastor Robert Lucas, Jr. As he walked through the halls he gave the media a history lesson about the church on the way to the auditorium. Historic photos dotted the gray cinder block walls of the hallway; many of them taken in black and white decades ago.

One large photo showed a man who looked like he could have been the pastor's father standing alongside the Rev. Martin Luther King. "My father Pastor Robert Lucas, Sr. was a proud friend of Dr. King's," the pastor told the assembled crowd of journalists. "He stood on the same stage when King gave his iconic *I Have a Dream* speech on the national mall."

Photos revealed that other civil rights leaders had visited the church too. One showed a younger John Lewis who himself would eventually be elected to Congress. A color photo showed a visit to the church sanctuary by the Rev. Jesse Jackson, Jr. when he had given a sermon there. There were several other photos of people Tomas knew must have been important but who he didn't recognize.

"This is one of my father with Marion Barry." Tomas didn't know about the former controversial mayor of Washington, DC who was once busted in a cocaine sting.

Another photo in particular did grab his attention. It wasn't just because it was one of the few photos in color. It was because of where it showed Pastor Lucas, Jr. standing and who he was standing with when it was taken. He was in the Oval Office where he and former President Donald Trump were standing together with the President's son-in-law and adviser Jared Kushner.

"You met with Trump?" Tomas asked inquisitively. This was the last place he expected to see a photo of Donald Trump.

"I was invited to a ceremony to witness the signing of the President's criminal reform bill. Many local black religious and political leaders were invited, but I was one of about a dozen to go. Many did not."

"But you did?" Tomas asked.

"Yes I did. Let me tell you all something," Pastor Lucas said almost defensively while stopping for a second and then turning to the camera crews. "When Trump held his prison reform summit I was one of the community leaders who was invited. Some said I shouldn't go but I went anyway. Now I've lived in this town my whole life. Got to meet some powerful and important people from the time I was a child. Met many a politician in my lifetime. But the Trump administration was one of the few where I was invited to give input in a room where a bunch of white people didn't think they already had all the answers. They listened to what I had to say, and when I saw what they did afterward I felt I had been truly heard. I'll never vote for the man, but I've always believed that when someone does something positive for the people no matter how you feel about his politics, then you look him in the eye, shake his hand and say 'thank you' for his good deed. That doesn't happen nearly enough in this town."

The Pastor turned and started walking again. "What about Repre sentative Taylor-Brown?" Tomas asked following up. "What are your thoughts about her?"

"I get that she's here today for a photo-op," Pastor Lucas responded still walking forward. "But she's been here when there have been no cameras around too. She cares about the people in this church and in this community and in this country. I think she would make a very good president."

The hallway gave way to the auditorium. It was just large enough to fit one basketball court with hoops on four sides, not just two. On the near end were the serving tables and the rest of the room was packed with rows of tables and folding chairs. About half the chairs were filled with people enjoying a hearty Christmas Day meal.

The male aide walking with them who had seemed to blend into the building's walls walked over to Taylor-Brown and led her over to the assembled camera crews. Wireless lavaliere microphones were quickly attached to an apron she was wearing.

With mics attached and cameras rolling, her dark and grayish black hair pulled back from her face in somewhat of a ponytail, Marilyn Taylor-Brown thanked Pastor Lucas for inviting her. She then talked about the importance of service and helping others and said that government should be a partner with churches and charities like these. At least that's what Tomas thought she said. He wasn't really listening because nothing the Congresswoman would say about the event would make his story. Tomas was only focused on the first question he would ask her about what had happened earlier that morning—and then he'd follow up with another question and then follow up after that.

He also decided that he should not ask the first question of the makeshift press conference. He didn't want to hit the Congresswoman first thing with the news that her ex-lover's body had likely been found in a car at the bottom of the Potomac River.

"I will now be happy to take any questions you may have," Taylor-Brown told the reporters.

A female reporter Tomas did not recognize spoke up. "Polls show you up in Iowa and New Hampshire but trailing in South Carolina because of lack of African-American support. How do you fix that?"

"Well it's not a matter of fixing anything," Taylor-Brown responded. "I think it is more about doing a better job of letting black voters know who I am and what I stand for. Pastor Lucas and the congregation here and many in this community know how I feel and what I've done in the past for the black community, and I know they will help me take that message to South Carolina." Pastor Lucas was standing beside and slightly behind the Congresswoman and nodding enthusiastically.

"Some have suggested that you pledge to naming an African-American to the ticket to broaden your support," the same reporter followed up with another question. "Have you given that any consideration?"

"We're still six weeks to the Iowa caucuses," Taylor-Brown reminded her. "I think it's premature to be discussing running mates at this time."

Tomas could hold back no more. "Congresswoman, the car of your one-time congressional aide Jason Young was found in the Potomac River this morning, and some human remains and some of his belongings were found inside. I was wondering if you had any reaction to this tragic discovery."

Without any hesitation she responded. "Sad news. As I've said in the past I had real feelings for Jason, and still think of him and the mystery of his disappearance a lot. My only hope is that the discovery will help finally bring some closure to his loved ones. I know they've been wanting answers for some time."

Something wasn't sitting right with Tomas. The answer she gave was too cold, too calculated and too fast. It seemed to him that she almost knew that question was coming. He followed up. "So may I ask Congresswoman you don't seem very surprised by the news. Did someone tell you about the discovery of Jason Young's car this morning?"

Taylor-Brown's demeanor changed. She was giving him a stone-cold stare and more color was coming to her lightly made-up cheeks. "Did someone tip me off is what you're asking?" Tomas had come to learn that politicians, especially politicians, would typically repeat a question back to him when they weren't completely prepared to answer his question.

"Yes," Tomas pressed. "Were you made aware of what police found this morning before now?"

"No! Well, yes—I guess sort of. A police officer called a member of my staff this morning to say they had found Jason's car. That's all I know," Taylor-Brown stammered through her answer.

"I'm talking to the family of Jason Young this afternoon," Tomas pressed. "Any message I can give them from you?"

In the span of 30 seconds Rep. Marilyn Taylor-Brown's demeanor had gone from calm and controlled to flustered and visibly angry. "No. Well. Um, as I've said before, I know they've been in a lot of pain for many years. There is nothing I can do to change that other than to say I'm sorry for their loss. Jason was special to me but that was many years before his suicide."

"So you believe it was a suicide?" Tomas was digging in now, taking full advantage of any little nugget of information Taylor-Brown had that he didn't have.

"Of course I do. At least that's what police have told me they suspected happened. I mean I don't *know* he committed suicide. I'm just going off what I was told. That's all."

The other reporters in the room could feel themselves losing complete control of this interview and their interviewee, who appeared to be getting angrier and angrier with every question Tomas asked. And it was all on a story none of them knew anything about. Another reporter chimed in with a question before Tomas could get another follow-up question off. "Tell us about this event today?" he 'soft balled'.

"Sure," Taylor-Brown replied while attempting to compose herself. "No, wait!" She turned back to Tomas. "Look, I don't know what happened to Jason Young. I can only tell you that we had a brief affair which I deeply regret and have apologized for. It was inappropriate, but it was also a long time ago and I'm not going to stand here and pretend to you that I haven't put that part of my life behind me and moved on. And that's all I've got to say about this now, okay?"

Tomas got exactly what he was looking for. A flustered nationally known politician running for president, no less, giving him the soundbite he needed for the big story he was going to break that very night.

To her credit Rep. Taylor-Brown stuck around for a few more softball political questions before being politely pulled away. The news crews started packing up their gear and retreated back down the hallway. Tomas and Al were taking up the rear when they both heard what sounded like someone with the clickity-clack of high heels running after them.

"Excuse me! DC Channel 3. Excuse me!" Tomas and Al turned around to see a petite woman in high heels running down the hall attempting to catch up with them. *"Excuse me!"* the woman was yelling at them in a voice so loud Tomas was certain they could hear her all the way back in the auditorium. She was a brunette woman dressed far too well for a Christmas Day event to feed the hungry at a local church. She was wearing a silk blouse with a pencil skirt of some sort, a pearl necklace with earrings to match and black high-heeled pumps that she likely wore often but did not run in very well. At the pace she was approaching Tomas thought she might be at high risk for breaking an ankle.

Tomas used to joke that he could spot a public relations person, or what people in the media liked to call 'PR Flaks' a hundred yards away. But in no time flat this one was within three feet of him screaming at the top of her lungs "Excuse me, but who do you think you are and what was that all about?"

CHAPTER 6

JOURNALISTS AND PR FLAKS exist on opposite ends of the information spectrum. You might say a good journalist cares about what matters to people and a good PR Flak wants journalists to care about what matters to them and their client.

A good journalist seeks facts. A good PR Flak spins the facts.

A good journalist looks to tell two sides of a story. A good PR Flak supplies only one.

A good journalist is objective. A good PR Flak is paid to be subjective.

A good journalist tells a story. A good PR Flak pushes a narrative.

A good journalist is credible. A good PR Flak gets paid a lot more money than the journalist whether they are credible or not.

Tomas disliked engaging with PR Flaks but he was apparently being confronted by one now. He looked over at Al to see if he could confirm that the person was indeed who he thought she was but Al just shrugged. He had no idea who she was either.

"Were you tipped off? Do you believe it was a suicide? What kind of crazy freakin' questions are those?" the yet-to-be confirmed PR Flak screamed at him from three feet away.

Tomas thought he would take down the temperature a little bit by responding in a normal tone of voice. "What kind of questions? Well in my defense," he answered her, "they did all end with question marks." The normal-tone-of-voice-strategy didn't work.

"Oh, we're being cute mister reporter now, are we!" replied the petite woman with apparently incredibly large lungs. "Who are you anyway?" Tomas was a little amazed that anyone much less a petite white woman in high heels would/could yell at him so loudly and at such a high pitch in a place of worship. If they weren't in a church he was certain her questions would be laced with lots of expletives.

"My name is Tom Stein and I'm a correspondent for *The Industry Tonight*."

That was indeed his on-air name and yes *correspondent* was his official title, but he had apparently just committed an act of name dropping in Washington, DC. Even this young woman screaming at him appeared to know what *The Industry Tonight* was and that fact alone seemed to stop her cold. The encounter went from her berating him to silence in seconds.

"He's new," Al chimed in.

"And may I ask who you are?" Tomas asked the woman he assumed was a PR Flak.

The woman suddenly appeared to be very uncomfortable. She looked down for a second and then tapped her fingers around her skirt as if she was looking for a pocket with a business card inside. A reply finally came in a normal toned voice. "My name is Olivia Zhang. I'm a Senior Communications Consultant with the Taylor-Brown for President campaign."

Tomas looked her up and down for a second. Senior Communications Consultant? She could not have been older than twenty-five. But then again he was technically a Washington, DC news correspondent about to turn twenty-nine, so who was he to judge? *And what was with the last name Zhang* he thought to himself. She was as white as he was. Not a hint of Asian anywhere on her body.

"Your questions ... they were ... they were ... were ... inappropriate," she stammered on.

"How so?" Tomas asked.

"Just because police gave us a heads-up on what they found does not mean she was involved in any way," Zhang continued trying to compose herself. "And as far as suicide is concerned, it is my understanding that this case has been treated as a suspected suicide for some time."

"I'm not implying anything Ms. Zhang," Tomas replied. "I just want to know what Ms. Taylor-Brown knows because she's a pretty big piece of the story, yes?"

"No sir!" Zhang replied. "She made a terrible mistake by having an affair with a staff member many years ago. That's it. No puzzle pieces here."

Tomas found it interesting that a PR Flak was attempting to explain something which happened likely before she was even born.

"Look Ms. Zhang. I asked the questions because I wanted to know if police felt that they had found Jason Young. She confirmed that. As for suicide, she brought it up and I wanted to know why she believed that way. She answered the question and I'll make sure her side is included in my story. Okay?"

"I'll be watching," Zhang replied with what appeared to Tomas to be a completely empty sounding threat. She then turned and walked back to the auditorium with her high heels loudly marking every step. It was at that moment that Tomas noticed that she was really attractive. He had no time to gawk. It may have been Christmas Day but he had a real scoop to get on the air.

"Dude, that was awesome!" Al told him grinning ear-to-ear. "You just used your 'TIT Power'!"

"TIT power?"

CHAPTER 7

ON THE DRIVE BACK to the station Al was giving Tomas his first TIT intel briefing.

'TIT' was short for *The Industry Tonight* and it was what insiders at DC-3 used as shorthand for anything involved with the hour-long program. The name fit in part because everyone understood that *The Industry Tonight* was the baby of station owner Marjorie Midas. Some would even refer to her as "The Big TIT" behind her back of course.

Al didn't usually work with *The Industry Tonight* correspondents by choice. Political news bored him. He would much rather be driving around the city videotaping police pulling cars out of the Potomac. Yet he still understood 'TIT Power' well.

The Industry Tonight may have had a small audience but it was an influential one. No Congressman, no congressional staffer, no White House aide, no administrator, no senior military member, no political party leader or political consultant, no lobbyist, no one on the *Who's Who of Washington A-listers* wanted to be caught off guard by a news report on *The Industry Tonight*. And no one certainly wanted to make an enemy of the program. There was even a vulgar term used when someone did that. 'TIT and the 'F' word!'

"That's what happened with that PR Flak," Al explained. "The last thing the Marilyn Taylor-Brown campaign needs is negative press on the

TIT. I'll bet you that young lady calls you to apologize."

"Don't know how she could," Tomas replied. "I didn't even have a business card to give her."

"She'll find a way," Al replied confidently.

On a normal weekday at *DC-3 News* Tomas and Al would be up against a pressing deadline. After all, the station aired news pretty much all day. Only a couple of syndicated talk shows and overnight infomercials broke up what was otherwise a 24/7 round-the-clock news operation.

But not on Christmas Day.

The station had not only produced some special Christmas Day programming involving a combination of local church choirs and non-denominational messages from local clergy, but a local college basket-ball team (Tomas couldn't remember which one) had been invited to a Christmas week tournament and *DC-3 News* had picked up the rights to their games. There would be very little time for news that day and being brand new, Tomas knew he would need all the time he could get to put his story together. Al would help him of course.

The first thing Al had to do when they got back to the station was to log Tomas into the newsroom content management system using his own ID and password. It was against station policy but he had no choice. Tomas hadn't been given his own ID yet because everyone in HR had taken the week off.

The video editing system at *DC-3 News* was almost the exact same one Tomas had used in Boise which was a nice break to help him get his story done. Tomas plugged his video box into the system and started downloading digital files while Al went into a video edit bay to down-load the video he shot from the field. Al also helped Tomas transfer the interview with the Polar Plunger from his smart phone into the content management system. "No," Al told Tomas, "it is not technically a union violation to shoot interviews on your smartphone."

The news employees at DC-3 who were not managers all belonged to a union, and there were strict rules for what Tomas could and could not do with video equipment. He had been hired as a one-man band reporter/ videographer, and so he was allowed to download video and sound bites onto story timelines and put them together with his own audio track to produce some semblance of a news story. But if he had not shot his own video, and on this day Al the videographer had, then Al or an editor had to do the editing by union rules. That included adding any post-production graphics or finishing touches Tomas wanted in the story. It would then be sent as a file to a computer server where it would be ready to air on a news-cast or post to the station's news web page. Tomas decided to 'cheat' on the union rules since Al wasn't familiar with the video he would be using from Boise nearly a year and a half ago. By the time Tomas had loaded the audio from his script onto the timeline the news story was virtually done.

Al was shocked. "Wow!" He had never before witnessed a reporter working so quickly with so many different digital editing tools at his dis-posal, especially in his first week on the job. All Al really had to do was walk into an edit bay, find the story file and send it to the server. They were both done with plenty of time to spare.

Tomas started working on his story for the station's web page although he would have no idea how to post it to the web. Someone on the news assignment desk would have to help him with that since the web page team was off for the holiday too.

Tomas also wanted to touch base again with Prudence Young. He called her as she was cooking Christmas dinner for the family since it was still early afternoon in Boise two hours behind the Washington, DC time zone. Everyone at the Young's holiday celebration had been anxiously waiting for an update, so Prudence put Tomas on speaker phone.

"I'm on deadline Ms. Young. I don't have too much time to talk. I'm about to go on-air with the story and put it on our website and I wanted to tell you to be on the lookout for it."

"Thank you Tom. We understand. It's been a very emotional Christmas

Day here," Prudence Young spoke loudly into the speaker.

"I bet. Would you be willing to do a video call interview later tonight?" he asked her.

Prudence paused. "Could we do it tomorrow? I would like to see your story first, and I need a little more time to digest all of this."

Tomas hated waiting to get something *tomorrow* that he knew he could get *tonight* because it increased the odds that he wouldn't get it *at all.* Prudence Young was a woman of her word though, and it was Christmas Day after all. He was sure she would come through for him tomorrow.

The 6 p.m. newscast producer had decided Tomas would pitch to his own story from a camera position in the newsroom. She figured that since it was his first week on the job, asking him to go out and do an actual live shot—either from the banks of the Potomac River or outside the Capitol Building—was just pushing him a little too hard.

Tomas sat in the chair with a remote-controlled camera in front of him and hooked up his earpiece to a cord that TV people call an 'ifb.' The device was used so that he could hear the anchor's voice pitching to him and also any commands from the news producer in the booth.

"Audio check. Tom, can you hear me?" the producer spoke into his ear.

"I can. Can you hear me?" he responded. "Do you need an audio check?"

"No, we're good. One minute to air."

Tomas took a deep breath. This would be his first story for *DC-3 News* and it was going to be a blockbuster even if the audience on Christmas night would be small. The only audience he really cared about anyway was Prudence Young and her family members who would be able to see the whole story once the video got posted to the station's website. The newscast was starting and the fill-in anchor, some guy he hadn't met named Brad, began reading the lead-in script Tomas had written for him.

"An unsolved missing persons mystery twenty-five years in the making is one step closer to being solved tonight. It's a story with a twist of political intrigue involving a woman who wants to be the next President of the United States. DC-3 reporter Tom Stein joins us with exclusive details you won't see anywhere else."

Tomas began to speak. "Brad, nearly twenty-five years ago a young staffer for Congresswoman Marilyn Taylor-Brown disappeared after admitting to having an extra-marital affair with her. This morning the Potomac River revealed what may be the first major clue to what happened to that missing man named Jason Young."

Tomas's video story then began rolling with sounds from the car being pulled from the river.

Tom Stein voice track: "Surrounded by a DC fire dive team, a car presumably lying at the bottom of the Potomac River for two-and-a-half decades was pulled back to shore. It was found by a group of men and women who took a frigid plunge into the river on Christmas Day to support their local Kiwanis Club. Carl Brookington was one of them. An experienced diver, he and some friends swam out from the shore."

Carl Brookington soundbite: "We were just diving into the water and some friends and me make a bet every year who can swim out the farthest in the cold water. I was wearing this diving mask when I looked down and saw what looked like a car."

Tom Stein voice track: "It was more than a car. Police confirm that when divers went down to check it out they found what appeared to be human remains and some personal items inside. On the back of the car was a rusted license plate providing a significant clue to who those human remains inside the car may be. Look carefully and you can make out the words *More-man* on the license plate, just like on this license plate. It's Jacob Young's personalized license plate from a photo taken nearly twenty-five years ago. Young's presumably last days alive were spent in the middle of a political firestorm. His wife had filed for divorce claiming that he was having an affair with his boss, then freshman Congresswoman

Marilyn Taylor. As rumors swirled, Representative Taylor was forced to concede they were true. Jason Young soon dropped out of sight and then went missing altogether. More than one year ago Young's family held a rare news conference. It was a last-ditch attempt to get some answers before Young's dying father passed away."

Prudence Young soundbite: "We are here today in hopes of fulfilling his last dying wish."

Tom Stein voice track: "The event featured large posters of Jason, his car, his vanity plate, and this unique locket he wore around his neck. It's the same locket sources confirm was found in the car taken out of the Potomac. They are the first real clues police have had in the case of a missing man mystery that's gone unsolved for decades even though investigators can't be sure a crime was committed."

Lt. Alvarez soundbite: "At this point we have no indication of foul play, but the car had clearly been in the water for quite some time and so further investigation will be needed."

Tom Stein voice track: "The discovery was made the same day that Congresswoman and Presidential candidate Marilyn Taylor-Brown was in DC helping out at a local soup kitchen. She says police tipped off her staff when they made the morning discovery and she offered her condolences to his family. But the gruesome find doesn't shed any new light on what happened as far as she's concerned."

Marilyn Taylor-Brown soundbite: "Look, I don't know what happened to Jason Young. I can only tell you that we had a brief affair which I deeply regret and apologized for. It was inappropriate, but it was also a long time ago and I'm not going to stand here and pretend to you that I haven't put that part of my life behind me and moved on."

Tom Stein voice track: "Prudence Young says she can never put the death of her son behind her. Jason's disappearance has been a lingering heartache for her for decades. But she has ruled out one possibility about what happened to her son. She concedes that her son Jason was depressed when he disappeared but she does not believe he would have taken his own life."

Prudence Young soundbite: "He would not have committed suicide!"

Tom Stein voice track: "A car hidden in the Potomac for almost twenty-five years, human remains inside, clues to the victim's identity but not what happened to him. Was it an accident, suicide, or something more sinister? This gruesome discovery bringing new life to the question: 'What happened to Jason Young?'"

Prudence Young soundbite: "Please, tell us what happened to our son!"

End videotape.

The director cut away from the story and back to Tomas on camera in the newsroom. "Brad, I spoke with Prudence Young this afternoon about the discovery as she was at home for Christmas with her family. She asked for some time to process these new developments but has committed to doing an interview with us tomorrow. We'll have that for you then."

Tomas could hear Brad reacting in his earpiece. "That's a lot of Christmases to not know what happened to your son. Thank you Tom."

Tomas got up from his chair. He and Al would shoot and edit a couple of 'bookend' stand-ups with him on camera for versions of the same story in newscasts later that night and the next morning. But it was Christmas and he was getting double-time pay per union rules. He was under strict orders to be headed home by 7pm that night.

As he left the station, a cold mist had covered the city. It had been fairly warm until the daytime turned to night. Tomas got into his Camaro in the station's parking lot and suddenly felt very hungry. Doing what most every hungry Jewish kid does on Christmas, he looked up a nearby Chinese restaurant on his smartphone and ordered takeout online.

The restaurant was only a few minutes' drive from the WWDC Broadcast Plaza. He pulled up to find that the restaurant was surprisingly busy—at least if you counted all the cars in the parking lot. Tomas walked in the door and could see that the restaurant had a seating area to the left and a takeout window to the right. He walked over to the line for takeout and that's when he saw her. Right up there at the front of the line was none other than PR Flak Olivia Zhang.

Oh Geez! he thought to himself. His day was over; he was hungry and the last thing he wanted was another confrontation with her. How was it even possible that in a city this size that they could be in the same place at the same time twice in one day? Should he just turn and leave? Maybe hide in his car until she left? It was too late. Olivia grabbed her bag of food, turned around and immediately spotted him a couple of people behind her in line.

"Tom!" she yelled, not quite as loudly as she had in the church. "Tom Stein!" Tomas waved meekly at her.

Olivia looked back at the cashier. "Has he paid? His name is Tom Stein. Has he paid?" Olivia took the credit card still in her right hand and flicked it at the small Asian cashier behind the counter so hard that she had to at first duck and then go retrieve it. Olivia was apparently buying him dinner.

She then walked up to him. "Look, I want to apologize. Ah, do you have a minute to talk?"

CHAPTER 8

"THE CHINESE TEA HERE IS AMAZING," Olivia told him. Even though they both already had their takeout food she had talked Tomas into sitting with her in the dining room. A waitress approached as they were both pulling their already purchased meals out of paper bags. Olivia appeared to talk to the woman in Chinese even though Tom was pretty sure the waitress spoke English. She went away to fetch their tea.

"You speak Chinese?" Tomas asked in a 'Captain Obvious' moment.

"My parents are Chinese. Or should I say my adoptive parents. They spoke it a lot around the house and so I guess I just picked up some of it."

"And that's where Zhang comes from?" Score two for Captain Obvious.

"Of course. Olivia Zhang. Kind of floats off the tongue, doesn't it?"

"It's unique. Where did the name Olivia come from?"

The waitress arrived with the tea and Olivia poured it into two small teacups for them. "It was my name when they adopted me. They tell me I was only a few months old but they liked my given name and didn't want to change it." Olivia grabbed some chopsticks like a pro and started digging into her vegetables with rice. "They got me through a Russian adoption agency and that was the name on my portfolio."

"Oh, so you're Russian?" Captain Obvious was in rare form tonight.

"Eastern European. I don't know much more. I was told some distraught mother just dropped me off one day at an orphanage and ran off.

Will probably never know my real roots for sure."

"An Eastern European baby adopted by Chinese parents and living in America. What a country!"

"Adopted by wealthy Chinese parents. See, it gets better!" Olivia grinned.

"Wealthy, huh?" Tomas responded.

"My parents own a mining corporation. That's how I met Marilyn. My parents mine copper on some of Marilyn's family's land in Minnesota and it's worked out well for both sides. A lot of people think the Taylors of Minnesota made their fortunes from farming and ranching, but it was the mining rights on their land that was the big money-maker."

"And your rich Chinese mining parents always dreamed of adopting an eastern European white girl?" Tomas was looking down and digging into his dinner now with his chopsticks. He usually ate Chinese food with a fork but since Olivia was using chopsticks he might as well use them too.

"Not a lot of Asian girls at Russian adoption agencies so I've been told," Olivia replied. "My mom says that she couldn't have any more children after my brother was born and she wanted to raise a girl. Someone got them in touch with someone who got them in touch with someone else; money changed hands, and here I am having dinner with you!" Despite their loud run-in earlier she seemed to be relaxed and enjoying herself now.

"What a country!" Tomas repeated.

"What about you? What's your story Correspondent Tom Stein with *The Industry Tonight*!"

"Just a stupid Jewish kid from Richmond. Born and raised a pure-blooded Jew. No gentiles like you in my family tree! Or Russian orphans adopted by Chinese parents either."

Olivia smiled in between bites. She must have been hungry because she had almost finished her meal. "Jewish kid, huh? Are there many Jews in Richmond?"

"Not where I come from," Tomas smiled. "I was a suburban kid. Chesterfield County Virginia. My parents moved there and built a home in this planned development. It seemed like the whole county just built up around us. But no, not many Jews," Tomas confirmed.

"So how did your parents end up in suburban Richmond?"

"*Greed*!" Tomas confessed laughing. "Maybe you've heard that about us Jews? But that wasn't it really. My grandparents owned a small number of successful jewelry stores in the New York metro area. It was very lucrative and my dad and his brother could have stayed there and done well. They just wanted to do something on their own to get out of their father's shadow. They agreed to head south to Richmond and started their own line of jewelry stores. The Stein Way Jewelers."

"The Stein Way Jewelers, huh? Your dad should sell pianos on the side," Olivia opined.

"Yeah. I heard there was talk of a lawsuit at one time by the Steinway Piano Company but I guess it never materialized," Tomas laughed. "It worked though. They opened their first store on Hull Street Road just outside of Richmond. My dad would work way past closing every night. Still does many nights even at his age. Before we knew it he owned about a dozen jewelry stores in Virginia and franchised out about a hundred more throughout the southeast. It has made him a bit of a local celebrity in Richmond."

"Really! How so?" Olivia asked pushing away the empty boxes of Chinese food.

"He and Uncle Izzy used to do their own TV commercials together. It was pretty kitschy stuff as us Jews like to say." Tomas sat straight up and cleared his throat so as to do his best Yiddish New Yorker impression. "First we cut the diamonds and then we cut your price. That's the Stein Way!" he said while imitating a man cutting a diamond. "My dad is actually much better on television than I am."

"So TV runs in your family!" Olivia concluded.

"No, just Dad and me I guess."

"And Uncle Izzy I suppose!"

"Izzy died when I was young. Had an embolism. They found him in his bed with blood everywhere. Honestly never knew him very well. After Izzy died my dad was a one-man show. He would drag me to the television studio where he shot his commercials. He later told me that he took me there because he just couldn't stand to go alone without Izzy. That's when I first fell in love with television."

"And here you are in the big time!"

"Is this the big time?" Tomas asked. He knew it was a big job, but the big time? Here he was in a city crammed with all sorts of national journalists and even local ones with far more stature and more impressive credentials. He was just offered a great job and he took it. Maybe he was on the path to the 'big time' but he didn't feel he was even close to that yet.

Olivia wasn't so sure. "You'll see," she assured him. She looked down for a second and started playing with her chopsticks. "Hey look, I do want to apologize for my behavior earlier today. I wanted to explain to you what happened."

"You were just doing your job. I'm cool with that." Tomas really hadn't been cool with that at the time, but that was several hours ago and this was now.

"No. Look, I love Marilyn like a family member and I'm here because I think she would make an historic and amazing president. But I'll tell you she also has claws. That woman can show a white-hot temper and you were getting her really upset. I knew that if I confronted you that would calm her down. I was trying to diffuse the situation a bit, not elevate it," Olivia explained.

"Why, what did you think she would do?" Tomas wondered aloud.

"Oh, just rant about it for the rest of the day. Make all of us on her staff miserable. Who needs that on Christmas Day?"

Tomas accepted her apology and the two chatted about their

backgrounds for a while longer. Tomas told her about going to journalism school at Arizona State University and then landing his first job in Boise.

Olivia had gone to Creighton University in Omaha and was considering law school there when she decided to take some time off to help with the campaign. Her adoptive father was not only a family business partner and friend to MTB but also a big donor. Marilyn and Olivia were very close too. Marilyn was grateful for the young woman's help on the campaign even if she didn't have any political campaign experience. Olivia was excited to be a part of the campaign team that could very possibly get Marilyn elected president.

It was getting late and Tomas could not hold back a yawn. "Sorry, long day."

"Me too," Olivia replied. She had paid for the tea and tipped the waitress in what seemed like hours ago.

They exchanged phone numbers and then got up to go. Tomas opened the front door of the restaurant for Olivia as she put on her coat and they both stepped into the cold DC winter air. She then turned around to face him as he exited behind her. "I am so glad you had dinner with me. It was great getting to know you."

Olivia then stepped toward him and gave him a loving, warm embrace followed by her standing on her toes to give him a quick kiss on the cheek. Tomas wasn't quite sure how to respond so he placed his arms on her back holding her less tightly than she was holding him. After a few moments of hugging each other in the cold, he then stepped back.

Olivia smiled awkwardly, grabbed his left hand with both of hers and rubbed it for a moment while saying in a soft voice, "Thank you again." She then turned and walked over to her SUV.

Tomas stood and waved as she drove away. It had been an awkward end to an enjoyable night and it was all his doing. The truth was that he was trying to at first prevent and then hide the fact that Olivia was giving him an erection.

CHAPTER 9

"GOOD MORNING MS. YOUNG," Tomas said as he and Prudence Young connected on the video call. It was actually 1 p.m. Washington time but 11 a.m. in Boise. They had texted each other earlier that morning to set up an agreed to time for their interview. Tomas wanted to spend some time catching up before he hit the record button.

"Good morning Mr. Stein," Prudence Young said mocking his formality. After her husband's funeral Prudence had asked Tomas to come over to their home a couple of times to his surprise. She had even given him a tour of Jason's old bedroom still left very much the way it was after he had moved to DC. Family members would tell Tomas it was an honor of sorts because she rarely took guests there.

The room was neat and clean which was just how Jason liked it. On the dresser was a trophy case of sorts with various awards and medals. On the end sat a plastic, square box. In the box was a running show covered with blood inside and a gold nameplate which read *The Legend of the Bloody Shoe*.

"What's with the shoe?" Tomas asked.

Prudence smiled. "Jason ran cross-country in high school and he was a good runner. One day he was passing someone on a course and they tripped him up. Jason swore it was intentional. Jason fell and a stick somehow pierced his ankle." Prudence pointed to her own ankle to show

Tomas where he was hurt. "Blood started gushing out of the cut but Jason was near the front and wanted to finish the race. He finished first but then fainted as he crossed the finish line. His shoe was covered in blood. We had to take him to the emergency room where they told us he had lost so much blood that they were going to keep him overnight, but he was fine. The whole school could not stop talking about it and so was born The Legend of the Bloody Shoe.

Prudence had remained grateful to Tomas for bringing some light into a dark moment of her and her late husband's lives and a casual friendship blossomed. She also single-handedly changed some of his notions about Mormons.

Growing up in Richmond Tomas had never really had any interaction with members of the Church of Jesus Christ of Latter Day Saints. He had always thought of it as sort of a western 'cult' movement and one time in high school had to be corrected by a teacher when he had inadvertently confused it with Scientology. To him Mormons stayed clustered among their own, somehow afraid of the temptations of the outside world.

Prudence Young was anything but that. She was in her seventies now but still quite active, vivacious and really pretty. She had longish gray hair that she wore pulled back in public but let flow freely in private. She chatted up others easily just like she did with Tomas. Putting him on display at her husband's funeral revealed her dramatic side. To put it plainly, her name may have been 'Prudence' but she was no 'prude'.

Prudence Young also genuinely loved her church. She and Tomas didn't talk too much about it but when he had questions about Mormons, she answered them frankly. Whenever she did talk about her church her eyes would light up. The church had made her a better person, a better mother, a better friend, and the clergy there had showed her tremendous support even at those times when she was in need and no one else seemed to understand.

Prudence told Tomas the story of one of her best friends in the world.

Years earlier she had been widowed when her husband and her five children died in a car accident. "They hospitalized her on a suicide watch," she told Tomas during one of his visits. "But all that woman really needed was her faith. The church community completely rallied around her. That's why she's still here today, and I'm grateful to have her as one of my best friends. She really helped me get through Edward's illness and death."

Prudence had taught Tomas that Mormonism wasn't really all that different from Judaism. There were the fringe sects and some strangeness that went with both religions—all religions really—but for the most part it was made up of regular people whose lives were enriched by their faith.

"You never told me that you had moved to Washington, DC. My goodness!" Prudence said through the computer screen during their interview.

"I know," Tomas replied sheepishly. "It just happened so fast and around the holidays and I'm sorry I didn't have time to call and tell you about it."

"You called when it mattered Tom." Tomas smiled and Prudence smiled back. "They are going to rule it a suicide, aren't they Tom?" she asked with surprisingly little emotion.

"I don't know. Maybe." Tomas had given it a lot of thought that morning. Human remains but no actual body to speak of and no signs of foul play according to police. Any possible evidence had either disintegrated in the water or floated downstream. It seemed that finding cause of death would be difficult if not impossible.

"I know it. I fear the truth will remain hidden at the bottom of the river," she now said in a tone of semi-despair.

"You still believe Jason was murdered," Tomas replied.

"I remember that he was very depressed before his death, but he was also very afraid."

Tomas wanted to hit the record button to get this exchange between them on camera, but he also wanted Prudence's permission first and this didn't seem the appropriate moment to ask. "Afraid? Afraid of who?"

"He was afraid of her."

Tomas knew she was talking about MTB. "But weren't they having an affair?"

"Jason called me a couple of days before he disappeared. His wife had just filed for divorce and the whole scandal had hit the headlines. He told his wife that he was going to leave the other woman and try to repair his marriage. But he also felt genuinely scared of her. Jason had experienced her temper before."

Tomas realized that Prudence Young believed that the woman who might be the next President of the United States may have murdered her son, and he wasn't recording *any* of it. It didn't matter. He wouldn't use the video even if he had been recording because she had no proof. It was better that he allowed her to keep her suspicions private.

"And he did not commit suicide!" Prudence Young added. "I want you to know that Tom because I know you want to find the truth. Maybe you can uncover what happened."

"Maybe." Tomas knew the likely end of this would leave Prudence disappointed. Maybe Jason did not commit suicide, but Tomas didn't know and had no real way of finding out. A police investigation would be done, its findings released, and that would be the end of it. After twenty-five years Prudence Young might get some of the answers she wanted, but not all of them. The Potomac River had washed all those answers away. "Ms. Young, I'm going to start recording now."

The interview with Prudence Young was fairly benign. Tomas didn't revisit her suspicions about Marilyn Taylor-Brown being a cold-blooded killer in political disguise. The interview focused on Jason instead. How he had become interested in politics while on a Mormon mission which included a stop in Washington, DC. He had volunteered for the campaign of a moderate Democrat running in Idaho's 1st Congressional District and was stunned when the man actually won against an unpopular first term incumbent Republican.

Jason had decided to leave school at Boise State to join the new Congressman's staff in Washington. Once there he met a woman at his local Mormon church and they were married in a whirlwind. Prudence still vividly remembered traveling to the DC area for the first time in her life for the marriage ceremony. Jason was still in his early twenties and had this brand-new life which she barely recognized. Her other two sons had stayed in Idaho, but here was Jason working thousands of miles away in a strange city in the political center of the nation. Prudence would never return to DC again.

Living in DC as a young married staffer was tough on Jason. Money was tight even though Prudence and Edward would help him out financially. Jason was also politically savvy enough to know it was going to be a short run in his current position. His boss, the Democratic Congressman, did everything he could to endear himself to his constituents in Republican-red Idaho, but everyone knew his win had been a fluke. Almost as soon as they got to Washington some of the Congressman's staff including Jason were looking for their next gig.

Jason's way out was Congresswoman Marilyn Taylor. She and Jason's boss were both part of the freshman Democratic Caucus with their offices close to each other, and that's where Jason first met her. She was not that much older than Jason and she seemed very kind. Jason and Marilyn would talk in the hallways of Congress about how crazy it seemed for each of them to even be standing there chatting in the hallways of Congress.

Unlike Idaho, Taylor's district, which included part of Minneapolis, was deep Democratic blue. Her re-election was virtually assured even if some complained that she had virtually bought the seat by out spending her Democratic Primary opponents by a margin of 5-to-1. Jason wanted to stay in Washington and he also wanted to work for Marilyn.

Prudence would recall phone calls with her son where he gushed about Rep. Taylor. Yes, she was a freshman and a bit idealistic, but also inspiring in her own way. Jason felt serving in Congress meant more to

Marilyn than just holding and wielding political power. He said that she wanted to make a real difference for people. Prudence could sense that Jason idolized her in a way.

After Idaho voters returned a Republican to the 1st District Jason decided to go work for Rep. Taylor after she won her reelection easily. Prudence knew nothing of their affair. She couldn't say when it started, how it started or even why it started. It just started, and she learned about it at around the same time when everyone else did.

That was when an attorney leaked Jason's wife's petition for divorce to a member of the media. Most reporters had no idea who Rep. Marilyn Taylor was, but everyone loves a juicy sex scandal and so the news exploded. It was not until then that Jason first told his mom and dad about what had happened in a phone call, his voice choked with emotion, his tone filled with regret. They didn't know it at the time but Edward and Prudence would never talk with their son again.

Tomas cut off the interview there. He didn't want Prudence speculating on camera about what had happened to her son although she probably would have willingly done so.

"Ms. Young, this has to be a very emotional time for you and yet I noticed you've been very calm and collected today. Tell us a little bit about how you are feeling?" So far the interview had been a bit dry. Tomas hoped that Prudence would let a little emotion come through.

"I made my peace with Jason's death a long time ago. Whatever had happened to him it was clear to me that he had moved into the afterlife and made his peace with the Lord. There is great comfort in that for me. Do I still keep his room ready for him should he show up one day? I do! But not in some vain hope he will. It's just my shrine to him, my place to remember the flesh and blood son who I can no longer embrace like I can his brothers. I miss that terribly! I miss *him* terribly! But my faith tells me that he awaits me in a better place. I'm very thankful for that."

Tomas ended the interview there. He had the soundbites he needed.

He would spend the rest of the day putting together a few stories featuring Prudence Young for that day's newscasts and those for the upcoming weekend. He knew it was a slow news week and he had plenty of material to spread out over a few days' worth of stories.

He took the rest of the week off until Monday when *The Industry Tonight* would return from its Christmas week hiatus. The program would even air on New Year's Eve focusing mostly on the campaign season ahead. The Iowa Caucuses were now just five weeks away.

But in the meantime Tomas wanted to unpack. His parents had offered to come up to help him, but he wasn't sure what they would make of the neighborhood he was living in. He told them he just needed some time to himself to get settled. He was also excited to get started as an *The Industry Tonight* correspondent.

CHAPTER 10

ON HIS FIRST 'OFFICIAL' DAY at work Tomas was learning that getting to his assigned cubicle at DC-3 was a bit of an adventure. He had only worked in the main newsroom up to that point. The station had given him a temporary security badge to get into the building but that was where his adventure began.

Like many television stations first built in the 1950s, WWDC had started as a small building and then gradually added on and added on and added on. When the Midas family bought the station, they began renovating virtually every square inch of the place. That included building an annex on an open area next to the main building which would become home to *The Industry Tonight*. It was built apart from the rest of the station by intent. Getting from one building to the other required either walking outside across an open-air courtyard or using one of two causeways which hooked up to the main building's second floor.

In other words it was easy for the new guy to get lost, and it apparently didn't occur to anyone that maybe they should escort him to his new assigned space. Tomas went to where he had gone the week before into the station's newsroom to learn that not only was he in the wrong place but that he wasn't even close to being in the right place. A morning producer who was wrapping up her shift led him up a flight of stairs, down a hallway with several offices, across a glass-encased causeway and around a corner. And there it was. The newsroom and studio specifically built for *The Industry Tonight.*

"Where's your desk?" the producer asked. Tomas had no idea. "Okay, well they'll be meeting in the 'Nip' down there," the producer said motioning to what appeared to be a conference room encased in glass on one side.

"Wait, the what?" Tomas asked, but the producer had already turned and started walking away. She looked tired and anxious to get home. Tomas walked down the stairs and made his way to the conference room.

The newsroom for *The Industry Tonight* was open and airy with a studio desk and cameras on one end and a wall of flat screen monitors on the other. Marjorie Midas had gotten the idea for the wall of monitors from a television station in Miami where she and her husband had a winter home. At the moment all the screens were dark.

The newsroom was both a working news center and a backdrop for the set. Tomas could see about a dozen cubicles for the correspondents, all of them empty. He assumed one of them was his. On one side was a raised hallway which connected to the stairs he had just walked down and an elevator. On the other side were glass offices with panels that rose up all the way to the second-floor ceiling. It was an impressive sight and looked like no newsroom he had ever seen before.

Tomas opened the door to the conference room and immediately saw a familiar face working on a laptop computer. She looked up at him. "Tom, you're here!"

"Hey Nan. Good to see you again."

Nanette Kendry's title was Executive News Producer for *The Industry Tonight.* It was a fancy way of saying that she was the boss of the newscast. She had a bit of a stocky build and a round face with curly, brown hair and very warm eyes. Tomas had interviewed with her when the station flew him out to DC a few weeks earlier. He and Nan seemed to hit it off immediately. Tomas didn't know it but Nan had been lobbying for some 'new blood' and agreed with Marjorie Midas that hiring someone like Tomas might bring a 'spark' to their pet nightly newscast.

"Have you logged in yet?" she asked Tomas.

"I don't know where I'm supposed to sit, and no one's given me a login," Tomas replied shrugging.

"I'll get you set up after the morning meeting."

Tomas pulled out a chair that was a few chairs down the table from Nan. They were the only two in there. "So why do they call this the 'Nip'?"

Nanette looked up at him with a faint look of disgust, but before she said a word, a tall, well-dressed man burst through the glass doors. "Good morning Nan," he said in a distinct Australian accent. Tomas recognized him immediately as nationally renowned *The Industry Tonight* Correspondent Lachlan McKnight. "Did you have a nice holiday?" McKnight was tall with longish but not too long graying hair which flowed back in waves from his forehead. "And what do we have here?" he said as he pointed his paper coffee cup toward Tomas. "Look Nan, it's the 'Boy Wonder'. Nice scoop last week Boy Wonder." Apparently somebody actually had been watching his reporting last week.

"Scoop? What scoop?" Nan replied. Apparently somebody else had not been watching his reporting last week.

"Why Boy Wonder here broke the story of the identity of the man whose body was found in the Potomac River. A twenty-five-year-old missing man mystery solved by the six o'clock news," McKnight told her. Tomas was really, *really* hoping the Boy Wonder moniker would not stick.

"Really. I'll have to see that," Nan replied looking over at Tomas. "First week on the job and you're already scooping the competition."

"Careful Nan," McKnight responded. "'The Big House' may want him!"

The Big House? Tomas thought to himself. These people speak in code.

Other correspondents started walking in, introducing themselves to Tomas as they sat down. The situation was so overwhelming for him that he would not remember any of their names by the time the meeting ended. There were only five correspondents today. The rest of *The Industry Tonight* news team was either still on vacation for the New Year's week holiday or out reporting on the presidential campaigns in Iowa or New Hampshire.

"Okay folks, let's get started," Nan began. "Elsa and Andrew will be going live tonight from Iowa." Tomas had no idea who Elsa and Andrew were, but he guessed they were in Iowa covering the run up to the caucuses. "Mr. McKnight, what do you have?"

Lachlan sat back in his chair. "The five biggest law changes for the New Year," he said while taking a sip from his paper coffee cup.

"Gripping," Nan responded sarcastically.

"Oh you'll love it Nan," Lachlan responded with a hint of sarcasm. "You'll get to see me juggle."

"For real?" asked one of the people seated at the table whose name Tomas could not remember asked.

"For real! Video at Seven!" Lachlan responded with a wide smile.

"I know everyone here has met our newest correspondent Tom Stein," Nan continued as if unimpressed by Lachlan's juggling boast. "Tom, I'm going to start you off with an "Industrial Art" profile."

"Industrial Art" was typically a feature piece done on various artists in the Washington, DC area. Most of the correspondents hated doing them but it was well known within the building that Marjorie Midas loved the feature stories. She would often pitch "Industrial Art" ideas to Nan after meeting an artist or going to an exhibition or show of some sort.

"Jay the Gay Comi-Queen is in town this week to perform on New Year's Eve. He's agreed to interview with us after a local show tomorrow night."

Tomas was somewhat familiar with his work. Gay Jay, as he called himself for short, had experienced a meteoric rise in the comedy world over the past few years in part because he was funny but also controversial.

He prided himself on wanting to get the nervous laugh. That was the joke no one really wanted to laugh at but they just couldn't help themselves. His jokes pierced narratives, which ranged from politics to celebrity culture to the social justice movement and even gay rights. Nothing and no one were off-limits.

And as far as the 'cancel culture' which had cowed so many other of his contemporary comedians, Gay Jay would do whole sets on how he would not and could not be canceled no matter how outrageous some of his acts had become. Any criticism of him seemed to just animate him more. He had developed an almost cult-like following of fans who would show up at his performances wearing *Jay is Okay* T-shirts which he would sell at his events and online. It was based on a routine Jay did about how ridiculous he found it that the okay sign people had been making with their hands for as long as anyone could remember had somehow now become seen by some as a symbol of white supremacy.

Booking an interview with him revealed an aspect of Nan's rebellious streak. She would often tell people that *The Industry Tonight* was different because it courted controversy. Everyone in the room knew an interview with Gay Jay would bring both viewers' complaints while capturing viewers' eyeballs.

Lachlan started humming the tune to the Prince song "Controversy" just to let Nan know that he knew what she was up to. "First day on the job and she's throwing you right into the fire!" he said.

"We'll have plenty of time to work the story over," Nan replied with a smile, "and besides, we need to get our newest correspondent noticed."

Tomas didn't know what to make of it all. He was still trying to figure out why they called this conference room they were sitting in the 'Nip'.

Tomas planned to do some research on Gay Jay while settling into his cubicle and trying to get comfortable. There wasn't much to do on his first day and so he took time to 'work the room' and introduce himself, and also shadow some of the other journalists and production crew.

He was also excited to watch his first *The Industry Tonight* broadcast from his cubicle in the background of the set. He had heard so much about it. That's when Tomas learned a new rule. *The Industry Tonight* mandated that anyone in the building at 7 p.m. had to sit in their cubicle during the 7 p.m. broadcast so that the room didn't look empty. That night there were only a few people around so it looked pretty empty anyway, but the experience was impressive to him still. He was glad to be there. He knew that he had made the right choice.

Tomas came in late the next day since Gay Jay's show wasn't until later that night. He spent the afternoon getting used to his new computer and thinking up questions for his interview. On a typical day in Boise, Tomas would be rushing around from news scene to interview to news conference to a place to get video which TV news people referred to as 'b-roll.' Most days went quickly because they were filled with activity and deadline pressure interrupted on occasion by a breaking news story, which brought even more activity and deadline pressure. This was differ-ent. There was deadline pressure but there was also lots of time to do your work. No rush, no fuss. It left Tomas at times with no idea what to do with himself having all this extra time.

"You must be the new guy." A tallish, thin, athletic African-American man was reaching over from the next cubicle extending his hand. Startled a bit, Tomas got up and shook it. "My name is Randall and I'm your next cubicle neighbor." Randall was dressed casually in jeans and a nice cotton pullover shirt. Tomas guessed by his attire that he wasn't working that day.

"Tom Stein," Tomas said reaching out his hand for a handshake.

"Nice to meet you Tom Stein. Randall Larson. Hey, I'm off this week but had to stop by the office because I've lost my other cell phone charger. I'll be in next Monday though. Looking forward to learning more about you."

"Thanks, me too!"

"And hey, nice work on that missing man story. You nailed it," Randall said while walking away. Apparently at least two people had seen his story on the discovery of Jason Young's car in the river. "See ya!" And as quickly as he had introduced himself the tall black man named Randall was out of the newsroom. Bored, Tomas decided to look up his bio on the station's website and read it to himself aloud in a soft voice.

"Randall Larson is a correspondent for the WWDC-TV 3 nightly newscast *The Industry Tonight* where he focuses on covering Congress. Randall is a native of Southern California who came to DC-3 from a television station in Kansas City where he was their top investigative reporter and broke stories on a regular basis. He's also worked at television stations in Sacramento, CA and Boise, ID."

Tomas sat up. "Boise?" They would have at least one thing in common. The bio didn't mention which station, but Tomas did a quick Google search and found it was not the same station which he had just come from.

Tomas found Randall's past a bit odd because there just were not a lot of African-American journalists in Boise—mainly because there were not many African-Americans there at all. Hispanics were the largest minority in the area and there weren't all that many of them either. It was one of the 'whitest' areas of the country he had ever visited much less lived in.

There was more on the bio including that Randall had been an accomplished tennis player in high school and college and had a wife and two kids. Tomas skimmed over the rest of it. He had already found the connection that he was looking for.

He then decided his remaining time in the afternoon would be best spent getting to the comedy venue early and getting set up. The show was still three hours in the future but Tomas was new in town and figured he would find something to keep him occupied.

Gay Jay was performing his comedy routine that night at a place called the Atrium Warehouse. It was an old warehouse down by the old Potomac Docks which had been converted into a restaurant, bar and performing arts center. Tomas was surprised at how the restaurant, bar and stage area kind of blended together into one. Dinner started at 5 p.m. and went until 8 p.m. Performances on the stage came afterward and the bar was open until 2 a.m.

The stage area was surrounded by dinner tables on three sides. Tomas thought it almost looked like a really, really wide catwalk. There were also two large balconies which surrounded the stage on three sides. Customers could gather to eat and then look over the balcony railings to watch the show. The bar was in the very back and the kitchen was in an enclosed area behind it.

The manager, a woman named Beth, pointed out to Tomas where he could set up once they moved around a few dinner tables. She also showed him where to find an audio input so he could get a direct feed of sound from the microphone on stage. The venue did a lot of videotaped events including a recent cable channel special in part because it was well equipped for the media. It was also a nice, cozy venue for comedians like Gay Jay to do some warm-up work before performing at a bigger arena. Jay had been booked on a national cable network to participate in their New Year's Eve special programming from Washington, DC, and he was using this performance tonight to help prepare.

"If you need to use the bathroom feel free to use the service door," Beth told Tomas. "It's right over there. When they built this place they made a special bathroom area for staff, but there is a door into the main men's bathroom if you need it."

"That seems kind of odd," Tomas replied.

"It's an old building. There's lots of strange stuff in here," she responded shrugging. "One more thing," Beth said. "You see over there?" She was pointing to a round table where six men and a woman were seated. "Do you know who that is?" Beth asked him. At first Tomas did not. "That's the Reverend Benjamin Rivers."

"Really?" Tomas replied. "What's the Governor of Illinois doing here?"

The Reverend Governor Ben Rivers insisted people put his title of God before his title of office and he *was* more than the governor of a state. He was also now a candidate for President of the United States seeking the Republican nomination. The former college offensive lineman was nicknamed 'Big Ben' by some because he was quite large. He had seemed a long shot for the Republican nomination at first, but was gaining traction in the Midwest and South. Many now saw him as the odds-on favorite to win the Iowa Caucuses. If he did win he would be the first African-American Republican Presidential candidate to do so. But why was he eating dinner in Washington, DC the day before New Year's Eve?

The table where Big Ben was eating had been placed apart from the rest of the atrium. That meant for Tomas that just walking up to the Reverend Governor, introducing himself, and asking what he was doing there seemed a bit unrealistic. Tomas didn't see signs of security people anywhere, but he knew there must be some somewhere. Maybe it was one or two of the people sitting with him.

Tomas moved over to the bar and ordered a diet drink and an appetizer, attempting to be inconspicuous while looking over frequently trying to figure out how he could meet the Reverend Governor. Then Big Ben got up and appeared to excuse himself. He was heading for the bathroom. A security guard followed him and blocked the main restroom door. Tomas waited a minute, got up and headed for the service door where there was no guard. He then walked through the service door entrance into the main restroom where Rivers was. It was a small restroom—a few stalls and five urinals, and it appeared Rivers was the only one inside. Tomas unzipped his pants and pulled up to a urinal two down from the Reverend Governor.

"How you doing?" Tomas nodded to Rivers.

"I'm good. And yourself?" the man politely replied without looking over. He seemed a little surprised that there was another entrance to the restroom and that someone was in there with him.

Tomas wasted no time. He was just going to have to go for it at this point. He was there under false pretenses after all. His bladder had nothing to give. "Reverend Rivers, my name in Tom Stein. I'm a correspondent for a local TV station for the news program *The Industry Tonight*." The Reverend replied with a heavy sigh but kept looking forward. "What are you doing in DC?" Tomas asked him.

Rivers smiled. "If I told you that I would have to kill you. Or have someone else kill you."

"Okay then. Well while you are in town could I arrange to get an interview with you?"

Rivers looked over and then looked Tomas up and down. "Is it my imagination or are the reporters here getting younger and younger?"

"I'm new," Tomas sheepishly replied.

The Reverend moved away from the urinal, zipped up his pants and started heading for a nearby sink. "Sorry son but I pay people good money to manage my media for me. You're free to call my campaign office to schedule something."

Tomas knew that was a dead end but he had to give it another shot. He moved over to the sink just to complete the false impression that he was in the restroom for a reason other than to ask Rivers for an interview.

"So tell me, are you enjoying your night out?" Rivers asked. He could sense a feeling of disappointment from Tomas and wanted to depart on friendly terms.

"Actually, I'm working. I'm doing a story on the comedian performing here tonight, Jay the Gay Comi-Queen."

"You're doing a story on Gay Jay?" the Reverend said with a sense of interest. "When I heard he was performing here I pulled a few strings to get a front row seat."

Tomas found it odd that a man of the cloth would pull strings to see an openly gay comic whose calling card was being outrageous due to his politically biting performances—especially against Republicans. "Yeah, well I'm going to interview him after the show tonight."

Big Ben's face lit up. He looked at Tomas and thought for a moment. "I'll tell you what son. If you let me come with you for your interview and watch it, then I'll give you an interview before I leave on Friday."

It was an incredibly odd request and Tomas wasn't sure what to make of it. He had never had anyone request something like that before, much less a candidate for President of the United States, but there was no way he was going to turn the Reverend down. "You got a deal."

The Reverend gave out a hearty laugh. "Okay. Come to my table when his show wraps up." He kept laughing as he exited the bathroom leaving Tomas attempting to comprehend the bizarre chain of events which had just occurred.

Tomas headed back to the bar, finishing his food slowly while using his smartphone to catch up on the news. He had never seen Jay the Gay Comi-Queen in action and waited with anticipation as the eight o'clock hour approached.

At 8:05 the lights went down a bit in the room and an announcer came out on stage to warm up the crowd. It wouldn't be long now. Tomas had no idea what to expect.

CHAPTER 11

THE WARM-UP HOST TOLD THE AUDIENCE a few jokes and then read the rules of the club. Everyone was listening but no one was really paying attention to him. They were here for the main attraction.

"And now!" the host said with a dramatic raising of his voice, "The Warehouse Atrium along with Comedy First productions presents the one, the only—and Thank God for that—Jay the Gay Comi-Queen."

Jay pranced out. That's the only word Tomas could think of to describe it. He pranced onto the stage from a side entrance waving his arms to loud applause and cheers. Tomas looked over and even the Reverend was getting into it with some very loud claps. After saying "Thank you" a few times and taking a couple of bows Gay Jay grabbed a microphone from a stand and got to it.

"So how are you all doing tonight?" Gay Jay asked a bit too enthusiastically.

As if on cue the audience raised their hands to show the 'okay' sign and then shouted in unison "Ohhh kay!"

"God help me; that never gets old," Jay shouted back. "As you can see I dressed up for you tonight." Jay did an imitation fashion-model walk down the catwalk showing off his skin-tight pinkish leather pants and a black leather vest which were somewhat reminiscent of what you would see in a bondage video. Jay was in good shape and his outfit accentuated his toned body. Tomas would almost go so far as to say that he looked kind of *hot*.

After he finished doing a twirl to loud catcalls and whistles from the audience Jay turned back toward the audience and started his act. "You know, a wise older man once told me that my dress was too tame. That while I do act and dress flamboyant, what people really want out of Gay Jay's dress is to be fla-ming! And I thought about it for a moment and then I replied, 'Maybe you're right Barack Obama, but I'm just not that kind of girl.' "

The audience replied with the type of nervous laugh Gay Jay so relished. *Where was this going?* Tomas thought to himself as he continued to videotape the act.

"Ah, Barack Obama. Remember 'Hope and Change'? Doesn't that seem like decades ago? I mean several of you in this audience might be surprised to learn that he's actually still alive." Jay started walking around the edge of the catwalk surveying the audience as if he were looking for someone in particular.

"So did you all see the Democratic debate a couple of weeks back?" Jay stopped. He had found what he was looking for and it genuinely seemed to surprise him. He was looking directly at the Reverend Governor. "Wait, I know you! Do I know you?"

"No!" Rev. Rivers responded loudly, Jay's microphone picking up his reply in the distance.

Jay stared at him for a second longer and then it hit him. "Oh my, *oh myyy*! We have political royalty in the room. Is it really you? Ladies and Gentlemen, the Reverend Governor Ben Rivers."

There was applause best described as a *smattering* of applause. There were also some boos. "Oh don't boo him because he's a Republican!" Gay Jay protested. "Boo him because he's a black man who's a Republican!"

Gay Jay hadn't realized that while he had just arrived on stage most everyone else had been sitting, eating and drinking for a while. They had seen the Reverend Governor already. Many had pointed and mouthed softly to a companion, "Do you know who that is?" They did. Jay was the last to know.

"What are *youuuu* doing *heerrrre?*" Gay Jay teased the Reverend Governor.

"I'm here to see you!" Gov. Rivers could be heard to say in a raised voice from his chair.

"Wow!" Jay replied seeming a little surprised. "So how do you feel about gay men?"

"Live and let live," Big Ben yelled back. "Judge not lest you be judged!"

"Look, it's a *crazy* Republican!" Jay replied. "I mean I love a good party, but I don't think I'm joining yours!"

The audience laughed and clapped.

"You know what they call my party Reverend?" Jay asked.

"Ah, Democrat?" Rivers responded.

Jay shook his head *no*. "My party is L-G-B-T-Q," Jay replied. "My party is more fun than your party, but I confess that your branding is better. Jay then looked around at his audience. "I know, L-G-B-T-Q. Awful, right? That's our brand? Seriously? We can't do any better than that? I mean I thought we considered ourselves to be creative!"

Jay paused while the audience laughed again.

"And why does the *L* get to go first? Is it in order of importance or something? Because if it were a race, we know the trans woman would beat the lesbian every time!"

Another pause and more laughter.

"Now the trans movement is now trying to convince people that biological men can become pregnant. They now call anyone expecting a baby a 'pregnant person'. Does this now mean that us men will also need contraception? Because I have to tell you that if I'm going to have to take a pill before sex that's not the pill I'm taking!"

Jay broke into a wide smile as the audience laughed.

"L-G-B-T and don't forget the Q and that is *still* too exclusive, so we have to add a plus sign now at the end. Here's my idea. L-G-B-T-Q-F-E-E. Lesbian, gay, bi, trans, queer and *effin' everyone else!*"

Jay paused for the laugh and then after the laughter died down, he asked, "So how are you all doing tonight."

"Ohhh-kayyy" was the audience's obligatory response while once again flashing okay signs.

"Since the Reverend Governor is here, let's talk some politics. I was watching the Democratic Presidential Debate a few weeks ago in Iowa and was shocked—*shocked* to learn that every single candidate on stage raised their hand when asked if they believed that America is structurally racist!"

Jay paused and pointed out toward his audience. "*Racist!*" He then looked over at the African-American Reverend Governor, pointed at the audience again and asked, "Racist?" Governor Rivers shook his head in a *no* motion.

Jay continued, "I don't think America is structurally racist. No, I think America is accidentally racist. Let me tell you what I mean." Jay began to pace back and forth on the stage as he continued with his story.

"My extremely wealthy brother lives in one of those gated communities. You know, the ones where black and Hispanic people build magnificent houses for rich, white, privileged people to live in."

More laughter.

"So one day I'm walking near his home when I see a house under construction. A magnificent house and sitting outside under a tree were a small group of black carpenters. It was a beautiful day and they were outside eating lunch on some lawn chairs and a makeshift table. I waved to them and they waved back as I passed. So I'm visiting again a year later. I love my brother but once a year with his family is *plenty!*"

More of an understanding collective chuckle came from the audience this time.

"And I'm walking by the same house. It's finished; the construction workers are all gone; and as I'm walking by that same tree I notice something in the area where those workers were having lunch probably day after day one year ago. It was a wild watermelon patch."

Jay paused for a moment as if to trick his audience into thinking that might be a punch line.

"I told that story to a friend of mine," Jay continued, "and he told me, 'You can't use *that*! It's racist!'

I respond, "But it's the truth. I'm not making that up. Some black workers who took a lunch break outside every warm day obviously enjoyed watermelon, spit out the seeds, and one year later nature did its thing. That's not racist. It's being observant."

"But my friend—he's not buying it. 'You know, *blacks* and *watermelons*. It's a stereotype.' And I look him in the eye and I say, 'the only way that story is racist is if I exaggerate it just a *little* bit and add that I also noticed a flock of *fried chickens* nearby!'"

The joke brought one of those reluctant audience laughs that Gay Jay seemed to enjoy more than any other. The laugh no one wanted to make but couldn't help themselves.

"Accidental racism. Truth is that if you look hard enough for something in society, you're going to find it. You could all be racists just for laughing at that joke, right? Take comedy for instance. I as a non-professionally trained comedian have an eye for finding humor in the things you experience every day. Right? Same with racism, or sexism, or *homo-phobia*." Jay pounded his chest as if to emphasize that the last one particularly applied to him. "Look hard enough and you can find it pretty much everywhere. Let me give you another example."

Jay looked back over at Reverend Rivers. "You like fried chicken Reverend?"

"I'm trying to cut back," Tomas could hear Big Ben reply in the distance.

"What is it about black people and fried chicken? Why do blacks get to corner the stereotype on liking fried chicken? White people *love* fried chicken. Gay white people, namely *me*, savor fried chicken! I love it when I bite into some freshly fried chicken and the chicken juices and the oil explode all over my face and my hands suddenly get really greasy and I get so greasy I just rub it all over myself!"

Somehow Jay had managed to palm a plastic ball filled with grease in his hand so that when he bit into it while faking eating fried chicken, the grease exploded onto his hands and face. He then proceeded to rub it all over his body in sort of a mini-burlesque imitation while the audience clapped and cheered him on.

"But you know what I don't like about fried chicken?" he continued. "I don't like the whole process of buying it from my favorite fried chicken restaurant. Because in order to get the chicken I truly love I have to walk into a restaurant with some old white codger's face plastered all over it who has an honorary military designation of Colonel which traces its roots to the Confederate Army while wearing the white suit and string tie of the old plantation south. Then I go inside where a group of—let's be honest—mostly black men and women working for *slave wages* listen intently to my orders and then serve me delicious food. I mean seriously, that's not a comfortable experience for me!"

The audience was laughing and clapping and nodding their heads. Tomas could see that Jay had hit a chord with many of them and he had made his point.

"You're all *accidental racists*!" Jay shouted at them as if he weren't actually sure he had made his point.

That kind of joke was one of the reasons Tomas was there. Gay Jay liked to take stock of the ironies of society and politics and no one was immune. Beyond 'accidental racism' his act that night would include other skits including;

Advice from Gordon Leach of *Lifestyles of the Rich and Famous* to

Black Lives Matters leaders buying million-dollar homes. (One joke went "Capitalize on your investment by pitching a new reality show sitcom set in one of your mansions called *The Beverly Hip Hoppies.*")

When woke tweets from young Republicans go horribly wrong (including one fake tweet "How my life changed forever the day we lost Tupac.")

Quizzing rioters on current events. ("I asked one young man why he was trying to tear down the statue of Andrew Jackson and he told me it was because he was a mean father who screwed up the life of the King of Pop.")

And so on. Gay Jay was part funny man and part social commentator. He was relevant to people because in a world where many saw political correctness and cancel culture run amok he seemed to be especially unafraid. That's why Tomas had been sent there to interview him.

Before the act was over the young woman named Beth, who had shown him the double bathroom door earlier, came back to help him carry his equipment to a back room where the interview with Gay Jay would take place. Tomas told her that the Reverend Governor Rivers wanted to observe the interview and so she left to escort him back to the room as well.

Tomas could hear that Gay Jay's set was wrapping up with his signature ending, "So how would you rate my act tonight?" to which the audience responded in unison, "Ohhh-kayyy!" and erupted into laughter and applause. It wouldn't be long now.

It was at about this time that Governor Rivers entered the room while his guard stood watch outside. He seemed genuinely eager and excited to meet Jay. That sort of surprised Tomas because they weren't really two people you would expect to see in the same room together, much less enjoying each other's company if they did happen to be in the same room together.

"Where would you like me to sit?" he asked while scoping out the interview area Tomas had set up.

"How about in that chair in the corner over there?" Big Ben nodded and walked over and sat down.

"That was some show," Rivers said while getting seated and watching Tomas finish setting up his lighting for the interview.

"Would it surprise you if I told you that it surprised me that you enjoyed it?" Tomas replied.

At that very moment Gay Jay burst through the door. He didn't enter; he burst. "Wasn't that just *fabulous*!" he exclaimed. He then did a double take when he realized the Reverend Governor was sitting in a chair along a far wall.

Rivers stood up to shake his hand. "That was great Jay. I thoroughly enjoyed your act."

For once Jay was silent, clearly stunned and unsure how to respond.

Rivers continued saying, "I just love how you speak truth to power."

So that was the connection between them Tomas thought to himself. All night he had been trying to figure out why a man of the cloth who was also a Republican candidate for President would attend the comedy show of a performer who described his own work as provocative, sexual, sometimes obscene, openly gay and devilishly funny. It was because Jay pushed back comically the way Rivers pushed back politically. Two very different men rebelling in their own unique ways.

"Thank you," was all Jay could muster in response. "Thank you for coming to my show." Jay paused for a moment and then gave him a quizzical question. "Ah, why are you here?"

"This reporter graciously allowed me to sit in on your interview. Is that, is that, *ohhh-kayyy*?" Rivers said while flashing the okay sign with his right hand.

This time it was Jay who was laughing. He then shook his head in seeming disbelief that a presidential candidate was flashing the okay sign at him. He headed for the chair Tomas had put out for him and from where they would do the interview.

Once Jay sat down Tomas put a mic on him, double-checked the framing on the camera and sat down in a chair opposite to him. He could see out of the corner of his eye Reverend Rivers returning to his chair. He tried to push out of his mind the strangeness of a candidate for the Presidency of the United States sitting in on his interview with a comedian.

Tomas liked to start one-on-one interviews with provocative questions. In his mind it helped set the tone of the question-and-answer session and was also a bit of a time saver. Why wait to get to your best questions when you could just ask them from the start? "I know a lot of people in the gay community are outspoken about not liking your comedy."

Jay's back stiffened and he sat up in his chair and made a face. Had the question somehow insulted him? Tomas was unprepared for what would come next because in a near pitch perfect imitation of former President Donald Trump, Jay answered, "Only Rosie O'Donnell!"

Tomas could hear the Reverend Governor laughing at Jay's use of a line by Trump at his very first Presidential debate and he gave him a glaring look. Inviting Big Ben in was not the best idea. Rivers got the message and tried to choke back his laughter, but the response brought a big smile to Jay's face.

"Okay, seriously. You get flak from some members of the gay community. They don't think your brand of comedy is helpful," Tomas continued with his question.

"Helpful? Helpful!" Jay responded raising his voice. "No one ever paid me a dime to be helpful. I'm here to be *funny*, not *helpful*. And that's not what they mean anyway."

"What do they mean?"

"They're just upset because I'm courageous, and they don't want to admit that they're cowards."

CHAPTER 12

"Cowards?" Tomas asked Jay.

"Cowards of conformity. Rebellion discouraged. No dissent allowed. Some don't like it when I poke fun at the movement, like with the LGBTQ+ thing. I can make a joke about anyone and anything, but not about being gay? Some think that if I tell a joke about it that I'm somehow being divisive within the community and subjecting it to more ridicule."

"Do they have a point?"

"No!" Jay responded. "Look, there are pioneers in the gay rights movement who I adore. Names like Frank Kameny and Dick Leitsch and Barbara Gittings. Names you may not even recognize but who are giants for people like me who now get to do things that they never could. I can kiss a guy in public. I can marry. I can join the army. I can make millions by going on stage and just being me. I can be free! But I can't speak up? I can't criticize? I can't tell a joke? That's not freedom. All that is trading one life where I have to hide my sexuality for another where I have to conform because of my sexuality. That's not freedom. That's just trading one jail cell for another, although admittedly one with nicer guards in well-tailored uniforms and way better soap."

Tomas could hear Reverend Rivers chuckling in the background. Was there a joke in there?

"And look," Jay continued. "I get why some in the gay community may not like my act. It is over-the-top flamboyant on purpose. It's a part of the show. I mean look at how I'm dressed! And maybe they fear that I'm contributing to stereotypes that some people have about gay men. But I don't see it that way. I see where I get to pack a room full of straights and gays and trans people and blacks and whites and whoever else wants to show up and none of that matters to any of them. We're just having a big party where we get to laugh both with each other and at each other and just have fun. No one is ever going to be able to convince me that's a bad thing."

"Do you ever worry about being canceled?" Tomas asked him.

"You mean like with cancel culture?"

"Yes," Tomas confirmed.

"Every comedian worries about that. Why do you think no one plays college campuses anymore? All the stupid little Hitlers running around with garbage for brains intent on shouting down anyone who they are offended by or don't agree with."

"Little Hitlers. A little strong don't you think?" Being a Jew Tomas disliked Nazi analogies.

"Not when you think about the damage they can do. Think of everything that has gone wrong in human history when we censor opinions and cancel dissent!"

"Hitler and Nazi Germany," Tomas affirmed.

"Yeah. Burning all those books should have been a pretty big clue as to what was coming next. Here's another example for you. I have this theory that the Black Plague of the Middle Ages was caused by lack of dissent," Jay asserted.

"Huh?" Tomas had no idea where Jay was going with this.

"Absolutely. In the decades before the Black Plague the Pope decreed that all cats were evil. All of a sudden all over Europe people are torturing and killing cats. They even made public spectacles of them. Now you know there had to have been people back then thinking, '*You know, that guy in the pointy hat is kind of losing it with this cat killing thing.*' But no, they just went along with killing cats and so with the cats away, the rats came to play and then came the plague!"

Tomas had no idea if what Jay was saying was true so he tried to move the interview along. "So cancel culture has the potential to …"

"Cancel culture has the potential to destroy one of the most diverse, most tolerant, greatest forces for good in the world, because if we can't have honest discussions with each other without worrying about someone taking offense, then we in this nation are no longer free."

"You believe comedy can save our nation?" Tomas concluded.

"I do my best," Jay responded with a wry smile. "Or at least I push back. Take the whole 'Jay is okay' thing. People have been using the okay sign for as long as I can remember. And then one day I guess some white supremacists use it in a group photo before they go read passages from *Mein Kampf* around the campfire. All of a sudden if you flash an okay sign with your hand then you're a white supremacist too. It's ridiculous! It's like if I give you the middle finger and then tell you that it is the new symbol for gay pride, you wouldn't buy that, and you shouldn't!"

"When you make jokes about accidental racism, that's also pushing back? That's dissent?" Tomas asked.

"It is. My point is that as a comedian I look for humor in those moments others find mundane. I can make a joke out of most anything really. If you are someone who benefits from the notion that everyone and everything is racist then you'll find it everywhere. Take this interview for instance."

"This interview is racist?" Tomas asked indignantly.

"Well, the way I see it there are two white men in the spotlight and a black man in the darkness in the corner," Jay responded and smiled.

Tomas could hear Reverend Rivers laugh and begin to clap. "Well said sir. Well said."

"So tell me *booooyyyy*, could you fetch me a Fresca?" Jay yelled mockingly over at Rivers in a slightly southern drawl.

More laughter and clapping from Rivers. Tomas could see the

attraction between the two men. They were for all intents and purposes on opposite sides of the political spectrum, and yet they felt a kinship in their ideas about freedom and the right to self-expression. There was a similar rebellious streak in both of them.

"And if you make everything racist then nothing is racist, right?" Gay Jay continued. "That's one of the points of my act. How ridiculous that some act in racist indignation over things that were never intended to be racist at all, just like with the okay sign. Accidental racism."

"But you're not saying there's no racism in America, are you?"

"No, of course not!" Jay answered almost as if insulted by the question. "Or sexism, or homophobia, and that's because there are idiots everywhere, right? There are idiots that look like you, pray like him ..." Jay said gesticulating toward the Reverend, "... and there are idiots who tell jokes like me," he continued while breaking into a wide smile. Then his expression turned more serious as he leaned into Tomas. "But in my day-to-day life most of the people I meet are polite and nice and more than tolerant; they're friendly. Are we really going to judge whole groups of people by the worst among them? Ain't nothing more bigoted than that!"

Tomas paused for a moment to take in what Jay was telling him, but Jay decided to fill the silence.

"I'll give you an example of an idiot among us in the gay community. Remember the whole Jussie Smollett thing in Chicago?"

Tomas did. Smollett was a popular black actor who was also gay who had staged a hate crime against himself in the streets of Chicago. He paid two Nigerian friends to fake attack him using bleach and a noose. Smollett was reportedly upset because he wasn't being paid more for his work, and thought news of the racist attack would bring him more sympathy from the producers of the television show in which he was a star at the time.

Jay continued, "Here's a guy who pays two Nigerians to fake attack him in the middle of the night in Chicago so he can claim two racist white guys did it." Jay stopped for a moment and stared into the TV news camera.

"And Jussie, if you're watching, take my advice. Don't quit your day job because casting clearly is not your strong suit!" And then he winked. "Oh wait, Jussie, you no longer have a day job!"

Even Tomas laughed at that one.

"It became a full-fledged national outrage until people started to realize it was all fake. Here was a man trying to use made up racism to further his career. And you know what I really hate about what he did?" Jay continued.

Tomas did not know.

Jay said, "It's that it gives every idiot white cracker out there one more reason to look sideways at black and gay people." Jay sat up again and went back into his rural drawl. "Martha! You need to watch out for them there gay, black people. They might try to fraaaammeee you! Especially if you're handling a noose while carryin' bleeeacchhh!"

"You should use that in your act," Tomas shot back smiling.

"But here is the thing," Jay continued. "How often have we seen people claim bigotry not because it was really there but because in some way it worked to their advantage. It's a shame because it really waters down those moments when it is actually there."

"The boy who cried *wolf*'" Tomas responded referencing an old fairy tale.

"And in the United States today there are far fewer wolves in my opinion than some would lead you to believe," Jay responded.

"But some do accuse you of 'punching down' with some of your jokes. Can your comedy be too controversial at times?"

"I don't punch *down*. I punch *line*! I use my comedy to point out some of the absurdities in life and I'm an equal opportunity offender. Look," Jay continued, "I don't deny that my comedy has gotten more edgy and controversial in recent years. I'm a more confident comedian now and in comedy, if you don't evolve you die!"

"Die?" Tomas asked.

"Yes, think of it this way. If you go to a Rolling Stones rock concert and if they don't play the song "Satisfaction" you might just demand your money back. It's a decades-old classic! But there is no such thing as a classic joke. I need to be continually coming up with new material for my audience. And as that audience grows bigger and bigger and I make more and more money, not only has my confidence risen, but I've gained new perspectives from interacting with a wider circle of people who I didn't know much about before. I've learned a lot from them these past few years and that's reflected in my comedy."

In a way Tomas too was on a similar journey. He was in a new city in a completely new environment and he felt he was learning a lot too. But needed to wrap it up. Tomas hated long interviews for a very selfish reason. He found logging long interviews a chore to break down into soundbites for a news story. Tomas asked a few questions about how Jay got into comedy and the origins of his act, but it was getting late. This was supposed to be primarily a political interview for a 2-minute story and Tomas felt he had what he needed. He thanked Jay, grabbed the mic off his shirt and started packing up his gear.

The Reverend emerged from the shadows to shake Jay's hand and then handed him a business card of some sort. "I would appreciate your support," Rivers asked almost surprisingly. *Would Gay Jay ever vote for a Trump-loving Republican* Tomas wondered to himself? Probably not but Jay was gracious about it. He looked at the card in the TV lighting which was still set up. Rivers then added, "You'll find my assistant Annie's contact information on the back. Please reach out to her if you ever need to contact me."

Rivers then turned to Tomas. "Same with you. Here's my card. Annie's contact information is on the back. I want to thank you for letting me sit in."

"Well, I did keep up my end of the bargain," Tomas replied.

The Reverend Governor smiled. "Yes you did. I have to leave town to go to New York for New Years. I have family there and they asked me tonight to come celebrate with them. But I'm coming back to DC to preach at a local church on Sunday. We can do your interview then. Call Annie on Saturday and she'll set it up."

Tomas was a bit disappointed. In his experience interviews scheduled that far out tended not to happen at all. It was more of a delaying tactic where something would come up in the interim and the interview would be canceled. He didn't have much of a choice though. "I'll call her Saturday," Tomas told Rivers.

It was late and Tomas had already arranged to take the news car home that night. WWDC used unmarked news cars so no one would be the wiser about the unfamiliar vehicle parked in front of his apartment. The only mandate was that he had to unload his camera gear and take it inside the locked apartment.

Tomas thought about an outline for the Gay Jay story when he got home, but as he went to bed he started reading the Reverend Governor's autobiography. Rivers like many who burst onto the presidential candidate sweepstakes had written a book to introduce himself to the American electorate. True to his rebel instincts, he chose a title which raised some eyebrows and probably sold a few more copies. He named it *The Donald and Me. My Enlightened Journey Into Trump-ism.* The cover had a photo of him and former President Trump appearing on a stage together.

The first chapter had gotten some play in the press as well. It read in total like this.

"I am by all accounts a black man, but I am not an African-American. My parents were both first generation-born Americans. My father's family came from Jamaica and my mother's from the Dominican Republic. My roots may lie in Africa as does all of human civilization, but I have no direct way by which to trace them back there. And if anything I have just written about my race and heritage matters in the least little bit to you then this book probably is not for you. Chapter 2."

Tomas smiled. The words of a rebel.

CHAPTER 13

IF THE REVEREND GOVERNOR BEN RIVERS had made one mistake in his autobiography it was that he wrote it chronologically. The book began with his childhood and it took him a few chapters to get to present day. Thankfully those first chapters were short as if the Reverend Governor's early years somehow happened in fast forward, but they were also pretty mundane.

Rivers wrote about how he had been born in Chicago as the only child of an Air Force veteran and his wife. Both his parents' families were rooted in New York, but after being an Air Force mechanic for several years, Ben's father was recruited first to an aircraft maintenance facility and then to a major airline's operations center based at O'Hare Airport.

Rivers was born in a neighborhood not far from O'Hare, but as he grew, his parents became concerned about his education and the state of the local public schools. Rivers had never known a day when his father did not work the overnight shift. His parents came to realize that navigating Chicago's daily gridlock wasn't going to be an issue no matter where they lived because the elder Rivers was commuting at such odd hours when traffic was light.

The Rivers ended up buying a modest home and settling in a more rural subdivision in northern Illinois between the city of Rockford and the Wisconsin state line. It was just an hour's commute down the tollway to

O'Hare. Traffic was almost always non-existent when his father left late at night and returned from work the next morning. As a result of their move most of the Rivers' neighbors were white, but there was also a smattering of blacks and Hispanics.

It was overall a very welcoming and tolerant neighborhood. The Rockford area was still a manufacturing hub even as manufacturing went into decline. Most of the homeowners had good paying jobs making components for all sorts of things including aerospace parts.

Rivers' childhood seemed normal enough for a suburban kid, even a black suburban kid. His parents were God-fearing people who took him to church each Sunday, although not to the same church every week. Some Sundays it would be a black church closer to downtown Rockford; other Sundays it would be the white church nearer his own neighborhood, but it would always be a Baptist Church.

Many assumed it was his upbringing that led Rivers to pursue the ministry, but Rivers wrote that it wasn't that at all. It was football.

Ben Rivers was always a big kid even though his parents were not. By the time he was a freshman in high school he was already 6 feet 2 inches tall and pushing 200 pounds. Rivers had always dreamed of being a football quarterback and wrote that his first real brush with racism came when he tried to pursue that dream in high school. The head coach of the varsity football program was a man named Baldy Pierce. No one knew his real first name. He had reportedly gone bald as a young man and the nickname stuck.

Rivers wanted to try out for quarterback, but Pierce told him the team needed him to play on the offensive line. Ben was devastated! He complained to his father that the only reason he wasn't getting a chance at QB was because the head coach couldn't envision the team having a black quarterback. Rivers wrote that his father's reaction surprised him.

"Do you really think I work the overnight shift because I like it?" Rivers' father asked him. "When I went into the Air Force I only had a high school education. That meant I couldn't be an officer who flew planes but I could learn to fix them. And when I got out of the military there were good opportunities to make a good living repairing amazing pieces of machinery if I was willing to work overnight, so that's what I did. You don't know if what you're facing is racism! And if you think everything that doesn't go your way is racism then you'll be nothing but a victim for the rest of your life. So don't whine to me about the opportunity you can't have. Suck it up and make the most of the opportunity you can have and you'll be successful just like I am!" Rivers wrote that it was some of the best advice he ever got from his father.

Rather than sulk at a slight he blamed on racism Rivers decided to embrace becoming the best offensive lineman he could be. He worked hard on the field and in the weight room bulking up his body even more. The result was that by his senior year in high school he was being offered a full football scholarship to a number of colleges.

Football also brought him closer to God. He and some of his teammates would regularly attend events sponsored by the Christian Athlete Club. Various speakers would come to talk to the young players over breakfast about how religion impacted their daily lives, and Ben began to see what he called "The living God." He recognized how belief in Christ could change lives and motivate men and women to be a better version of themselves through the Lord. It convinced him that he wanted to help be that change for others and football could help him achieve that. He would use his scholarship opportunities to pursue becoming an ordained minister.

Rivers ended up attending a small Baptist college in Iowa. Despite being small the school was remarkably able to man an entire football team. To say he dominated on the football field would be an understatement. At one point a few NFL scouts even showed up to check out his play.

Big Ben had other plans. The school he attended had a partnership agreement with a larger public college for ROTC, and Ben decided to follow in his father's footsteps and join the Air Force after graduating. The big difference for him was that rather than enlisting as his father had, he would be entering the military as a college-educated officer.

Rivers would serve in the military for eight years as a transport pilot. He loved flying. Being in the air brought him closer to the majesty of the heavens and to God. While many of his fellow officers planned to parlay their flying skills into lucrative positions as airline pilots, Rivers' dream of joining the ministry never wavered. By the time he was set to leave the Air Force he had already enrolled in divinity school.

Tomas was bored. It was late at night and Rivers' book was putting him to sleep, a result he was pretty certain was not the intended outcome. Maybe Rev. Rivers' roots did appeal to some potential voters out there but that didn't make it good storytelling. Tomas as a journalist had always been taught to 'lead with his fist' when telling a story. Start with the most compelling information you could to gain the reader's interest and then work to hold it throughout. Whatever this biography was it wasn't that. Tomas decided to skip ahead a few chapters.

That was until he came to the chapter which started like this.

"I became a political acolyte of Donald J. Trump at the scene of a riot." Now Tomas thought he was getting somewhere.

CHAPTER 14

"I BECAME A POLITICAL ACOLYTE OF DONALD J. TRUMP at the scene of a riot," Chapter 5 began.

"I had been in the Illinois State Senate for nearly ten years when Donald Trump announced his candidacy for President. Like many I thought it was a publicity stunt. I had never much cared for 'The Donald' up to that point. Never watched a single episode of his reality television show 'The Apprentice' or stepped inside a Trump Hotel, not even the one in Chicago. To me he was the multi-millionaire showman, a P.T. Barnum for his day and his presidential campaign would be little more than a political circus."

"And yet as Donald Trump was opening the door to his political future, I was considering closing the door on my own. My personal political odyssey had started in a fit of rage. My father had suffered a stroke and was forced to retire. I returned home to help my parents out for a short period of time and ended up never leaving. As I started to manage the family finances, I was shocked to learn that my parents were paying nearly $1000 per month in property taxes for their modest, four-bedroom home. A $1000 a *month*! And for what?"

"Even worse, the local school board was pushing a referendum on the ballot for the next election to take even more tax money. I could not believe it. What middle class family can afford to pay $1000 per month in property taxes. And they wanted *more*?"

"I went down to a public forum where school officials would try to sell voters on the tax increase and gave one of the best sermons of my lifetime," Rivers wrote. "I told the story of my parents and how hard they had worked to make a home and raise their only child. How I never knew a day in my life that my father didn't work the overnight shift until he could work no more. How the government was draining them of a lifetime of dreams achieved and goals acquired by taking what little money they had been able to save. Raise taxes on them? You should be lowering taxes instead!"

Rivers continued to write, "When I finished my sermon of sorts I could feel the anger in my face and my black skin did little to hide it from others. Some applauded as I sat down. School board members looked at me scornfully. They knew I had cost them some votes.

"I was approached by Coach Baldy Pierce after the meeting, not realizing he was also in attendance. He told me that after he had retired from teaching and coaching that he had begun working for the Republican Party. He also let me know that the local State Senator was retiring and asked if I would be interested in seeking the seat. 'No!' I told him. I didn't know anything about politics. I didn't even know if I was a Republican. Coach laughed. 'If you hate high taxes,' he told me, 'you're probably a Republican.'

"People think of Illinois as a blue state and it is a Democratic stronghold, but that is because it's dominated politically by Chicago. Where I lived," Rivers wrote, "whoever won the Republican primary would win the seat. I was a big underdog to win that primary, but with Coach Pierce's help my campaign gained traction. People could see I was something different. I was not the same-old, same-old politician but a man with passion to achieve things for them. The local religious community also lined up behind me. Even the local Catholic church community while not outright endorsing me spread the word of my campaign, and on primary night we pulled off the biggest political upset win anyone could remember. I arrived in Springfield that winter full of big dreams and desires to bring change only to learn that in Illinois Republicans can't accomplish much.

"Imagine my frustration sitting in my seat at the Statehouse day after day as liberal Democrats passed laws that the liberal Democratic Governor would sign that they would then crow about to their liberal constituents. But they weren't helping anyone except themselves and their cronies. They would hand out taxpayers' money to this or that so that they would make the people more dependent on them. 'Don't vote for me in November,' they would tell them, 'and there'll be no more government goodies for you!' And by making people even more and more dependent on government they were only making them worse off. Crime was still rampant in the neighborhoods they represented. Their schools were still bad because they needed to placate the teachers' unions to stay in power. Government got bigger and bigger because of the power of the state workers' unions to elect Democrats who would then reward them with lush contracts that just got more and more expensive. Corruption was rewarded everywhere you looked while the taxpayers got the shaft.

"Now it was ten years later and I was feeling frustrated seeing all this happen and being powerless to prevent it. Working as a State Senator was a decent part-time job, and I was also working as an Associate Pastor at a local Baptist Church. My life was 'congregate on Sunday, legislate on Monday.' It was a routine I had worked hard for and yet had become weary of.

"My father had mercifully died the year before having suffered for some time with serious health problems and my mom wasn't doing that well with it. 'My dad died of a heart that was broken', I would tell friends, 'and now my mom is dying from a broken heart.' I would preach the hope and promise of the gospel and looked to God for guidance, but I confess that my heart at that time was full of sadness. I loved preaching but my words lacked inspiration. In Springfield I was little more than a 'placeholder politician' keeping the seat warm for the next Republican who would be in the exact same powerless position against a Democratic majority. Life was not working out the way I had expected."

Tomas had only just met Reverend Rivers, but the man he was describing in his book at that period of time seemed much different from the man with a reputation for being politically boisterous and even at times outrageous. He continued to read on.

"I was also wary of the upcoming election of 2016 at the national level. It would be Hillary Clinton's election to lose despite the largest and most diverse field of Republican candidates running for president. The truth was I wasn't sure I liked any of them that much.

"The early money among my political friends was on Jeb Bush, the son and brother of two former Presidents. My feeling was he would be perceived as just more of the same from Republicans, and he could not defeat Clinton. Others were early supporters of Sen. Ted Cruz of Texas. Cruz was what I would call a 'red meat' Republican—one of the leaders of the right wing of the Republican Party which I didn't believe had the popular support it once did. He was another candidate who I felt could not beat Clinton. Sen. Marco Rubio of Florida was an intriguing choice. I thought him to be among the smartest of the many candidates for the Republican nomination, but I could not convince myself that he was ready for the big stage. My conclusion like that of many others was that President Hillary Clinton was an inevitability.

"And then one day I was watching cable news with my mother. She had never been political throughout her life until I ran and won public office. She was tremendously proud of that and she made more of an effort to keep up with the news so that we could have dinnertime conversations about politics on those nights when I was home. The cable news channel was carrying a speech by candidate Donald Trump in Arizona. Except they were not just covering the speech. They showed live pictures of cars lined up for miles to see him while large numbers of protesters tried to block their access. 'Can you believe this?' I asked my mother in amazement. 'Hootie supports him you know,' she replied. I was speechless. 'Mrs. Hoover supports Donald Trump!'

"Barbara Hoover, who lived next door, was better known as 'Hootie' to everyone. She was an older white woman with short gray hair. She had been recently widowed and my mom and her had bonded in their grief over losing their husbands. She was also the epitome of the older, blue-collar matron of the family. Her husband had worked in manufacturing. So did one of her daughters. She was best described as a 'normal,' humble, Midwestern American, and if she supported someone like Donald J. Trump for President, I thought that maybe I should take him more seriously too.

"Among my political friends there was one State Representative who also was an early supporter of Trump. He was a retired cop who found Trump's sometimes incendiary rhetoric to have an odd sort of 'truth to power' appeal in a nation which had become too politically correct for him. He invited me to attend a Trump rally scheduled to be held in of all places—downtown Chicago. It would be an event where the Trump the lion would be walking onto the center stage of the Democrat Colosseum.

"The event turned into a clash of thousands of Trump supporters inside and thousands more anti-Trump activists both inside and outside. I could not believe my eyes. I could feel the intense energy and the passion of people from all walks of life, both pro-Trump and anti-Trump. I had never in my life seen one man able to create such a spectacle and he didn't even have to show up to create it. He ended up canceling his appearance in the interest of public safety to prevent a full-fledged riot. But the event was riotous enough.

"And as I observed all this I thought to myself that this is exactly what the Republican Party needs. Populist passion! We needed to toss aside the staid political meekness of former presidential candidates like Mitt Romney. Or the false flag of the so-called 'rebel' politician named John McCain who in truth was a traditional politician. Or the cozy conservatism of the Bush years which got us into wars we didn't want and nearly wrecked the economy. Trump wasn't just railing against Democrats; he was hitting back hard at other Republicans who he felt had no winning constituency left, and he was right about that.

"I became a fervent Trump supporter that night. I still didn't think he could win but I did think he could transform my political party into the party of real people. The party of hard-working men and woman who ask little more of their government than to protect them from harm while not taking too much from them in taxes. The party for the 'Hooties' of the world.

Tomas could not help but notice the extreme change in Rivers' tone as he wrote those words in Chapter 5. He saw it as the political version of being 'born again.' Donald Trump had reinvigorated Rivers' passion for politics which has begun as a fiery anti-tax speech a decade earlier. It explained how a preacher from Northern Illinois had been transformed into a politician who some liked to refer to now as 'Trump 2.0'

But it was late and Tomas could feel the 'sleepies' taking hold. He put his phone down and rolled onto his side. He would read more of Rivers' autobiography but for now he knew enough. More importantly, he now understood a little bit more of the man. As he dosed off he pondered questions he would ask Rivers when they next met.

CHAPTER 15

TOMAS DIDN'T TELL NAN ABOUT the possibility of a one-on-one interview with Rivers. Even as she helped him with the Gay Jay story Tomas did his best to keep from her that Rivers had also been in the same room with them. At one point she even heard Rivers laughing in the background but didn't ask Tomas about it. He assumed that she assumed it was a security person or someone like that.

Tomas wasn't happy with the Gay Jay story. He felt that he could have been much more aggressive with how he presented the comedian by highlighting some of his more controversial comments. He had left out the 'coward' answer for instance. Tomas concluded after seeing the final cut of the story that he had pulled some punches that Jay would have been completely comfortable with him throwing.

Maybe it was because this would be his first report on *The Industry Tonight* and Tomas didn't want it to be too controversial. Maybe it was because this story was at its a heart a 'feature story' that wasn't really his expertise. Maybe he was thinking ahead to the interview with the Reverend Governor that he still wasn't really sure would happen.

Nan liked the story. She said it hit all the marks when it came to Gay Jay. Funny, a bit outrageous, controversial and interesting. "You think it's hard-hitting enough?" Tomas asked her.

"Hard hitting?" she replied with a quizzical look on her face. "He's a comedian. This is a feature story Tom, not an investigative report. If I wanted hard-hitting we would run it in the first block of the newscast, not in the "Industrial Art" section."

Tomas didn't like the story any better after Nan's critique, but he was done with it and she liked it and that was really all that mattered. His story would be the last story to run in the newscast on a holiday week on the least watched night for *The Industry Tonight,* Friday. Even if it was his first story at his new gig there would not be many around to see it. Far more would probably catch it later online. "Sometimes," he thought to himself, "you just have to put the pencil down and turn in the work."

Besides, Tomas was really hungry. It was 6 p.m. on a Friday and his story didn't air until 7:50 p.m. when he would introduce it live from *The Industry Tonight* newsroom. He decided to run out to grab a quick bite to eat. That took longer than expected. By the time Tomas got back it was 7 p.m. and *The Industry Tonight* newscast was just starting. Almost immediately as it began Tomas felt like he had taken a punch to the gut.

The newsroom was in 'Breaking News' mode with all the monitors turned bright red with the words 'Breaking News' written in black. It bathed the entire newsroom of *The Industry Tonight* in a freakish red glow. Tomas would joke with friends that if you replaced the words with swastikas you might mistakenly think you were at a Nuremberg rally, or in hell!

The monitor nearest him had the sound on so he could hear everything that was being reported by the anchor on set, someone who Tomas did not recognize. "Breaking News on the political front. A tabloid newspaper has released photos on its website of Illinois Governor and Presidential candidate Reverend Ben Rivers sitting in a chair with a woman they report is a high-priced call girl. Reporter Evelyn Carden joins us with more. Evelyn."

Tomas didn't know Evelyn Carden. She worked over at The Big House, or the main newsroom at the TV station. It was rare for *The Industry Tonight* to use Big House reporters, but it did happen from time to time, especially when there was breaking news.

"George, the photos were posted online less than an hour ago by *The Tabloid Times*, a tabloid newspaper known to focus on celebrities and gossip. The photos show Rivers and a woman identified as 'Chastity' dressed in a revealing swimsuit sitting on the Reverend's lap. We're going to show you some of those photos now. According to the story posted with the photos Chastity is a sex worker for a high-end call girl operation, one which has serviced other politicians in the past and in some cases helped bring an end to their political careers. The article reports that Rivers also spent some time with the young lady in private on the boat where the photos were taken. Rivers was reportedly on the boat a few months ago when fellow Republicans were attempting to convince him to drop any ideas of running for president in exchange for being considered for vice president, an idea we are told Rivers rejected. The story goes on to say that the woman is now working as a paid staffer on the Rivers for President campaign although they did not use her full name. *DC-3 News* cannot confirm the information and calls to Rivers campaign office were not immediately returned. A source of mine who was on that boat does confirm that Rivers was on that yacht named *Lover's Escape* and so too was the woman identified as 'Chastity'. We will of course continue to reach out to the Rivers campaign for comment. George."

George, the anchor whom Tomas did not recognize, continued with a comment in the form of a question even Captain Obvious would love. "Evelyn, Rivers is an ordained minister and a self-proclaimed man of God. These photos cannot be helpful to his image."

"It could be devastating to his campaign George. Rivers' faith is a big part of his appeal to the religious right of the party and news like this could be a serious setback for his presidential ambitions."

As the back-and-forth between George the anchor and Evelyn the reporter continued a couple of thoughts raced through Tomas's mind. First, for a reporter to get confirmation of what happened from someone actually on the boat within an hour of the story breaking was either amazing reporting, incredible luck, or something more insidious. The second thing was that there was no way Rivers was doing his one-on-one interview with Tomas on Sunday now. Tomas was upset but he was also glad that he hadn't told Nan about the planned interview with Big Ben.

As Tomas got ready to front on camera his own story on Gay Jay, another thing crossed his mind. You've got a blockbuster sex scandal story on a preacher running for president and you break it on a Friday night? Running stories on a Friday is what those who manipulate the media do when they want to bury stories, not break them. It didn't quite add up to him.

After the newscast Tomas walked over to The Big House to find Evelyn in her cubicle. She was a night shift reporter and so she still had a good part of her workday left ahead of her. She didn't even see Tomas approaching. "Hey Evelyn, Tom Stein. I'm new here."

"Hey," Evelyn responded while typing and not looking up. "I really liked your story on Gay Jay," she added.

"Thanks." Tomas could tell she was in a rush and in no mood for small talk so he got right to the point. "Hey, on the Reverend Governor story, I was just curious; who is your source?"

"Yeah," Evelyn smiled while looking up. "I had to burn a favor for that one. I'm sorry but I can't divulge my source."

Tomas nodded and thanked her. He understood. Under those circumstances he wouldn't have revealed anything either, even to someone in-house.

It's been said that history repeats itself, and the incident with Rivers was remarkably similar to a 1980s sex scandal Tomas had read about which sunk the presidential ambitions of a senator named Gary Hart. Hart had been accused of having extra-marital affairs and he dared the press to present any evidence that was indeed true. That's when photos surfaced of him with a younger woman aboard a boat named *Monkey Business*. It doomed Hart's campaign and his political career.

But the predicament with Rivers seemed even worse. In this case the woman was a prostitute, he was a man of the cloth, and the alleged concubine was now working for him. Tomas believed this one revelation alone had pretty much doomed Rivers' chances for the nomination of the Republican Party— that is if it was true. Tomas found with stories like these from a questionable source that it was best for him to be a 'Doubting Tomas' about the information.

The good news from the breaking news on Rivers was that Tomas would get his weekend back. He still took camera gear home in the faintest hope that Rivers would still do the Sunday interview, but he had no illusions about that. Tomas would go through the motions as if the interview still might occur but he knew that Rivers would be crazy to go through with it. The Ben Rivers for President campaign was now going to have to be in full damage control mode to save his presidential ambitions. Doing a one-on-one interview with a young reporter just starting out at a local TV station in Washington, DC was not in that playbook. More likely Rivers would either hold a news conference or seek out a one-on-one interview with a more prominent journalist than him, most probably one who worked for a big news network.

Friday night turned into Saturday morning which turned into Saturday afternoon. Tomas did as he promised and reached out to Rivers' assistant Annie. She actually answered the phone and in a tone of familiarity after he introduced himself. "Hello Tom, thank you for your call."

"Hi Annie," Tomas responded as matter-of-factly as he could given the circumstances. "The Reverend Governor asked me to call you to confirm the details of our interview tomorrow." Tomas was trying to act as if no sex scandal existed or that somehow Annie might be unaware.

"The church service starts at eleven o'clock at the West Valley Baptist Church in Chevy Chase. Reverend Rivers will have a few words for the congregation during the service and then you can conduct the interview with him afterward. I'm sure you have many questions," Annie instructed him.

Tomas couldn't believe it. It was all he could do not to blurt out, "*You mean he's going through with it?*" Instead, he paused for a second, composed himself and replied, "Thank you. Will you be there?"

"I will," Annie responded, "and I look forward to meeting you."

There was a pause. It all seemed surreal, and Tomas wondered if there might be some sort of misunderstanding. "Annie, look, in light of recent events will any topics be off the table for the interview?"

"No," she replied. "You may ask him anything you wish."

Tomas was dumbfounded. "Okay. Well thank you Annie and I look forward to meeting you tomorrow." After he got off the phone Tomas sat in silence and disbelief. "What is Rivers doing?" he thought to himself aloud. Here was a man whose presidential political ambitions were hanging by a thread and he was going to spend time and energy at a critical moment in his campaign conducting an interview with him? It made no sense at all to Tomas. There had to be a catch.

Tomas was deep in thought as he began making himself some kosher hot dogs for dinner. Tomas wasn't really an actively practicing Jew, but still felt a kinship to being Jewish that had him eating mostly kosher. He was not strict about it. It was just something which gave him more of a sense of his religious identity. He pondered whether to call Nan about the interview. He still wasn't certain it would happen. Did he really want to bother her on a Saturday about something he remained relatively uncertain would occur?

As the water boiled and he stuck the franks in the pot it suddenly occurred to him that he hadn't gotten past Chapter 5 of the Reverend Governor's book. The interview that Tomas was still convinced would not happen would be all about the breaking news sex scandal. But if the interview did happen, he wanted to know as much about the Reverend Rivers as possible, and so he began reading more of his autobiography.

Tomas skipped past the Trump campaign and Trump years and instead went straight to Chapter 9 and Rivers' account of his successful run for Governor, the run that famously—some would say infamously—helped cement his reputation as 'Trump 2.0'.

CHAPTER 16

"I WAS RECRUITED HEAVILY during the Trump years," Rivers started writing in Chapter 9 of his book. "The national Republican Party was on a quest to recruit more minorities, more women, and more military veterans for public office. I checked two out of three of those boxes. At one point I was asked to mount a primary challenge to the incumbent Republican in my own Congressional District. Like me, he was an Air Force veteran, but he had politically lost his way. The truth was that as far as I could tell he was a 'never-Trumper' from the very beginning. During the 2016 primary he endorsed Jeb Bush, a losing political bet if there ever was one. Now many in the party wanted *him* out!

"The Trump presidency seemed to annoy the Congressman as much as it did the Democrats and his political fortunes faded fast. He would be one of the few Republicans to vote to impeach Trump after the Capitol riot in what was hailed by many on the left as his act of political courage and conviction. It was neither. He likely knew he was on the way out of public office, hated Trump, and so he voted for an impeachment he knew was unwarranted and would never succeed. I believe he did it out of a sense of spite and disillusionment.

"That Congressman like me had also become a 'placeholder politician' during his many years in Washington. His legislative record wasn't just unremarkable; it was non-existent even when Republicans did hold power in our nation's capital. It seemed to me it was as if he held office simply because he had nothing better to do. It would have been a personal joy to be the one to send him on his way and perhaps use that very powerful Congressional seat to accomplish something. If I were to unseat him I was determined I would no longer be a 'placeholder' but rather a change-maker.

"I said 'no'. My mother was ailing and still needed me at home. The farthest I was willing to go politically at that point in my career was where I had been for the past decade, and that was Springfield. That's when Coach Pierce brought up the idea of running for Governor."

"'It's a political suicide mission,' I told him. The last Republican to become governor was a billionaire businessman who practically bought the seat and beat a Democrat incumbent who was very unpopular. That Republican's four years in office had been a disaster for a state already on life support because he refused to use the levers of political power effectively. His strategy was to hold the state budget hostage to get concessions from the powerful Democratic House Speaker. His aides would seek my counsel. I would tell them that if they were going to use such tactics the Governor would have my support, but they could not go halfway. I would tell them, "The longer this drags on the weaker your position becomes."

"The Governor did not take my advice. The end result was a budget battle where it seemed that no one felt any real pain. State workers stayed on the job. Pensions were still paid. The only thing that got worse was the state's putrid balance sheet. In the end, as I predicted, a group of Republican legislators abandoned the Governor and left him politically empty-handed. He was so inept that even I almost voted against him the following year."

Tomas could not imagine Rivers voting for a liberal Democrat. And of course he didn't.

"The Democrat who succeeded him as Governor was also a billionaire businessman who in my opinion also bought the seat," Rivers wrote.

"A true liberal who bought into the fallacy that you can fix things with just more and more tax revenue, especially if you get it from the wealthy. That never works because I've found there is always a justification to find a better way to spend new tax money rather than pay for what you've already purchased. That was the Illinois way."

Rivers went on to write that what Democrats discovered was that Illinois residents were already 'taxed out'. A Constitutional Amendment to allow the state to implement a so-called 'progressive' income tax where the wealthy paid a higher tax rate failed at the ballot box. Even worse, Illinois residents were also voting with their feet. The state was going through a massive out-migration of population branded *The Illinois Exodus*. One study had found that a large majority of the people leaving were minorities living in urban areas who were mostly loyal Democratic voters. Rivers would point out that the very people who had created the dark blue political hue of Illinois were now leaving in droves for 'redder' states like Texas, Florida and Georgia because of the opportunities there. He would joke that the Republican Party in Illinois could be the first to regain power not by their addition of their voters but by the Democrat's subtraction of *their* voters.

But could he win the Governorship? Were things so bad that the state was willing to take a chance on him? Rivers decided that if he was going to take on what seemed like by any political calculation a Herculean task, that he was going to do it his way. This wasn't going to be a campaign but rather a crusade in which he vowed he would hold nothing back. That's when he began to apply the lessons he had learned from Donald Trump. The first lesson was to keep things simple.

Rivers' campaign would focus on three planks. The first was the elimination of all toll roads statewide. The need for new highways paired with no money to pay for them had created a boom in toll roads across Illinois and especially in the Chicagoland area. There was even talk of putting tolls on existing longstanding freeways. Rivers created a slogan complete with red hats which read 'Don't Toll on Me'. "Nothing, *nothing*," he would tell supporters, "hurts the poor and working class more than a toll road. Rather than opening a path to opportunity, it shuts them down because people can't afford to pay the price. We have isolated whole communities, especially in Chicago by placing tolls all around them that they can't afford to pay rather than by managing our budgets so that mobility for all is a top priority."

The second plank was a bit obscure politically, but it was an issue Illinois voters understood well, especially if they owned a home. "No Property Taxation Without Representation."

For decades the response by many communities to solving a political problem was to create a property taxing district for it typically run by a board appointed by local elected officials. As a result some homeowners were paying property taxes to twelve, thirteen, even fifteen separate entities and it added up financially. It was one reason why Rivers himself was paying nearly $1000 per month in property taxes for a house which was worth barely more than $200,000. His proposal would be that any taxing district that was run by an appointed and not an elected board would be dissolved. Its responsibilities would be given instead to the most appropriate elected body, typically a county board with a supervisor or a city council with a mayor. "Let the elected officials raise your taxes," he told beleaguered homeowners, "and if they do then vote them out!"

The third plank was purely Trumpian. If Rivers was elected Governor, then the state would fully cooperate with the federal government when it came to enforcing illegal immigration and would punish and outright outlaw so-called 'sanctuary cities'. "Few things hurt the poor in America more than the illegal importation of workers willing to work for less than them," he would say at rallies. "It's a race to the bottom. If I told you that immigration policy must protect U.S. workers against unfair competition from foreign workers, with an appropriately higher level of protection to the most vulnerable in our society, then you might think that was the

Trump in me talking. No, that's the exact sentiment from the former liberal Congresswoman from Texas named Barbara Jordan. She was an African-American who understood well how the scourge of illegal immigration harms the most vulnerable. We should *stop* doing stuff like *that*!"

One political pundit branded it "The Reverend Rivers Dry Hole" writing that there was no way he would get any part of his platform passed in deep Democratic blue Illinois. Rivers admitted in his autobiography that was probably true, but wrote that his candidacy was a long shot to begin with so he reasoned why not set out a bold agenda?

There were other things in which pundits drew comparisons to Rivers and Trump, the main one being his rallies. As news of Rivers and his campaign spread many people were naturally curious. Here was a black minister politician whose run for Governor was inspired by the presidency of Donald J. Trump. That plus years in the pulpit had taught Rivers how to rally a crowd. He never held rallies at venues the large size of Trump's, but he packed smaller venues nonetheless with people often turned away. Those who did make it inside would break out in chants during Rivers' speeches such as "We love Trump! We love you!" as the Reverend beamed onstage.

Rivers found that he appealed to a unique cross section of voters. Trump voters were drawn to him. There was of course his appeal to religious voters, not just the religious right but blacks and Hispanics who were Christian or Catholic as well. His views on immigration were even embraced by a section of the Hispanic community concerned that the situation with illegal immigration was getting so out of control that it was now a crisis, and their communities were suffering as a result.

But there was more to it than that. Here was a man who didn't act, talk or seem like any other politician in Illinois. He was an oddity that many could not stop talking about—much like how the cable news networks could not stop covering Trump during his 2016 campaign. No one really knew what to make of Rivers, but he seemed fresh and different and for the news media noteworthy.

Winning the Republican primary was surprisingly easy for Rivers, but it was a hollow victory. Truth was that there were not many other Republicans who sought the nomination because they knew the end result would be to lose in the general election. Rivers feared that was his likely fate as well. He just didn't care. Rivers felt that if he could move the needle with ordinary people who had never voted Republican before then it could be the start of something bigger. He underestimated himself.

The Reverend ended up facing a former Democratic Congresswoman from the western part of the state. She had retired from her seat for fear of being redistricted out of it following the previous census. As one newspaper columnist described her, "She's a moderate who doesn't seem to inspire any single faction of the Democratic Party. If Biden won because he wasn't Trump then she'll win only because she isn't Ben Rivers."

But she didn't win. Polls had hinted at a possible upset in the weeks leading up to the election and the voters confirmed it. Rivers would win the election by a slim margin and also increase the number of Republican seats in the legislature. It was a mild surprise but by no means a mandate. From that day on supporters and even detractors would refer to him as 'Reverend Governor'. God first—just the way Rivers liked it.

The Reverend Governor had a bit more success early on politically in his administration than he expected. Hurting from Rivers' attacks on taxation Democrats agreed to participate in a legislative committee to look at outlawing certain types of property taxing districts. His proposal to get on a path to eliminate toll roads went nowhere because the Illinois Tollway Authority was far more politically powerful than even Rivers realized. His executive orders to eliminate sanctuary cities were thwarted by the courts.

It was Rivers' political antics which gained him more headlines. Rivers spotted some protesters at one of his rallies who were against his proposed sanctuary city ban. They were standing in line to get inside a large auditorium. Rivers brought some of his bodyguards over toward the obvious protesters and asked his guards to help those in line behind the protesters cut in front of them. At first the protesters were bewildered, but once they realized that Rivers was going to have people cut in front of them until they until they might not get in at all they started objecting loudly to what was happening. Rivers smiled. "What's your problem? Because that's exactly what the illegal immigrants you support are doing. They're cutting in line in front of people who are willing to do what it takes to come into this country legally. They're illegal line cutters." From then on Rivers would refer to illegal immigrants as 'illegal line cutters' and the phrase stuck especially with some in the more right-wing media.

Rivers also made headlines at another event following destructive protests in Chicago. The headlines concerned a white police officer who shot to death a black armed robbery suspect who was holding a knife. During his speech Rivers pulled out a plastic knife which was obviously a toy and then charged a part of the crowd with it in his right hand. As they recoiled, he then returned to the lectern and recounted what had just happened. "Here I am the governor of the state holding a plastic knife and yet when I came at you with it, I still saw people pull away in fear. You have nothing to fear from me. So imagine what a police officer feels when he is facing a man who is a real threat to his life holding a weapon which could take his life. Do you think he feels no fear? A wise man once told me that courage is not the lack of fear, but courage is being fearful and showing courage anyway. I will always support the courage of our police officers when they are threatened with the prospect of not returning home that night to their wife and children."

The stunt got Rivers some criticism in the press. One newspaper editorial said it was beneath the actions of a governor. But Rivers would point out that the video of it got lots of news play and more than a million hits on his social media page. He felt he had made his point.

Tomas realized as he became sleepy that all this reading might not matter. If Rivers was really going to go through with the interview on

Sunday there would really be only one topic, the sex scandal. Tomas hated that his interview might be the one to bury the political campaign of Big Ben over something so tawdry as a sex scandal, but it was what it was. He drifted off to sleep impatient for what the next day might bring.

CHAPTER 17

Tomas listened to the cable news Sunday morning programs on his satellite radio as he drove out toward Maryland. The Rivers sex scandal was the big topic on all of them and some pundits were almost gleefully predicting the Reverend Governor's campaign for president was over. Even a conservative news channel agreed. It all seemed very premature to Tomas, especially since no one had heard from Rivers yet.

If everything that had been reported was true then Tomas didn't quite understand why Rivers would interview at all right now—much less with him. The facts as Tomas knew them seemed pretty damning. What could possibly be his defense? And if he had a defense then why would he interview with a local reporter who had barely been on the job for a couple of weeks? Nothing added up to Tomas and in the back of his mind he still felt Rivers would bail on the interview.

Tomas had never been to Chevy Chase and so he left early and arrived at the church *very* early. So early in fact that he caught the first church service leaving at around 9:30 a.m. There weren't many people at that service from what he could tell. Rivers was the main attraction at the 11 a.m. service, but surprisingly the church's congregation had managed to keep his appearance top secret from the media. Tomas could see no other media besides him around the large building.

He decided to grab his gear and make his way inside early. As he walked in the main door a short, white woman in a skirt suit was standing in the entry as if she were there just for him. "Tom Stein?" she asked as if the camera gear Tomas was carrying did not give him away.

"You must be Annie," Tomas replied. He put down a camera tripod to shake her hand.

Annie smiled as if she were completely unaware of the hit job Tomas was about to put on her boss. "During the service we thought we would have you film upstairs in the video center. The Reverend Governor will speak with you afterward." Annie was smiling in a way that made Tomas uneasy, sort of like a gambler at a poker game who wanted you to believe she really did have the better hand.

She led Tomas up some steps to the second floor of the church and to an area that overlooked the sanctuary. In the room up there were a couple of static cameras, some digital video recorder machines, and a controller. A man who introduced himself as Dave was preparing to videotape the next service and offered to let Tomas use whatever video he recorded. Tomas was wary because he hated relying on the work of someone else for his news stories, but he figured if he videotaped Dave recording the service in addition to what he shot of it himself then he would have enough video to provide all the footage he needed for his story.

He and Dave chatted about the church's video setup to pass the time. The church streamed their services live on the web. Their impressive setup included three remote controlled cameras and a computerized control room of sorts. Dave controlled everything from there, switching to shots from the pulpit to the choir to the organist to the parishioners. Soon it was almost 11 a.m.

Tomas watched as parishioners filled the pews to overflowing and standing room only. The Reverend Governor could still pack a room. The organ player serenaded the arriving crowd with various religious songs as those who could find a seat in the pews sat down. A choir assembled on the church stage and opened the service with a religious song which

Tomas did not recognize. Rivers entered through a side door with a man Tomas assumed was the church minister. They sat down in some chairs behind the pulpit when the choir was done singing. The parishioners were then seated with others standing on the outer walls of the church when the minister stepped up to the podium at the pulpit and began to speak. Tomas made a point of getting his comments on video.

The minister told the assembled crowd, "I know that many of you came to hear a sermon by the Reverend Rivers. Due to some recent events which you may have heard something about …" The minister smiled and paused while some in the congregation laughed. "… Reverend Rivers is limited in what he can say today but he does have some words he wishes to share with you. Reverend Rivers."

Despite the sex controversy the parishioners stood and applauded loudly as Rivers approached the podium. The Reverend Governor smiled and motioned to the congregation to be seated but they continued to stand and applaud. Finally, after about a minute of applause and even cheering, they took their seats.

"Thank you," Rivers said acknowledging the crowd. "I'm sorry I cannot share my sermon this morning. I have been advised against it by both my campaign and Republican Party officials. In fact they would prefer I not be here at all this morning in light of recent news reports about me. But I did ask if I could at least recite the Lord's Prayer and they said I could. What they didn't realize is that I have my own version of the Lord's Prayer." A sheepish smile came over Rev. Rivers face. "And so I am going to respectfully ask that you do *not* repeat after me as I recite it."

There was murmuring in the room. The congregation suspected Rivers was up to something and their anticipation grew. Tomas trained his camera lens on Rivers and started rolling.

"Our Lord who art in Heaven," Rivers began. "Hallowed be thy name. Thy Kingdom come, thy will be done on Earth as it is in Heaven. Give us this day our daily bread and forgive us our trespasses as we forgive those who trespass against us as hard as that can be. For Lord there are so many human souls on this planet who will trespass against us. They will use lies to hurt our hearts and those of our loved ones and damage our hard-fought reputations. They will pretend to be virtuous and righteous in revealing misdeeds when it is *they* who are committing grievous sins and perpetuating lies. I have witnessed this Lord, and I have witnessed it very recently."

Rivers paused and nodded to the crowd as if to confirm that they all knew what he was talking about.

"But Lord, I know that you work in ways that no man or woman can understand. And that you in your wisdom Lord are testing me. But Lord I know that you have also sent me a lifeline." Rivers voice grew louder and bolder. He was full on preaching now. "For among us today is a Gabriel. A man with a modern-day trumpet to let all know the *truth* of the virtuous and bury the *lies* of cowards and sinners. A man among us who will share a story with all that shall enlighten rather than denigrate, build up rather than tear down, and let you know the true *Glory of God* that the Lord has inspired in me and I know all of you!"

Rivers pointed straight at Tomas, his finger shaking. "That man right there. You see him. I trust in him because God tells me that he will tell the *truth*! For he is an *honest* man. He is a *professional* man, and his calling is nothing more than to tell you what is *right* and what is *not right*! To all assembled here I ask that you watch closely what *he* does and you too shall see the *truth* and the *light*!"

Everyone was staring back and up at Tomas now as two thoughts entered his mind. The first was that this was the second time in two years he had been singled out in a church and he was really hoping this was not becoming a trend. The second was why was Rivers so confident in his abilities? The two had literally just met. It made no sense.

Rivers continued. "Lord, do not lead us into temptation, but do deliver us from evil as I know you will me soon, for thine is the kingdom and glory forever and ever. Amen."

"Amen" the somewhat bewildered congregation repeated, many still looking back and up at Tomas who was attempting to take video of the service. The pastor shook Rivers hand as he replaced him at the lectern. He then smiled. "I really like that version of the Lord's Prayer," to which the congregation laughed in response.

Tomas would shoot some more video of the service as it progressed but his mind kept wandering to Big Ben's remarks. "What was that all about?" he thought to himself. Did Rivers somehow think that by challenging him in front of hundreds of parishioners that maybe he would go easy on him? Is that why you invite the cub reporter from the local TV station to be your first interview after a major sex scandal breaks? It was all mystifying and his emotions would gravitate between anger and dumbfounded curiosity. What was going on?

Annie tapped Tomas on the shoulder. The service wasn't quite over yet but she wanted to get him into a room downstairs for the interview before the crowd started shuffling out. "What was all that about?" he asked her as he assembled his gear. She helped out by picking up his tripod.

"You'll see soon enough," she answered.

"I don't understand what I'm doing here. What are his expectations of me?"

Annie turned and faced him at the top of a stairwell. "There are no expectations. All he asks is that you be fair and truthful—like a good reporter *should* be and do your job." She paused. "Are you religious Tom?"

"Sort of. Not really," he replied.

Annie looked straight into his eyes. "Then this is going to be hard for you to understand but sometimes God really does speak to the faithful in mysterious ways. Me, I wanted someone else to do this interview; perhaps a network anchor or a White House correspondent, but the Reverend saw God's work in his promise to interview with you. That's why you are here now."

Tomas understood. Sort of. Not really.

He was determined as he followed Annie down the stairs and through a hallway toward a back office where he would do the interview that he would pull no punches with Rivers. The tough questions he would ask Rivers once the interview started began racing through his mind as he followed the clicking heels of Annie's stilettos. Annie stopped at a door, opened it and stood outside it so as to waive Tomas inside. He walked in and immediately did a double take. There was not one person, but two people were sitting, awaiting him side-by-side in two chairs placed in the middle of the room. On the left was the Reverend Rivers and on the right was 'her'. The woman from the photo. The woman the world in an instant had come to know as *Chastity.*

She was dressed modestly in an outfit which seemed appropriate for church but a little light for a DC winter. Her hair was different and she wasn't wearing much makeup, but it was definitely her. She was a stunner to be sure. Long legs, a shapely body and large, inviting saucer-like eyes with an air of innocence which did not in any way convey her chosen profession. She was obviously nervous, her eyes meeting his and then darting across the room before turning to Rivers who gave her hand a reassuring grip.

She was the one who would be in the spotlight for this interview. Tomas set up his camera gear and pulled out a second lavaliere microphone to give to her so he could record her words. What in the world could she possibly say?

CHAPTER 18

"*NAN, PICK UP NAN!*" Tomas yelled into his phone as Nan's voicemail message played into his ear. He waited for the beep. "Nan, it's Tom. Mayday! Emergency! I need your help and I need it *now*! Please call me back ASAP!"

Tomas hung up realizing he didn't say exactly why he needed Nan's help and that reason might be a motivator for her to respond, and so he texted her. "Just ended interview with Rev. Rivers. *Major* exclusive. Please call me!"

Nan apparently responded to texts better than voicemails for she called back 2 minutes later and without even bothering to say "hello," she asked Tomas, "You got an interview with Rivers?"

"It's even better than that Nan!"

"How did you get an interview with Rivers?"

"He was at a church service in Maryland today and, well, it's a long story."

"And what are you doing working on a Sunday?" Nan interjected.

"Nan, stop. I'll explain it all later but it's even better than you can imagine!"

"Why? What did Rivers say about the sex scandal?"

Tomas smiled and laughed as he drove. "Not one single word!"

"Wait, you got an interview with Rivers and you didn't ask him about the scandal?" Nan replied incredulously.

"Didn't have to Nan. It's even better!"

There was a pause. Nan was clearly confused about the direction of this conversation. "Better? How?"

"Because Chastity was there too!"

Tomas could hear an audible gasp from Nan on the other end of the line. For the next 30 minutes as Tomas drove in from Maryland toward the television station the two discussed their strategy for handling the story. Both knew it would be major national breaking news, especially on a Sunday Night, and they wanted to unveil it in a way that would get the story maximum impact. Nan made a point of never coming in on Sundays but today she would make an exception. She would make calls to a couple of Associate Producers to help out as well. And of course she would have to call The Big House to discuss how they wanted to handle it. This was major news and there would be no trying to hold the interview until Monday's *The Industry Tonight*.

In other words, they were bracing for a glorious media feeding frenzy and Tomas needed Nan's help to make sure he had his stuff in order. He was excited because he had never had such a big story in his lifetime. This story would be the lead story nationwide and Nan was excited too. At one point during their conversation on his drive in Tomas could have sworn he heard her giggle.

Nan arrived at the station about an hour after Tomas did and found him working in his cubicle logging the interview. He had already downloaded all his video into the station's computer video editing system. Word had reached over to The Big House about what he had, but in his 'TIT' cubicle he could be alone and focus away from the buzz. Nan interrupted him briefly and they went over their plan.

They would begin by tweeting out and posting online and on social media some excerpts from the interview with Chastity. Tomas would also do some teaser hits in the 4 p.m. and 5 p.m. newscasts, but the 6 p.m.

broadcast was where his blockbuster story would first fully air.

Nan knew that when word leaked out about the Rivers story the station would be inundated with calls from the networks, the cable nets and plenty of other news outlets seeking permission to use clips from the interview. She had a team of associate producers ready to help field the calls and send out video clips which they had prepared with *DC-3 News* branding in the corner of the video clip. They had video gold and Nan wanted to make sure the station got proper credit for it.

If the internet was any guide, then the impact of the story would be immense. Hits on the station's website blew up into the tens of thousands almost instantaneously once teasers for the story were posted. Public and media interest wasn't just high. It was at a frenzy.

Tomas was new and so Nan did watch over him, but she had already developed trust in him. She knew the story would be solid. She would help him craft it for maximum impact. Nan also did her best to run interference for Tomas so he could focus on his work and not be distracted by the serious amount of noise which would surround his scoop.

By sheer coincidence Ron Stone was anchoring that night. As well staffed as DC-3 was a lot of its anchors were still on vacation and Stone was filling in. Nan counted that as a lucky break as having Stone on the anchor desk would be more familiar to Tomas and give the story a bit more *gravitas*.

That's because Stone had been a fixture of television news in DC for decades. He was a tall African-American man with the slight pudginess which came with middle age. He also dressed so well you could barely notice that. He wore black-rimmed glasses on-air and his hairline had receded over the years but on set he had a presence like few others. Ron Stone brought a comfortable intensity to every news story he read. He could also flash a dazzling smile when appropriate. Stone was on the air a lot because DC-3 did so much news including his anchoring of *The Industry Tonight* weeknights but never seemed unprepared.

Stone could also be 'off the cuff,' throwing in personal observations about stories while anchoring without ever showing his politics or bias. He was a straight shooter who was also willing to say out loud what everyone watching might be thinking at the moment. Stone would anchor the 4 p.m. and 5 p.m. news that night, but it was anchoring the 6 p.m. news which he was anxiously looking forward to. The newscast with the big scoop. It took a few hours for Tomas to get everything done and yet it went by in what felt like seconds when the 6 p.m. news began.

"Good evening, I'm Ron Stone. Our top story tonight is the response from a Republican Presidential Campaign to the sex scandal which threatens to derail it. And that response I must tell you is mind-blowing. *DC-3 News* and *The Industry Tonight* correspondent Tom Stein is live in the newsroom with a story you will see only on DC-3."

Tomas was a little bit nervous knowing how closely his story would be watched. He was also experienced enough that his TV news training kicked in:

"Ron, after the publication of pictures showing governor and presidential candidate Ben Rivers with a scantily clad sex worker on his lap on a boat named *Lover's Escape* on Friday, many jumped to conclusions about what happened between them. The Rivers campaign now had a full-fledged sex scandal on their hands. What I learned today is that there wasn't any sex and certainly should be no scandal."

The video story then played beginning with video of Chastity in tears.

"It's been a nightmare," she said weeping.

Tomas began his narration. "You may know this woman as Chastity, the highly paid sex worker seen in this photo on the lap of Illinois governor and presidential candidate the Reverend Ben Rivers. Her real name is Brenda Caruso and she interviewed besides Rivers to let you know what really happened that night months ago, a night she says unexpectedly changed her life for the better."

"I cannot say enough about how much Reverend Rivers has helped me," she said dabbing her eyes.

More narration. "Caruso says she was working for a high-end call girl operation at the time when she was given an assignment."

Caruso sound bite: "They sent me and a couple of other girls to entertain some men on a boat."

"And you were told to focus on one man in particular?" Tomas asked her.

"Yes, a black guy. The only black guy on the boat."

"That was Reverend Rivers," the story narration continued, "But when she tried to tempt him first by flirting with him and then by offering sex, she says something unexpected happened."

"He flat turned me down. He wasn't turned on at all. He just started asking me questions."

"What kind of questions?" Tomas asked.

"Where did I grow up? What's my favorite place to visit? How are my parents doing? Just regular questions as if he wanted to know more about me."

More narration. "Rivers and Caruso say they then retreated to a room on the boat to speak in private. Both say it had windows and that everyone outside could see that they were doing nothing more than having a conversation inside."

Caruso soundbite. "He asked why I did what I did for a living and I was honest with him about it. It's the money and the power and the drugs and it is freeing in a way that I never experienced before. But I wasn't proud of what I was doing. And that's when he asked me if I would consider giving it up to join his campaign. That he was going to run for President and he needed good people on his staff, people he could trust."

"Caruso agreed to that and more," Tomas continued with his narration. "She would attend church as well at Rivers' urging and go to meetings and help out at church events."

Caruso soundbite. "He set me up with a local church. It's been amazing.

I feel that I have like a million friends now and I realize how truly lonely I was before. It's a brand-new world for me."

Tomas response. "He's really helped you."

"In just a few short months he has so changed my life," Caruso continued. "People need to know how amazingly caring he is even to someone like me, and he has never asked me for anything in return."

Tomas voice track: "But it was an encounter which would never have happened had someone not hired Brenda Caruso in the first place, presumably to immerse Rivers in a sex scandal. So who hired her?"

"I honestly don't know," Caruso answered. "It was all handled through the agency. I didn't want to know."

The interview moved to Rivers. At this point Tomas had pulled out an old trick called a 'reversal question on camera'. Once the interview was complete he turned the camera on himself and then re-asked Rivers questions he had asked him earlier to simulate a conversation.

"Someone set you up?" Tomas asked him.

"I'm glad someone set me up," Rivers responded.

"Who set you up?" Tomas continued.

"I don't know and I don't care because they did me a favor. They introduced me to a wonderful woman who just needed a little help from God with her life. And God-willing that was me. And people ask me why I do the ministering and the politicking, and it is because God put me on this earth to serve him by serving others. So maybe it was God who set me up!"

The story ended and switched to Tomas back on camera in the newsroom. "Reverend Rivers says there were about twenty-five people at the gathering on the boat and he will not speculate about who may have hired Caruso. He tells me he plans on holding a news conference tomorrow to answer more questions about what happened on the boat that night. Ron."

Stone seemed a bit awestruck by what he had just witnessed over the air and paused for a moment to compose himself. He had a scripted question for Tomas in the Tele-Prompt-Ter and started to read it. "Tom, what about Brenda Caruso? Does she plan on staying with the Rivers for President campaign?"

"Yes Ron, she does. She tells me her family was not aware that she had worked as a sex worker and so she's going to take some time off to spend with them before returning to the Rivers campaign. She also says she is so inspired by Rivers' example that she would like to run for public office herself one day. Ron."

"Well she's got my vote!" Stone eagerly replied and then immediately appeared to realize he probably should not have said that. "Just wow!" Stone shook his head back and forth. "I mean folks, isn't that something?"

Another pause and then Stone moved on to the next script.

"Tom Stein is the newest correspondent for DC-3's *The Industry Tonight* team. Tomorrow night at seven o'clock *The Industry Tonight* will spend the entire hour on the Rivers controversy with more new developments like you just saw tonight. That's on *The Industry Tonight*—tomorrow night at seven o'clock here on DC-3. And DC-3 will continue to follow developments in this breaking political news story. You can also catch more clips from tonight's interview on our website DC3-dot-com."

Tomas stood up from the camera position once the newscast hit the first commercial break and that's when people in the newsroom began to applaud. Nan came over to give him a big hug. He would do a few more 'hits' that night in later newscasts but the big moment was over. Now the fallout from his exclusive story was set to begin.

Tomas could hear the phones in the newsroom ringing incessantly as he made his way from the newsroom in The Big House back to the newsroom in the TIT. It was quiet there; the monitors were all turned off and while the lights were on the whole room was darker than usual and very empty. When he got to his desk he noticed that his cell phone had gotten so many texts that it had vibrated off the desk and down onto the floor. He would check the messages later.

He sat down, leaned back in his chair, put his feet up and let a wave of pure exhaustion roll over him. He had not slept well the night before but the adrenaline at covering the biggest story of his young career had sustained him until now. Now at that very moment he felt really, really tired and he still had three more newscasts to appear on before going home.

Tomas shook his head violently as if wanting to snap out of his tired funk and walked over to the coffee station at the edge of the newsroom. Tomas never ever had coffee at night but this night he would pluck a K-cup into the coffee machine and watch the black energy drink collect into his mug. That's when he spotted Nan hurriedly coming down the stairs from the causeway that led to The Big House.

"Dude!" she yelled over at him as she rapidly approached. "*Dude!* You just single-handedly set the entire political universe on fire! It's blowing up over there. I have never ever seen so many hits on our web page! You might just break the Internet."

Tomas smiled. "Yeah, yeah."

"Well try to sound a little less excited," Nan scolded him. "Enjoy the moment. It's a big one!"

Tomas smiled again. "You know what I enjoy Nan? I enjoy telling the truth. That's the only reason I really got into journalism. Not to blab out speculation about things that I really know nothing about or to tell people what I think, but to just tell them the truth. Journalism is such a cesspool right now. I mean for two whole days American journalists all over the country repeated a lie because some *tabloid paper* came out with some incriminating photos and fake news. I was listening to some of the morning news shows where some predicted the Rivers campaign was *dead* based on a *tabloid news report!*"

Nan understood. "You know Tom I've been working in TV news for twenty-five years, most all of it in this town. That means I can remember when the *Post* and the *Times* were respectable newspapers, not the partisan rags they are today. I read a headline in a Sunday paper online this morning which read "The Reverend Governor's Steep Fall from Grace." What really struck me was that the article was almost celebratory. It was as if the writers were elated to see that the closest person to Trump-ism in the presidential race was now failing, even disgraced. I wonder what they'll write now?"

Tomas smiled, shook his head and then looked over at Nan after pausing for a moment. "You know the school where I studied journalism is called The Walter Cronkite School of Journalism and named for a man who was once considered the most trusted man in America. Could you imagine a journalist being considered that today?"

Nan could not.

"That's what I want to be," Tomas continued.

"You want to be the most trusted man in America?" Nan replied.

"No, just one trusted man in America."

"Well you told the truth tonight when no one else would, and you did a great job!" Nan responded encouragingly. "Ron seemed really impressed with your reporting. That's a big deal around here. But I do have a question for you. Why did Rivers interview with you? I mean you are brand new here. If it were me I would have picked a bigger named journalist."

Tomas looked over at her again. "I was told by his assistant that God told him to do it," and then he shrugged.

Nan started laughing. "That's awesome! I think Rivers may have an 'in' with that guy."

"Yeah," Tomas responded. "He's certainly working in mysterious ways tonight."

"Alright, well enjoy your coffee but then I need you back over at The Big House, okay."

Nan left and Tomas made his way back to his desk. He started looking at all the text messages on his phone. There must have been hundreds of them—friends, former colleagues, anyone who may have had his number—all congratulating him on his big interview. But one of the texts especially stood out to him as he scrolled through his phone.

It read, "MTB is soooooo mad at you right now!" with a winking smiley face punctuating the sentence. Tomas immediately knew that MTB was Marilyn Taylor-Brown and that the text must have been from Olivia Zhang.

He decided to reply to her, texting, "Your boss is upset that I exposed a lie?"

She immediately texted back, "In this town people get upset when you expose a truth that might hurt them." She then followed up before Tomas could respond with a second text which read, "When can I see you again?"

"See me again? Why? What's up?" Tomas texted back.

A pause and then a new message. "Because when I felt that hard-on through your pants the other night I thought that there might be some interest?"

"*Noooo!*" Tomas blurted out to an empty newsroom. He had no response for her, so he just tried to cut the texting off before it became sexting. "I've still got a lot of work to do. Can we continue this conversation another time?"

Olivia responded with a "thumbs up" icon and then followed up with another text. "Loved the Gay Jay story btw."

Tom replied with a "TY". The Gay Jay story seemed like months ago to him now, but he was gratified that another person liked it. Coffee in hand, Tomas picked himself up and headed back over to The Big House. He still had a long night ahead.

CHAPTER 19

TOMAS COULD NOT REMEMBER ever feeling as exhausted as he did Monday morning when he walked into the 'Nip' 20 minutes late for the morning meeting. The whole crew was there including some reporters Tomas did not recognize whom he guessed had just returned from vacation. As he entered every last one of them stood and gave him an ovation. All morning the AM news shows including DC-3's morning newscast had been buzzing not only about the dramatic interview with Rivers and 'Chastity' but many also made mention of the new, young reporter named Tom Stein who broke the big story.

So many people were trying to get a hold of Tomas on his personal cell that he pretty much ignored them all because it was so overwhelming. He did make a mental note to return his parents' voicemail at lunchtime. The others would have to wait if he was going to be able to respond to them at all.

Nan had already warned him that tonight's entire hour of *The Industry Tonight* would be devoted to the Rivers story. The Big House would also put demands on him throughout the day. Rivers was still the biggest story out there by a mile and the news execs at DC-3 wanted to use his scoop to full advantage. Overnight ratings which had come in during the morning indicated that DC-3 had its largest Sunday night audience ever. Everyone wanted to keep that momentum going while the Rivers' news iron was still hot.

But Tomas was also dead tired. He had slept hardly at all for the second night in a row. The late-night coffee on Sunday had been a bad idea. Once his head hit the pillow, he tossed and turned over a combination of excitement and thoughts racing through his mind about what had just happened. He was going to have to just 'gut it out' today. For the moment Tomas just needed to get through the morning meeting without nodding off.

"Ladies and Gentlemen, I present to you DC-3's new 'Boy Wonder'," Lachlan told the assembled crew. It was met with a mixture of laughter and applause. Lachlan continued, "So my good man, is it your plan to break earth-shattering news stories every week?"

"No, only on holidays and weekends," Tomas shot back at him. "Less competition from you!"

Lachlan laughed and sat down. All the conference table chairs were taken so Tomas sat in one of the chairs which lined the perimeter of the room as Nan went through the news plan for that day. The rest of the day for Tomas was kind of a blur although one moment stuck out. An online news outlet known to lean conservative politically reached out to the station and asked if they could interview him. Nan wasn't against it but Tomas declined because he didn't want the story to be about him, although in some ways he was powerless to prevent that. Many were curious about this fresh face on the scene who had just broken the biggest story of the year—even though it was still very early in the year.

The Reverend Ben Rivers for President campaign had decided to hold off on a news conference until Tuesday morning. That meant another day where the only video of Chastity and Rivers would be coming from what Tomas shot. He and Nan would milk every frame of the interview for all they could. Tomas would continue to do news 'hits' throughout the day on DC-3 while Nan and her team of producers would shape *The Industry Tonight* broadcast at 7 p.m. They had booked political panels, had sidebar 'reaction' stories ready to go—even had arranged live satellite interviews set up from some of Rivers' colleagues in Illinois. And then the whole thing, all that planning, all that work, completely blew up in their face.

Tomas had walked back to his cubicle after fronting the lead story on Rivers for *The Industry Tonight* when his desk phone rang. It was a news producer over at The Big House and she was noticeably nervous. "Tom, Hi. I have a man saying he's Reverend Rivers on the phone and he would like to comment live on the air."

Tomas jolted upward immediately. All the work and all the planning and all the logistics of putting that night's *The Industry Tonight* newscast together and no one had even thought for a second to ask Rivers whether he would participate ahead of his news conference the next day. It was a massive oversight. "Put him through to the control room," Tomas instructed.

"But it could be a prank!" the producer protested.

"I know. Put him through. Tell Nan I'm on my way."

That night viewers of *The Industry Tonight* would notice a figure in the background behind anchor Ron Stone jump up and begin running at full speed toward and up the stairs and out of view. Less than 30 seconds later Tomas burst into the control room and ran up to Nan. "Let me talk to him," he asked her slightly out of breath. Nan put Rivers on speakerphone.

"Reverend Rivers. Tom Stein, how are you?"

"Tom! I hear that you are the toast of the town!"

"Same could be said of you Reverend!" Tomas replied. "Hey look, we can hear you, but we can't see you, and we need to confirm it really is you. Neither you or I would want to put an impostor on the air."

"No problem Tom. So how do you propose we do that?"

"At church yesterday. What did you do from the pulpit?"

Tomas and Nan could hear Rivers laughing through the phone line. "I gave my own version of the Lord's Prayer."

"It's him," Tomas confirmed to Nan. "Reverend Rivers, we'll be patching you through to anchor Ron Stone shortly."

"I'll be here," Big Ben reassured them.

Nan started barking instructions to those working the newscast in the control room. "After this story airs we'll be going to phoner line 2." She then pressed a button that put her voice into Ron Stone's earpiece. "Ron, I've got Reverend Rivers on the phone. He wants to do a live interview 30 seconds away."

They could hear Stone gasp through his microphone before he replied, "Wait, what?"

Nan ignored him and resumed barking orders to the control room. "I need a phoner super to identify him, and do we have any full screen graphics of Rivers? Move guys! We don't have much time." She had barely gotten the last word out when the video story ended and Stone appeared on camera. "Pitch to Rivers" was all she had time to say.

Stone did as he was told. "Folks, I'm told that Reverend Rivers has just called into *The Industry Tonight* to share his perspective. He joins us by phone. Can you hear me Reverend?"

"Loud and clear Ron. How are you this fine day?"

"I'm good sir. Certainly an eventful 24 hours for you."

"Ron, before you continue with your questions, can I say something?" Rivers interrupted.

"Of course, go ahead."

"I just want to tell your audience what a fine young reporter Tom Stein is. I've been in politics for a while now, and I can tell you that he treated me tough but fair, honestly and respectfully. You don't see a whole lot of that in the media these days and I think he's got a very bright future."

"Thank you Reverend. I'm pretty sure he's watching, so let's move on, shall we?"

The interview went on for more than 30 minutes. It was the worst form of television ever. An anchor interviewing a talking head that viewers couldn't even see. Nan tried to spruce it up by inserting video, asking the graphics operator to put on screen some of Rivers quotes soon after he said them, etc., but for the most part, it was just Ron and the Reverend having a chat.

And yet watching from the control room Tomas found it captivating. Topics ranged from more details about what happened on the boat to the reaction among Rivers' supporters and the campaign when the Chastity story first broke to the fallout after his interview with Tomas.

At times Rivers would fall back on scripture to describe the ordeal. He made an analogy about his encounter with Chastity to the story of Jesus and the prostitute who cried at his feet and used her tears to wash them. Rivers described the environment inside the campaign once the tabloid story broke. Many wanted to release a statement right away, but Rivers said that he prayed about it, and God told him to wait. "Let the pigs swim in their slop for a while," was his thinking he told Stone. "The truth will come out soon enough."

Rivers and Stone talked about the boat and who may have set him up. No one could find out anything about the boat because it appeared it wasn't docked in DC anymore. Someone had heard a rumor it had been recently spotted in Monaco. Rivers told Stone he didn't care. "You find out who sent Brenda Caruso to me, and I'll gladly shake their hand."

By the time Stone bid Rivers a good night no real new developments in the story had been revealed but there was more context to how it unfolded, and people were hearing the story from Rivers himself unedited and unfiltered. It was terrible television but it was compelling stuff anyway.

After the newscast ended Nan looked at her computer monitor and saw a sea of red. It indicated all of the carefully crafted stories, interviews and panel discussions that she had to cancel because of Rivers' surprise interview. She sighed, looked over at Tomas who had watched the entire rest of the newscast from the control room and asked, "Who is this guy?"

"He's certainly different," was all Tomas could say in another vintage Captain Obvious moment.

"You know something? There is only one other person on the entire

planet who could pull that off, who would pull off something like that!"
she replied.

"And that would be?" Tomas asked.

"Donald J. Trump."

Tomas thought about it for a moment and concluded that she was right.

And there would be something else Trumpian about that night. Rivers
proved once again that he could draw a big audience. When the overnight ratings came in the next morning, *The Industry Tonight* had pulled
its highest viewership numbers ever. They weren't *huge* as the 7 p.m.
newscast rarely posted big numbers, but they were substantial. From that
day forward Rivers would juice the ratings of any news network which
featured him whether it be carrying one of his rallies live or doing stories
on his campaign. It brought the kind of big numbers not seen since the
heady cable news ratings from coverage of Donald Trump's first presidential campaign. And it was for many of the same reasons. People who had
become rabid supporters of Rivers watched. Sworn enemies watched too.
Those in the middle watched for curiosity's sake and because they didn't
want to be stuck at the office water cooler and not be able to join in on the
latest conversation about what Rivers was up to now.

But covering Rivers also seemed more benign to news executives
because he wasn't Trump. Rivers didn't love the media. Who did really?
But he wasn't constantly calling it 'fake news' or turning his followers
against them. Rivers as a faithful man of God was also beholden to the
truth even if some didn't accept his version of the truth. He didn't re-tweet
conspiracy theories because he didn't tweet at all. He captured a lot of the
enthusiasm of Trump without some of the Trump 'noise'. Over-covering
Rivers on the news was a low-risk, high-reward proposition for television
newsrooms even if other candidates complained that the coverage was
drowning out their voices.

Nan had considered assigning Tomas to Rivers full-time, but when the
Rivers campaign made it clear that he would not be given special access

and that the interview was a one-time deal, she decided against it. Better she thought to pull the Tom Stein card on Rivers in those moments when she really needed to use it.

Tomas was fine with that. His first few weeks had been a whirlwind and because he had worked so many holidays and the past Sunday, Nan ordered him to take Tuesday off. The next day Tomas would watch Rivers' news conference, which was carried live by all the cable networks and DC-3 on the TV in his apartment. And then he took a nap. He thought things would calm down a bit now and that the frenetic pace he had been on could not continue. News happened in cycles after all and he was way overdue for a down cycle. He could not have been more wrong.

In just one week Tomas would find himself covering an explosive story in one of the most dangerous situations he would ever encounter in his life, much less as a journalist. And it was all because he accidentally took the wrong news car.

CHAPTER 20

WWDC-3 TV HAD TWO PARKING LOTS. One was unsecured for employees and the other was fenced and gated for the station's news cars, live vans, satellite trucks and even a remote production truck. Overseeing it all was a burly Hispanic man whose real name was Salvador Carmen Estes, but everyone just called him 'Car-man'.

Carman did everything for the DC-3 fleet of news vehicles. Routine maintenance, minor repairs, car washing, vacuuming, and more. He was also a bit of an innovator. When he had heard about technology that helped trucking companies track their vehicles by satellite, he thought it would be a perfect innovation to use at DC-3. It not only allowed Carman to better maintain the vehicles by tracking their use but a monitor on the Assignment Desk tracked the position of the cars in real time, making it easier to route the closest vehicles to a breaking news story.

It was a system that only worked if you knew who was in which car so that you could text the closest person to any breaking news scene and dispatch them to the area. And how *DC-3 News* did that was decidedly 'old school'. They used a whiteboard.

Carman would assign most of the vehicles himself based on which ones he knew were in service and which ones were not. Assignment editors who handled logistics would assign certain people to certain cars. Videographers and MMJs could even use the whiteboard to assign a car to themselves if they needed one. But every assignment went on the whiteboard. A car number went by each person's name when they had the car, and once they were done with it, they would erase it and put the car number in a space on the whiteboard labeled the 'stable'.

On a cold Tuesday in January Tomas came in to find himself assigned to what he thought was car 11. He went downstairs, grabbed his gear from a locker and took the keys to car 11 from a large key-chain board right next to the secure metal door to the parking lot. He was one of the first *The Industry Tonight* correspondents out the door that morning because he had a bit of a drive ahead of him. He was going up to the University of Maryland to meet with a political science professor. His story that day was on a system called Ranked Choice Voting. It was a system where people were allowed to vote for more than one candidate in order of preference in an election, so if there were five candidates on the ballot for a single race, they could rank each candidate with 1 being their favorite and 5 being their least favorite. Two Republican candidates in tight races in California had sued to end the practice for the primary election there.

The professor had recently written an article for a major business publication arguing that the system disenfranchised voters by forcing them to cast ballots for people they in no way supported or else risk having their votes go uncounted. Tomas planned to interview him and then go to the dorms where many students were returning after Christmas break. He would then have the students vote in a mock ranked choice election and then use flash cards to show how the candidate with the least support could actually win. Tomas had spent a lot of time both researching and preparing for a story which fate would determine would never make it to air, at least not today.

Minutes after Tomas left the station the police scanner in the newsroom crackled with reports of what appeared to be a major news story. Pretty much every police department in the country had gone to digital scanners. They left newsrooms blind when it came to tapping into the radio frequencies police used to dispatch news cars because they could no longer monitor them. But in Washington, DC, the police chief was trying to build a more trusting relationship with the news media, and part of that was providing the local news stations with the 'key' to their main digital radio channels so they could listen in as police dispatchers communicated with patrol cars.

This one sounded big. Experienced 'scanner hounds' on the assignment desk had determined that there had been an officer involved shooting which had left someone seriously injured. Immediately they started scanning Carman's whiteboard and then looking at the car tracker monitor to see who was closest. They thought it was Tomas. They were wrong.

In fact Tomas was a good 15 minutes away even though the monitor showed he was less than 15 blocks away. His cell phone rang and he was detoured to the scene. "You are right on top of it," an assignment editor told him. Tomas was confused because his own GPS said differently, but he did as he was told. He had the assignment desk on car speaker and they started yelling at him, "No, turn around. *What are you doing?*"

"I can't turn around," Tomas protested. "I'm on 295!"

"No you're not! You're in Deanwood," an assignment editor shot back. Tomas was so new he had no idea where Deanwood was but he was pretty certain he wasn't there. "Then it's got a nice, wide Main Street that looks a lot like I-295."

"Wait!" Tomas could hear the people manning the desk start to argue with each other. "He's not in 11. He's in 17. Look!"

"Oh wow, you're right. Who is in 11 then?" another person shot back on the desk. They decided to do a group text to the entire staff. "Whoever is in Deanwood call the desk now!"

It turned out Al was in Deanwood and he had car 11. He was heading out to the area to shoot video for a redevelopment story and that's when he couldn't find his assigned car 17. He thought he had misread the board so he took car 11 instead thinking the 7 was actually meant to be a 1.

By the time Tomas arrived at the scene police had not yet had time to set up a perimeter around the shooting, so he grabbed his camera and ran toward the area. That's where he found Al already shooting video.

The scene was surreal. There was a parked, running car with an open door and a body covered with a tarp about 20 feet away from it. Behind it was an unmarked police car, its driver's door also open and lights still flashing. Tomas counted about a dozen marked police cars with more arriving every minute. Sirens echoed through the area as if they were coming from everywhere around him. Near the scene was a huddle of officers and Tomas recognized Lt. Manuel Alvarez among them. "Pretty impressive," he thought to himself. "They already had the public information office at the scene."

As Al shot video Tomas knew The Big House would want a live shot ASAP and he noticed that Al had a 'Bond Box' with him. Perfect!

A 'Bond Box' was short for a 'bonded cellular' device. As Tomas would explain it to his parents one time, the device was essentially a cell phone on steroids. It was able to connect to several cell phone signals at the same time, split the signal into parts and then reconnect them at a receiver at the station. The result was that a news crew could go live from virtually anywhere there was cell phone service—inside an elevator, a moving vehicle, and of course any major crime scene, and do it within a minute or two of turning the box on.

Every television station had them now, but years earlier DC-3 was one of the first to deploy them, and someone in the marketing department decided it would be cool to call them 'Bond Boxes' after the mythical spy James Bond. Special graphics were made and music created for whenever they were used on-air which walked right up to the line of copyright infringement of the movie franchise. The boxes even had special 'Bond' wraps. They caught on so well that people would walk up to DC-3 crews in the field just to ask them if they could show them their Bond Box.

They only worked where cell phone service was good like in a metropolitan area. But they were faster to set up than a much more complicated 'live truck' which used a tall, pneumatic mast to shoot a point-to-point signal using microwaves — or a satellite dish to beam live pictures back to the TV station off a satellite thousands of miles in the sky. Tomas had the bond box plugged in and sending back a signal in less than 2 minutes. He had no information but he was ready to go live on-air holding a microphone as Al pointed his camera toward him.

"We have some breaking news out of east DC right now," Tomas could hear in his ear piece. "A reported use of 'deadly force' by a police officer in Washington's Deanwood neighborhood. DC-3's Tom Stein is live at the scene with a Bond Box. Tom, what can you tell us?"

"I'm standing here on a side street just off of Minnesota Avenue where police scanner reports indicate a police officer shot and killed a man just minutes ago. I'm going to ask my cameraman Al to pan over to the scene. You can see there is a body covered with a tarp near the open door of a gray sedan. The vehicle behind him is an unmarked police car. You can see the lights flashing and the driver's side door also open on that vehicle. It appears that the driver of the gray car may have gotten out of his vehicle for some reason and approached the officer and that is where he was shot and killed. We don't have any information from police yet including whether or not that man was armed. I'm going to take a few minutes and see if we can find anyone who witnessed the shooting and will be back with new information as we get it. For now, live in the Deanwood area of DC, I'm Tom Stein, *DC-3 News*."

Almost immediately after he was done a producer told him through his ear piece: "You're supposed to say 'live with the Bond Box'."

"Producers!" Tomas thought to himself but didn't say out loud. He needed to focus on getting any information he could. He saw a small group of bystanders down the block and made a beeline for them. "Anyone see anything?"

"Yeah, I did," an older African-American man said raising his hand. "Craziest thing."

"What did you see."

"The cop was pulling the guy over and then the guy got out of his car and started yelling at the officer. Well the cop starts getting out of his car and then this guy just charges at him. Head down. He was yelling and charging and pointing at him and the cop just pulls his gun out and shoots him."

"Did the guy have a weapon?"

The witness shook his head *no*. "Not that I could see. He was just screaming and running like a crazy man. I'm not sure I wouldn't have shot him too. It was crazy."

"Describe the victim," Tomas asked him.

"Black man. Kind of short and stocky. Was wearing jeans and a sweatshirt."

"And the cop who shot him?"

"You can see him right over there!" he said pointing. He was pointing at the group that Lt. Alvarez was talking with.

"Which one?"

"The guy with the mustache."

That's when Tomas realized that Lt. Alvarez wasn't there for public relations reasons. He was the shooter! "Thanks man. Can I get your name and number if I have more questions?" The man shook his head *no* and began to walk away. "That's all I saw man," he said as he turned away.

Tomas raced back toward Al and the 'Bond Box'. "New information," he yelled at him. "Need to get set up."

Tomas did another live shot with the new eyewitness information he had just obtained while making doubly sure people understood that none of it was confirmed. As he wrapped up he noticed a news chopper approaching and realized it wasn't theirs. He was feeling like it was going to be a long day. Tomas had no idea.

Police had set up a perimeter around the scene—about a block in each direction—but rather than being kept outside of the police perimeter Tomas and Al found themselves stuck inside of it. Other DC-3 crews were arriving and their news helicopter finally showed up as well, but Tomas was the station's only eyes at the actual scene at the shooting. His dilemma was that there was no more information to be had. Police had pushed back any civilians beyond the police lines and Tomas suspected he wouldn't be far behind them.

As witnesses emerged, crews behind the police lines were getting more information than Tomas was. Others expressed their anger that police would kill a man who Tomas had told viewers on-air that a witness said did not appear to be armed.

And then the rioting and the looting began.

For Tomas it was surreal. Here he was standing on a street corner surrounded by cops who were themselves surrounded by hundreds of very angry people. Some began loudly shouting profanities at officers. He knew that the next time he went live on-air his microphone would pick it all up. There was little he could do about that. By sheer luck he was the only TV reporter with a live Bond Box inside the crime scene. Newscast producers at the station would go to him again and again just so he could show and narrate what was happening in real time.

The situation was growing more perilous by the moment. At first it was only shouting, but then the crowd began throwing whatever they could find at the officers on scene. Rocks, soda bottles and other assorted objects. Tomas could hear glass breaking nearby as some in the crowd began smashing windows and breaking into nearby stores.

Amazingly the police were so intensely dealing with the escalating situation that none of the officers seemed to notice him or Al even during his live reporting. As the crowd attempted to push closer to the crime scene officers pushed back creating a manned perimeter and that's when one of them finally approached Tomas and Al.

"You need to get out of here!" he yelled at them above the loud din of the crowd.

"How?" Tomas responded looking around as if he himself felt trapped.

The officer looked around too. He had no idea either. "The riot squad is just down that street," he said pointing. "When they get here I want you two out of here with them. You are in grave danger!"

Tomas looked down the street where the officer had pointed and for the first time in his life he saw police fire a canister of tear gas and then another. Soon he could see through the crowd that officers in riot gear were approaching. "*Take me live now*!" he screamed through his microphone. He knew this would be his last live shot of the night, at least from that corner. Seconds later he could hear Ron Stone pitching to him from the studio. "Tom, what is the situation out there now?"

"Ron, the situation here is rapidly deteriorating. Police have moved the body of the man who was shot and killed. He was placed by an officer into a van and if you look down this way police in riot gear are now moving in our direction to help get officers safely out of here. I don't know if you can see the smoke but I believe that is tear gas they are firing to disperse the crowd as they form a line and march down the street toward us. You can see people in the crowd running from the scene but also, Al, look over there. Some people are throwing objects—whatever they can find really—at the approaching riot police. Oh my Gosh, Al, over to your left. Not sure if you can see that Ron but that's a man, a looter, leaving what appears to be a drug store with a basket full of stuff."

Viewers could see the tall, black man in jeans and a white T-shirt holding a shopper's basket full of stolen merchandise which no one could quite make out.

"The police are ignoring him Ron. Right now they are just slowly working toward our location so that they can get this crime scene under control. And they're almost here. Maybe half a block to go."

Tomas was cut off by anchorman Stone. "Tom, are you okay? Are you safe? Can you get out of there?"

"Ron, I think so. We've been instructed by officers to leave the scene with them once the riot police arrive. And we'll keep broadcasting live while we do so you'll know when we know."

"Tom, you should know there are reports of car fires and heavy looting nearby. As a matter of fact, if we can take a shot from DC Chopper 3, we can show you some of that. What are you seeing from where you are?"

"Ron, the police perimeter of the scene remains secure for now and we're just inside of that, but if you look around, it is chaos everywhere. People running and screaming, many throwing projectiles at police although mostly at the riot officers as they approach. You can hear a chant coming from a crowd over there using an expletive to describe the police. Again, police appear to have processed the scene. The body of the man shot and killed by an officer has been removed. I think officers are just ready to get out of here and so are we."

"Do what you can to get yourself to safety," Stone urged him.

Tomas and Al would eventually make their way out of the crime scene and keep reporting from a safe distance. The station played the video they had shot while inside the perimeter over and over again. Viewers could clearly see the glow of cars and buildings on fire behind him in the dark night sky; thick, black smoke slowly rising into the air.

It would be 3 a.m. before they would be relieved by morning show crews sent to continue the live wall-to-wall coverage through the over-night. The crowds had mostly been dispersed, but neither Tomas or Al could get back to their vehicles now. Both cars were trapped inside a large, established police perimeter. Al couldn't remember if he had left his car running. Tomas was fearful that his news car was one of those that had been torched.

They ended up hitching a ride with another *DC-3 News* crew headed back to the station. The excitement of the chaotic situation soon gave way to utter exhaustion by all inside who had been covering it. By the time Tomas had pulled his car into his apartment's parking lot it was after 4 a.m., and he had no memory of how he had driven there, he was just that tired. He didn't even have the energy to make it upstairs to his bed. The couch in his living room would suffice.

As Tomas slept, he relived the events he had just witnessed over and over again in his dreams. He had never been that up close to so much violence, so much anger, so much conflict. Those dreams so consumed him in his exhaustion that he didn't remember hitting snooze when his phone alarm went off at 6 a.m. Nor did he hear the phone ring and the voicemail notification at 10 a.m. It would take him 15 more minutes until he woke up in a sudden panic realizing he was very late for work.

The voicemail was from Nan. "Hey Tom, I know you had a long day yesterday so I hope you are doing okay. Let me know what time you'll be in but make it soon. We've got another busy day ahead."

Tomas picked up the phone and called her back. It was going to be another long day.

CHAPTER 21

THE CITY'S MAYOR AND POLICE CHIEF had just begun a media briefing when Tomas jumped in his car. He listened to it on the 'all news' radio station as he drove into work.

The chief identified the shooting victim as Lamont 'Shorty' Curtis, a lifetime DC resident who years ago had served as officer with the Capitol Police Department. He had died from a single gunshot wound to the head after being pulled over for a suspected DUI traffic stop. The chief was not yet ready to identify the shooter as being Lt. Manuel Alvarez even though everyone already knew that because of what Tomas had reported. He did confirm the officer who shot Curtis was on paid administrative leave.

And then came a surprise.

"I want to read you a statement from the officer involved in this shooting who we will identify at a later time," the chief of police told the reporters. Tomas could not see how many journalists were there through the radio audio, but it sounded like a lot. "The officer wants you to know the following and this is his statement. It reads and I quote, 'In the interest of transparency, I want you to know that Lamont Curtis and I did serve together on the capitol police force many years ago and considered each other at one time to be friends. Although we had drifted apart in recent years I came to know his family well and wish to offer them my sincerest condolences. I would give anything for this to have ended a different way.'"

Tomas then listened to the mayor discuss plans for anticipated protests that night. Yes, extra police would be on duty. No, they were not considering calling in the National Guard. No, there were no plans yet for a curfew.

Interestingly they refused to answer most questions even though there were a lot of questions. What was a public information officer doing making a traffic stop? Did the officer not have a less lethal option than to shoot the man in the head? And why would a man who was allegedly intoxicated charge the officer in the first place? Why were they both in that neighborhood? Why was the officer not wearing a body camera?

Tomas pulled into the station parking lot and headed inside having no idea what was expected from him that day. Nan immediately saw him and met him as he descended down the stairs. "Nice work last night. Everyone's talking about it," she told him.

"I gotta tell you I'm exhausted," he replied as if trying to manufacture an excuse for oversleeping.

"Everyone is exhausted and this is just getting started," Nan replied. "Look, because we anticipate more rioting The Big House is taking over everything. It's going to be 24/7 until things calm down. They've asked us to provide perspective content and so what I want from you is sort of a 'stream of consciousness' story about yesterday."

Tomas was confused. What is a 'stream of consciousness' story?'

Nan sensed his confusion and continued. "Just go through your video and put together a story of what happened as you saw it. Your deadline isn't until seven o'clock, so you've got some time."

Tomas had no clue what Nan wanted. What happened as he saw it? He sat down in an editing station, pulled up the files including his live shots and started going through them, but there was something nagging at him. The whole thing didn't make sense. It was a feeling that he had felt before as a journalist, a feeling that things as he knew them didn't quite add up. Sometimes his suspicions were correct but not always. Nonetheless Tomas did his best to do as he was told, exiting the edit bay from time to time to look up at the monitors for the latest on DC-3's ongoing coverage. It was clear that many in the city, and specifically the Deanwood area, were on edge and bracing for more violence.

It all tended to make the newscasts seem somewhat disjointed—police involved shooting; the possibility of more rioting; reaction to police shooting and the possibility of more rioting. Presidential candidates and other community leaders give their take on the police shooting and the possibility of more rioting, and now here's Brian with tonight's weather forecast.

By 5 p.m. protesters began to gather around a makeshift memorial for Shorty Curtis. By 6 p.m. they began to march urging all involved to keep things peaceful as the winter darkness fell.

Tomas fronted his 'stream of consciousness' story at 7 p.m. He hated the story but no one else seemed to mind. Right after him was to be a panel discussion about what happened the night before which included a community activist, a local newspaper columnist and to most everyone's surprise—Lachlan. What was he doing on a panel discussion?

"I'm Ron Stone here in *The Industry Tonight* newsroom with local Pastor Robert Lucas Junior, Kendrick McCann, columnist for the *DC Daily Express*, a website which covers the local African-American community and our own Senior Correspondent Lachlan McNight."

Stone turned to McCann. "I know after we're done here you are planning to head down to Deanwood where a march is scheduled for about an hour from now. Everyone in DC is very tense right now after what happened last night. Are you concerned we might see a repeat of that violence tonight?"

"I hope it is peaceful and urge everyone to show restraint, but people are upset Ron," McCann replied. "They're angry that these incidents of police use of deadly force against unarmed black men keep happening."

"Oh for heaven's sake, unarmed. Really?" Lachlan interrupted. "His weapon was his body! Eyewitnesses confirm he was charging the officer in an obvious attempt to tackle him and probably try to get his gun. So the officer either defends himself, or he tells his attacker after the man steals his weapon, 'Hands up, Don't Shoot'."

Tomas recognized the phrase *hands up, don't shoot* as referring to the police shooting of Michael Brown in Ferguson, MO years earlier. An eyewitness had told police that Brown put his hands up and said "… don't shoot" to the officer before the fatal shot was fired. It had become a rallying cry for protesters even though it was later learned that Brown had done no such thing and the eyewitness account had been a lie.

"We don't know that he was going for the officer's gun," McCann shot back. "Maybe he felt his life was in danger and that was all he could think to do."

"He could have complied, right?" Laughlin shot back.

"You cannot understand the fear many black men feel when confronted by police."

"If he complies, he's alive today. Seems to me most black men have a lot more to fear from another black man with a gun than a police officer with one," Lachlan proffered.

"Oh, here we go again. Justifying police violence against people of color by bringing up black-on-black crime." McCann was clearly getting irritated by the direction of the conversation.

"Because they're related!" Lachlan responded. "Every day we send cops into virtual war zones filled to the brim with guns and tell them to root out the bad guys who victimize everyone else. They go in there to *protect* black and brown people, not hurt them. But whatever you do, don't make a mistake. Don't shoot someone who looks like he's reaching for a gun. Noooo! Wait until he produces it and fires at you!"

"George Floyd was no mistake! It was intentional homicide by police," McCann said, nearly yelling now.

"No one defends what happened to George Floyd, and the police officer who murdered him is behind bars where he belongs! But what about Jacob Blake who admitted to going for a knife when a Wisconsin police officer shot him. Or Andrew Brown whose weapon of choice against Sheriff's deputies in North Carolina was a BMW 6 Series he bought with all the money he made selling drugs to addicts. Or Rayshard Brooks who not only struggled with Atlanta Police officers who were arresting him for being a felon who was driving drunk, but who grabbed an officer's taser and fired at him before being shot and killed." Lachlan was virtually standing now as he rolled off the names of black men shot and killed by police over the years.

"You're saying they deserved to die!" McCann shot back leaning forward to the point where both men were just 2 ft. from each other.

"I'm not saying that at all! I have no idea who deserves to die! But they certainly improved their odds of dying. And if I wrestled with officers and shot their own taser at them I suspect they would shoot my lily white behind too!"

Tomas was watching all this and not realizing his mouth was gaping wider and wider as he looked on. "He's going to get mail," he said to himself out loud.

"What's mail?" came a voice from behind him. It was Randall Larsen.

"I mean that some people are going to crucify Lachlan for what he's saying up there," Tomas responded turning around.

"I knew what you meant," Randall smiled at him.

Stone managed to calm down both men and get them back into their seats. The Reverend was now talking. Tomas wasn't really paying attention to him as much as Lachlan's demeanor. He looked genuinely angry. He wouldn't say another word during the segment and stormed off the set when it was over. He made a beeline for Tomas and Randall and told them, "Follow me boys. I need a drink."

Lachlan liked to drink at a bar called *The Hideout* because there was literally a 'hideout room' in the back. The room was usually closed off except for special events, but the owner would open it up for Lachlan so he and his friends would not be disturbed. They were sort of local celebrities after all, and he and Randall were steady business.

"That was some show you put on up there," Tomas told him while sitting at their table nursing a beer.

Lachlan took a sip of his scotch on the rocks. "It's time we start telling people the truth."

"*The* truth or *your* truth," Randall chimed in. Randall and Lachlan were known to be longtime friends who had sat together at this same table many times trading barbs like these.

"What's your truth sir?" Lachlan asked back.

"Don't look at me. I'm a suburban kid. Even my high school basketball team was mostly white! But I don't think my truth is your truth."

"Good thing all of them had a black friend they could claim when they were telling racist jokes to each other," Lachlan replied.

"I'm just saying you can't know what it is like to be a black man in America. It's a truth you can't see."

Lachlan smiled. "And you know what it's like to be a white Australian in America?"

"Well aside from the crazy accent which no one can understand it is probably a bit easier," Randall replied giving a fake toast to Lachlan with his own beer.

Tomas joined in the conversation. "You don't really think blacks have it as easy as whites, do you? I mean we're not *that* far beyond Jim Crow, separate-but-equal, redlining …"

Lachlan cut him off. "No, I do not. But times have changed and if some blacks spent as much time working to take advantage of the smorgasbord of opportunities this nation would afford them as they spend making claims of racial grievance, I think they would be better off. Look at Exhibit A right here," he said pointing at Randall. "Randall, did you get good grades in school?"

"I did," Randall confirmed.

"Randall, did you go to college on a partial scholarship for minorities who got good grades?"

"And a tennis scholarship. You know I did."

"Randall, because of that, are you now living the American dream?" Lachlan probed.

"I worked hard for all of it sir," Randall replied.

"And in the United States of America, my friend, people like you and me who work hard to take advantage of the opportunities presented to us will ultimately find success. And what I love about you is that you do it all without any excuses." Lachlan paused for a moment and then added, "But let us face facts dude. You're an 'Oreo'."

Randall laughed out loud at Lachlan's characterization of him as an 'Oreo,' black on the outside but white on the inside. "I'm calling BS on that one sir!" he told him smiling.

Lachlan smiled, took a sip of his drink, and then looked down while shaking his head. "Randall, did I ever tell you about covering my first murder?"

"No, all the time we've spent back here and you've never brought it up" Randall responded, the two talking as if Tomas weren't even there.

"It's not a good memory for me. When I first came to America I was working the crime beat for a New York tabloid newspaper. This was back before Giuliani became mayor when there was a lot more crime to cover in the city. But I'll never forget my first murder. It was late on a Saturday night and I arrived to find the body of a black teenager under a sheet. He had been shot to death. And right as I arrive, the boy's mother arrives at the scene too and just starts wailing. Cries like I had never heard before! Maybe she knew her kid was in a gang; maybe she didn't, but her grief was just so terribly real and it was heartbreaking!"

Lachlan paused. He had been staring at the floor while telling his story as if he were somehow under duress, but now he looked up. "I was so angry. There was nothing, nothing I could do to help that woman. Nothing to ease her pain. I had never felt so helpless. I would just go back to my newsroom, type up a few words about what happened and the editors would bury it on page twelve because it was one of a half dozen shootings that night. It was infuriating and I don't talk about it much because some nights I can still hear her screams."

"That's some story," Randall replied.

"In any case, that's what happened tonight. I was channeling her."

After another sip of his drink, Lachlan's tone remained somber even as he changed the subject. "I'm thinking of retiring," Lachlan blurted out. "Maybe head back to Australia."

"So that's what that whole panel discussion was?" Randall probed. "One last blast of the truth before you head off into the outback sunset?"

"My heart's not in it anymore," Lachlan conceded. Here was the crusading journalist who was a DC legend, the man more responsible than anyone for putting DC-3 on the journalism map, the man who was now sulking before Tomas about calling it a career. Tomas could not believe he of all people was sitting at this table and hearing it for himself.

"Can I ask why?" Tomas offered.

"Truth is my heart hasn't been in it for some time. Journalism has changed but I have not. It left me more than I'm leaving it."

"What do you mean?" Tomas asked.

"Randall knows," he said peeking over at Randall.

Randall rolled his eyes. "Oh here we go with Hunter Biden again." Hunter Biden is the son of President Joe Biden. During the 2020 campaign one of his laptops was dropped off at a local computer shop in DC and never retrieved. It contained a treasure trove of damaging information to both Hunter and potentially his father, but the mainstream media ignored the story in the weeks before the election. Even Twitter and Facebook banned the content from their social media platforms as 'Russian disinformation'.

Lachlan turned to Tomas. "Back in 2020 I had got word of the laptop and confirmed with a Justice Department official that Hunter Biden was under investigation by the feds. The Attorney General was trying to keep the story out of the media, but I had it dead to rights. We were ready to go with it when Marjorie killed it."

"Marjorie Midas killed a story?" Tomas asked incredulously. It was the exact opposite of what her reputation would have predicted.

"She told me to my face that she could put up with a lot but that she was not prepared to deal with the blowback she would get if the station helped get Donald Trump reelected. Her liberal snowflakes would kick her out of their chummy little social circle to the point where the only person she could hang out with was some lefty lawyer who had decided to defend Trump during his impeachment hearing," Lachlan said sarcastically. "It was a gut-punch for me. Here is a man who wants to be president who may have been compromised by the dirty dealings of his son. Had it been Donald Trump and Trump Jr. we would have been all over it."

"Wow," was all Tomas could say in response.

The table was silent for a moment. Then Lachlan continued, "In any case, my source at Justice was furious. Couldn't blame her. How do you explain to someone why you would cover two people seeking the same office so differently? I mean we're supposed to be the umpires in the game of life, right? But everyone sees through it. If candidate Trump threw a perfect fastball right down the middle, we would call it a 'ball'. If candidate Biden threw so wildly that he hit the batter, not only would we call it a 'strike' but we would applaud the outcome. It was deflating. I had become the face of fake news." Lachlan looked down again at his scotch and took a sip.

"He's usually more fun than this," Randall assured Tomas. "Just having a day."

But Lachlan wasn't done. "And then after the election we get hyperinflation and crazy gas prices, and so many people pouring over the southern border that they were shipping them as far away as New York City, and he's calling his Vice-President 'President Harris.' It was ridiculous, and people on the street would ask me, 'You had to have known. Why didn't you warn us?' And my only answer was that they wouldn't let me."

Lachlan looked down at his drink, took a sip and decided to change the subject. "So did I at least light up social media?" Lachlan asked with a smile.

"Oh yeah. It's burning up my phone," Randall replied. "You are either a crusading reporter finally telling the truth or the biggest racist on the planet."

"Well I know that when Nan reams me out tomorrow you'll assure her than I'm neither. I have to pee." Lachlan stumbled out of his chair and headed to the bathroom leaving Tomas and Randall at the table.

"You don't seem too concerned about him calling you an 'Oreo,'" Tomas observed.

"He's made that crack before and he knows that I know that he doesn't mean it. Just his way of needling me."

"And you're not offended?"

"He knows my story," Randall said smiling. "I once told him about how my mom would tell me a story about her childhood. Her dad was a famous sportscaster and she grew up in the suburbs surrounded by nothing but white kids. She played with white kids. She went to school with white kids. It was great for her because she loved to do the things and play the games that they did, but she was also different and unique. She stood out and she enjoyed that. And then one day out of nowhere, her dad pulls her from school and tells her they are moving back into the city. She said she cried and cried for days and never really seemed to fit in afterward in their new neighborhood."

"Really," Tomas interjected, "How come?"

Her dad was a celebrity. It wasn't a poor neighborhood but my mom had nicer things than everyone else. My mom had developed a love of horse riding. No one else in that neighborhood had ever ridden a horse. Many probably had never seen a horse up close. And so they teased her about it. My mom loved to read. She would rather read a book or a magazine than hang out on the street corner or the basketball court. That brought more grief and bullying. Suddenly she hated going to school and her grades started to drop. Granddad finally decided she would be better off in private school with mostly white kids, but they were not going to move back to the suburbs."

"How come?" Tomas asked while taking another sip of his beer.

"My mom told me that she asked him that before leaving for college. 'Why did they have to move away?' she asked him. Granddad told her that he was afraid she was becoming 'too white'."

"Wow," Tomas replied.

"Yep. She was pretty angry about that and my mom told me she would never, ever do that to me. That she and my dad would do the best they could for me no matter where that took them or who they encountered along the way. And 'F' anyone who told them that their beautiful brown child was becoming 'too white'."

"Did she actually use the 'F' word?" Tomas asked.

"Truth be told she used the 'N' word too!" Randall said laughing.

"She sounds like a really strong woman. I can tell that she really loves you and wanted the best for you," Tomas replied.

Randall smiled. He hadn't quite finished his point. "Did Lachlan ever tell you about his tabloid TV friend?"

"No, never brought him up."

"He's the guy who does DNA tests on men to determine who is the father of some woman's child."

"I've seen the show," Tomas confirmed although he could not remember the tabloid TV personality's name.

"In any case, you've got these so-called 'adults' acting up in front of a studio audience. Some are white and some are black, but all of them are arguing and doing all sorts of crazy stuff that would embarrass anyone halfway normal, and they're doing it all on national TV! And that's when they cut to a shot of the baby in another room. A beautiful, young innocent child at the center of tabloid TV fodder. And you look into that beautiful kid's childlike eyes—a child who has all the potential in the world, and you hope for the best, but you think that if this is how your biological parents really are kid, you're doomed!"

"Pretty exploitative stuff," Tomas replied. "Probably why I don't watch."

"Exploitative to be sure, but there's a strange honesty there about how life can be such a craps shoot that people like Lachlan will never be able to understand."

"What do you mean?"

"I mean that *my* kids live in a nice house with educated, professional parents. We often think of nothing more than their future and wellbeing while setting them up with all the things we know are important for their success. They go to a good school in a safe neighborhood where everybody watches out for everyone else. And when the time comes for them to go to college and out into the world, resources will be there to help them pursue their own dreams. My wife and I will make sure of that!"

Tomas nodded his head in agreement. "I don't doubt that for a moment."

"Yeah," Randall said leaning into Tomas a bit. "But those babies on that tabloid TV show. Odds are they will have none of that, right? Their parents love them but they probably won't have the ability to keep them from the allure of the streets; their school won't be able to do enough to educate them; their community won't be able to do enough to nourish them or protect them from all sorts of trouble. My kids will experience hope and promise and support. That baby on the tabloid TV show will likely only know a life of hopelessness and despair and privation. They are trapped in a bad place and they know it. There is no way out. No wonder they get so angry. No wonder they riot."

They both sat silent for a moment. Randall had given Tomas something to think about and he pondered what he had just heard.

Lachlan returned from the restroom and they sat and had one more round of drinks. There would be more rioting that night and the next but none of them would be utilized to cover it. It took a major snowstorm to help calm the streets. Lachlan's comments received a lot of negative publicity, but it had also been overshadowed by the evolving situation on the ground. He had been reprimanded by Nan, but that was it and he did not retire, at least not yet. He was in his early 70s now but he was not yet ready to go.

And something else would soon happen. Something terrible which would take all the attention away from Lachlan and put the media spotlight on Tomas himself. And all because he wanted to have sex.

CHAPTER 22

TOMAS AND OLIVIA HAD BEEN TRYING to make it a date for weeks. Things just hadn't been working out. She was out on the campaign trail many days of the week, and when she was in town they couldn't sync her availability with his schedule. They were also both a bit hesitant to be seen out together, the new crack reporter having dinner with the presidential candidate's senior political aide. Olivia was particularly concerned about MTB finding out.

Then one Thursday afternoon she texted him with an idea. "What if I cook for you this Saturday?"

Tomas was off on Saturday. "That could work," he texted back. "Your place?"

"No, I have roommates" Olivia texted back. Tomas had no idea she had roommates. "Let's have dinner at your place instead," she continued with a follow-up text.

Tomas thought to himself about whether he really wanted his first real date with Olivia Zhang to be inside his apartment in a complex some nick-named the 'Hijab Hilton'. "I don't think that will work," he texted back.

"Why not?"

Tomas had no real good reason to tell her 'no'. "Sure. What time?"

"I'll see you at 7 p.m. I'll bring the food; you bring the drink. Make it a good red wine." She added a few smiley face icons at the end of the text.

"I'll see you then." He texted Olivia his address.

Tomas was surprised at how anxious and excited he was for 7 p.m. on Saturday to arive. Olivia intrigued him in ways that no other woman really had in his young life. He did want to see her and learn more about her and if the chemistry clicked, maybe even have something more than that with her.

Saturday at 7 p.m. seemed like an eternity until he heard her SUV pull up to his front door. He opened the door to see if he could help her with the groceries. It was dark out and damp and cold but he could make out her petite figure in a long coat in the apartment complex lights. He went out to help her grab a bag of groceries but she was halfway up his front walk by the time they met. Olivia smiled with a "Hey" expression and walked past him. She was wearing a mid-length dark coat that fell just below her knees and leather boots which rose above the bottom of the coat. It was a sexy look, and Tomas almost thought she was 'strutting' past him.

Olivia walked into the house as if she had been there a hundred times before, stopped just inside the doorway and looked around to survey the room as Tomas closed the door behind them. That's when she turned to him with groceries still in hand asked, "Dude, what's with all the Muslims?"

"It's a long story" he replied smiling, "but on the other hand, it is safe here and my neighbors are really friendly."

Olivia smiled as she glanced up and down at him.

"Can I take your coat?" Tomas offered with an outstretched hand.

Olivia put the plastic bags of groceries on an end table and pulled her coat off to reveal a bluish mini-dress with the leather boots stretching up above her knees. Suddenly Tomas felt a bit underdressed. She was sexy to the nines. He was wearing jeans and a dress shirt. They didn't seem to belong in the same room together.

Instead of handing him the coat, she let it drop to the floor and then she charged him, pinning him against the closed door. All the excitement of seeing Olivia which had built up to this night was betraying Tomas now.

As hard as she was pushing her entire body against his there was no way she could not know how much he wanted her at that moment too.

Hard kisses became deeper longer kisses as four hands gripped whatever clothing they could find. Soon Olivia's dress and his shirt joined her coat on the floor. Her bra followed as Tomas at first lightly caressed and then firmly kissed Olivia's beautiful, bare breasts motivated further by her quick breaths and moans of joy.

Olivia tried to unbuckle his belt but Tomas instead pushed her back and onto his couch. He reached over and pulled her satin panties down over the long leather boots. He thought for a moment about removing the boots too, but they were fastened like makeshift chastity belts from the top of her knees to the bottom of her of extended stiletto heels. He would have to work around them.

Tomas slowly but firmly ran his hands up the inside of the boots until his hands hit the flushed, red hot skin of Olivia's inner thighs. She gasped as her head tilted back into the couch. His hands continued to firmly caress her thighs while Olivia at first squirmed and then pushed her body toward his hands.

Soon his head was lying against her between her open legs, his mouth so close to her burning spot of passion that every deep breath of his brought a short breath of hers. Olivia let out a soft whimper when Tomas touched her between her legs with his lips. She let out a low moan when he followed that up with his tongue.

Olivia tightened her legs around his head, thighs burning hotter than Tomas ever knew skin could. Her moans now were getting so loud and frequent that he attempted in vain to raise his hand up to cover her mouth. She bit it instead.

Oral sex with Olivia was a virtuous cycle for Tomas. The faster and harder the rhythm of his tongue pushed against her, the louder and higher pitched her expressions of intense pleasure would become, and so he would go faster and maybe a little harder still. Then came an unexpected moment when her body began to shudder uncontrollably. Her breaths quickened; her legs tightened, and Tomas could taste the warm juices oozing out of her as her shaking body held his head in a white-hot vise grip. It was a moment of complete sensory overload. Heat and skin tightly against his face. The smell of sex filling his nostrils. The taste of passion dripping against his lips, tongue, and chin.

And then Olivia wanted him again. Same chain of sensual events. Same overwhelming outcome.

A moment of rest and then Tomas could hear Olivia whisper to him "kiss me." It was a ruse by her for as he worked his way up to kiss her on the lips, Olivia's hands then went straight for his pants. "Take me," she whispered.

"No condom," he replied, but she shook her head in response and started fumbling for his belt and zipper. Tomas pushed himself against her as if to help her undress him. He managed to get his jeans and underwear down to his knees before she grabbed him and pulled him close. "Take me," she whispered again.

She then guided her right hand down his body until it found what it was looking for and guided him inside of her. "Please!" she begged in a whispered tone.

Tomas did what she asked but it was a blur. Hot breaths and moans as two bodies moved in sensual sync together until he began to shudder and the energy of sex drained from his body. He lay against Olivia with everything now feeling limp, his ears picking up the sounds of her long sigh of satisfaction.

They lay on the couch for a few minutes mostly still. Olivia would lightly stroke his hair, but she and Tomas were in a satisfying place of warmth and closeness and shared pleasure. Tomas could only enjoy the moment. He had no idea what more to do or say. It would be Olivia who would break the ice.

"I'm starving" she said in a matter-of-fact voice. They both laughed and Tomas got up, pulled his pants up and went to the bathroom to grab some washcloths bathed in warm water and some towels for cleanup. Olivia slipped back into her dress but left the bra and panties on the floor. She passed Tomas at the bathroom door as he brought out the towels and washcloth. There was a brief kiss on the lips as she closed the door behind him to use the bathroom.

Within minutes she was in the kitchen preparing dinner. It was a small kitchen, and when Tomas entered to help her and perhaps sneak a kiss on her neck she 'shooed' him away. He headed for the wine bottles on the dining room table, opened one and poured them both a glass. Olivia was so focused on cooking that when he gave her the glass of wine, she held a hand up to him, smiled and said, "All I need is 10 more minutes."

Fine.

Tomas headed over to his small stereo set and began playing music on his smartphone. He then cleaned up what mess was left on the sofa, sat down and sipped his wine. "What are you making me?" he asked.

"You'll see," came the reply.

It was only around 10 minutes later, but when Olivia emerged, it looked as if she had just cooked up a gourmet, restaurant-style masterpiece meal. She had made a crusted sirloin steak covered with a rich mushroom gravy and a caprese salad on the side that she had made ahead of time and brought with her. As Tomas sat down she put his plate in front of him and then sat down with hers.

"This looks amazing," he told her.

"Tastes better," Olivia assured him.

She was right. A perfect medium-rare steak with just the right tenderness against a mild crust and delicious gravy. "This *is* amazing!"

"Thank you!"

"I have a question," Tomas sheepishly asked. "What's with the boots? I could have broken out a crowbar and not gotten those boots off of you."

Olivia smiled at him. "I wanted to sexy things up for you."

"Great idea except for the sex itself," Tomas protested.

"You seemed to work around them okay."

"And no condom?" Tomas continued.

Olivia blushed and looked down as if she were seeking some sort of explanation from the floor. Then she looked up as if it had given her the answer. "Dude, if I wanted a piece of plastic inside of me, I would have brought a sex toy. Besides, if a professional reporter Jewish kid isn't safe for sex then there is no hope for us girls anyway."

Tomas looked at her with a smile. "Please tell me you're on birth control." Olivia nodded that she was.

"May I ask who taught you to cook?" Tomas asked amazed at a steak which could earn five stars even in DC's elevated culinary environment.

"Marilyn."

"Your boss taught you how to cook?"

"Oh she's much more than my boss." Olivia took a bite of the salad and continued. "She's my godmother."

"I had no idea," Tomas replied in a genuinely surprised tone. "You didn't mention that at the Chinese restaurant."

"Yes, the Taylor women have a reputation in the kitchen, and so growing up she would teach me all her kitchen secrets."

"She taught you well," Tomas replied while another piece of delicious steak was about to enter his mouth. "So you grew up with her?"

"My adoptive mom sometimes had to spend months in China, so I would go to Marilyn's retreat on the ranch and just hang out. She would teach me all sorts of things. Eventually she would even take me to Washington when I wasn't in school. Like her I learned to love this town."

"I'm still learning it," Tomas confessed. "It's different."

"That it is," Olivia agreed. Suddenly the music had caught her attention. "What band is this?"

"It's an alternative rock band named Irving."

"A Jewish kid who listens to a rock band named Irving. The stereotypes almost write themselves."

Tomas laughed. "Better brace yourself. The next song is by Uncle Izzy Osbourne."

Olivia smiled.

Tomas then began sort of semi-singing the lyrics. *"Remember when we danced with your mother. She was so drunk in the living room. When her profile turned a certain way, she looked how you will look forty years from today."* Tomas looked at Olivia.

"What?" she asked.

"Has anyone ever told you that you look a little bit like MTB?" Tomas told her.

"Oh yeah. And we also menstruate together as well!" Olivia countered.

"Seriously?"

"No of course not seriously," Olivia said annoyed. "That was a joke."

"Oh, sorry."

"You should be," Olivia told him. "You know that you telling your hot date that she reminds him of a middle-aged woman isn't going to help you score with her. You know that, right?"

Tomas smiled. "I think you're missing the point. I already *have* scored with her!"

Olivia laughed as if to say, "You did not just say that!" And then: "I'll give you this," Olivia continued. "When you spend so much time with someone you admire there is a part of you that wants to be like her. Maybe that's where the resemblance comes in."

Olivia looked down and then looked back up at Tomas. "By the way, I've been meaning to ask you. How did you get that interview with the 'Reverend Governor'?" Olivia said Big Ben's title almost mockingly while putting her fingers up in the air to accentuate that she was putting it in quotes.

Tomas smiled. "A tricked-out restroom."

"What?"

"When I was shooting the 'Gay Jay' story Rivers was there. It turned out the restaurant had a secret entrance of sorts into the men's room, so when the governor went inside to do his business I sneaked inside to meet him."

"And he agreed to interview with you right then?" Olivia asked.

"Only if I let him sit in on the interview with Gay Jay."

"What?" Olivia responded with genuine surprise.

"Yeah, he's a big fan. Big Ben wanted to meet him. I let him sit in through the whole thing and he turned out to be a man of his word afterward."

"Marilyn was so upset about that interview with 'Chastity'." Olivia was doing the quotation mark thing with her hand again but this time with Chastity's name. "You instantly turned Rivers from detestable sinner into glorious saint."

"You don't think MTB had anything to do with him being set up with Chastity, do you? You know. The whole prostitute on the boat thing?"

"No. She's got too many Democrats to fight off to worry about the Republicans right now. And besides, that's really not her style. Looks more like a Republican dirty trick to me."

Tomas agreed. But so far no one had been able to figure out how Rivers had been set up. He changed the topic. "So how is the Congresswoman dealing with the whole Jason thing?"

"That was a long time ago," Olivia responded with a sigh. "Honestly, she's more torn up about the situation with Alvarez shooting that black guy."

"She's that close to Lt. Alvarez?"

"Oh yeah, they go way back to her first term in Congress. Been close ever since. He's even an unpaid security consultant for the campaign right now."

"Like 'close' close?" Tomas asked Olivia.

"No, not like that. More like brother/sister or maybe 'protector' and 'protected'. He's very protective of Marilyn. I don't really know why he feels that way about her, but it has been that way for a long time."

"You've known him a long time then."

Olivia nodded. "Yeah, ever since I was a kid. It's not that we're close at all, but he certainly hung around a lot whenever we were in DC."

"Have you talked to him since the shooting?"

"No, no. It seems like he's kind of gone into hiding since the shooting. What do they call it? Paid administrative leave?"

"Has Marilyn talked to him?" Tomas asked—genuinely curious and wondering whether he could use any of this on the news.

"I'm pretty sure she has but she won't talk about it. She also knew the guy who Alvarez shot although not nearly as well. I think she's a bit confused about the whole thing."

"She knew Shorty? Did you know Shorty?"

"No. I only met him once—of all places at my sweet sixteen birthday party in northern Virginia. Marilyn made a big deal of it and for some reason he showed up. I even have a picture of him."

"You have a picture of Shorty from your sixteenth birthday party? Isn't that like forever ago?"

"Watch it buddy!" Olivia admonished as she began to scroll through what seemed like thousands of pictures on her smartphone. "Here. There he is standing next to me and Marilyn and Alvarez."

Tomas looked at the photo. He had seen lots of photos of Shorty which were shared by his family members after he had been shot to death, but in this photo he looked different. Shorty was not just younger and thinner but seemingly more full of life in this photo. Pictures taken later of Shorty appeared to Tomas to be of a man who was in some way just more 'run down' by life.

"I don't think Marilyn has seen Shorty for a while though," Olivia continued. "This may have been the last time. Really sad what happened."

"It's certainly a crazy coincidence that Alvarez and Shorty reunite during a traffic stop and one kills the other. A tragic but crazy coincidence," Tomas concluded.

Olivia decided it was her turn to change the subject. "I saw your diploma hanging in the kitchen. Who hangs their diploma in their kitchen?"

"I thought it would be where no one else would see it!"

"Yeah, good plan," Olivia said mockingly. "Your real first name is 'Toe-MASS'?"

"No, you pronounce it just like you would 'Thomas' but without the 'h'."

"Where did that come from?"

"My mom just never understood why people put an 'h' in the name. She would tell me that you don't pronounce it 'THO-mas'. When people spell my name for short, they don't spell it 'Thom'. She didn't see the need for the extra letter."

Olivia smiled. That actually kind of made sense to her. "So do I call you 'Tom' or 'Tomas'?"

"'Tom' is my TV name. 'Tomas' is my alter-ego."

"Your alter-ego?"

"Hmm-hmm," Tomas responded nodding. "'Tom Stein' is all business. He values facts; he values the truth, and he tries his best to tell it. 'Tomas' is more complicated, more personal, the real me. 'Tomas' has feelings and opinions and beliefs but they are his and his alone and there is a line between the two, and Tom tries his best not to cross it."

"You're saying that when you're working, you are 'Tom,' but here tonight you are 'Tomas'?" Olivia asked.

"I guess," he replied. "Have you ever heard of a news anchor named Walter Cronkite?"

"Sure," Olivia responded. "TV news legend."

"Cronkite would end every *CBS Evening News* program with the tag line 'And that's the way it is.' It was his homage to his efforts to be a truth teller no matter where the facts happened to take him. We've lost that in journalism today. 'Tom Stein' is my attempt to get some of that back."

"You don't think people want to get to know Tomas, the real you?" Olivia wondered.

"No, because if they learn that, then I lose objectivity with them. I lose credibility with them and people will look harder for any sign of personal bias. I cannot do my job well if I mix them together. I need them to trust me."

Olivia nodded as if she understood although it did seem like an odd construct to her. "Well I'm looking forward to getting to know 'Tomas' better!"

The rest of the night was sort of a blur for Tomas. There was talk, but there was also food, and there was wine. Neither would admit it but they were both exhausted. They ended up in his bed in what clothes they had worn to dinner including Olivia's immovable object leather boots. When Tomas next opened his eyes he saw Olivia getting ready to leave the following morning. She kissed him on the head and then she kissed him on the lips and whispered, "Gotta go." Tomas smiled and got up to walk her out in the clothes he had worn to bed.

When they both got outside Omar was there getting something out of his car. After Tomas opened and closed the door to Olivia's SUV, he looked over sheepishly at Omar who responded with a thumbs up gesture. He shrugged back with a 'What?' gesture and Omar replied with a smiling nod. It was clear that his neighbor and likely his wife and kids had heard them having sex last night. He retreated back into his apartment, buried his head in the pillow, and went back to sleep still feeling a warm glow from the night before.

Later that Sunday he would text Olivia. "Just want you to know I had a great time last night." He waited for hours but there would be no reply. Maybe that meant that it was nothing more to her than a one-night stand. Maybe she just missed the text. Or maybe the 'dating game' for her had just begun.

Tomas hated the 'dating game'. He hoped that Olivia wasn't playing with his heart now, but he fully suspected she was. Women!

He was wrong. He would not text her again, and by Tuesday he would learn why she had not texted him back.

CHAPTER 23

TOMAS HAD NEVER BEEN TO the main conference room of the television station before—only the conference room over at *The Industry Tonight* newsroom. The one he still didn't know why they called it the 'Nip'. He had been summoned there this morning and as he and Nan headed there together she filled him in as best she could.

"There are two police detectives who want to talk to you about an ongoing investigation."

"Investigation?" Tomas asked. "Into what?"

"Not sure, but the station's lawyer will be there. He'll watch out for you."

"Nan, what the …?" Tomas replied genuinely alarmed.

"Tom, I don't know," Nan interrupted him. "Let's just see what happens."

Nan opened the door and Tomas followed her inside. At a conference table were two black men in suits on one side and a white man in a suit on the other. Nan introduced Tom to the white guy in the suit first. "Tom, this is station attorney Leo Cairns." Tomas shook Leo's hand.

"Thank you Nan," Cairns replied. He then turned to the two gentlemen on the other side of the table. "These men are detectives Clark and Benson with the DC Metro Police Department. They are here to ask you some questions, and I've assured them that you'll be completely cooperative."

Cairns then looked over at Tomas and smiled as if to assure him things would be okay. "Gentlemen."

Tomas sat down. The detective Tomas thought was Clark started with his questions. "Mr. Stein, do you know Olivia Zhang?"

"We had dinner a couple of times," he responded trying to hide the heart-pounding panic he was feeling in his chest.

"Just dinner?" Clark followed up.

The lawyer Cairns stepped in. "Oh c'mon guys. Let's not play games. We're here to help."

Clark nodded. "Mr. Stein, we have just put out a missing persons alert for Ms. Zhang. She has not been seen or heard from since Sunday morning."

"Wow," Tomas replied in sort of a low whisper. This was bewildering news.

"We've obtained her phone records as part of the investigation and you are in them. That's why we're here."

Tomas nodded. "And you think she's the victim of foul play?"

"We don't know," Clark conceded, "but we are hoping you could help us determine what's happened to her."

"Am I a suspect?" Tomas asked.

Clark shook his head *no* but didn't exactly say *no*. "We're not going to rule anything out but I will tell you that one of her roommates saw her come home to her apartment Sunday morning and then leave to go on a jog. Several security cameras in the complex also caught her leaving. When did you last see her?"

"She left my apartment early Sunday morning."

"And you?"

"I went back to bed. I was beat."

"She stayed Saturday night at your apartment?"

Tomas squirmed at the thought of talking about his sex life in front of Nan and the station's lawyer, but he nodded. "It was her idea to come over to my place and cook. I don't think either of us had planned to have sex and for her to stay over, but it just sort of happened."

"The texts would confirm that," Clark offered. "Not only your texts to her but some texts to a friend after she left your home."

"What did they say?"

"I'm not at liberty to say," Clark responded, "but they were about you and the night you two spent together."

The detective could probably tell that Tomas was very nervous and upset, and he appeared to be offering an olive branch of sorts to calm him down. It worked. Tomas relaxed a little bit but was also overcome with a profound sadness that Olivia was now missing. They had not spent enough time together for him to fall in love with her, but he was very interested after Sunday in seeing where their budding relationship may go. He realized it was very likely she was now gone forever.

The questioning continued for about an hour. The detectives wanted a blow-by-blow account of every encounter Tomas had with Olivia, but especially that night *before* her disappearance and the *morning* of it. Tomas began telling how Olivia had talked about Lt. Alvarez when Detective Benson spoke up for the first time.

"Did she say anything about being afraid of Lt. Alvarez?"

The question caught Tomas off guard. "Afraid? No. Why would she be afraid of him?"

Clark looked over at Benson with an irritated expression. "No reason," Clark said. "Just curious how she described him."

The wheels started spinning for Tomas. *"Do they think Alvarez had anything to do with Olivia's disappearance?"* he thought to himself. *"And if so, why?"*

The detectives wrapped things up, thanked Tomas for his cooperation and gave him their card in case he remembered anything else which might be relevant to Olivia's disappearance. "Just so you're aware," Clark alerted them as he left, "there is going to be a news conference later today.

We feel this is high profile enough that we might be able to get some help from the public. Thank you again."

After they left Cairns, Nan and Tomas sat at the conference table and each took their own collective deep breaths. Finally, Cairns broke the silence. "I think that went about as well as can be expected."

"What's next?" Nan asked.

"I'm going to advise Ms. Midas to put Tom on paid leave for a while. You know, until things die down a bit."

Tomas objected. "I just *got* here."

"I know and the detectives as much as said that you are not under suspicion," Cairns reassured him. "Nonetheless, I don't think you working on-air here is a good idea until this dies down a bit."

"I agree," Nan offered. "A two-week vacation on the house!" she added trying to make the best of a bad situation for Tomas.

"Two weeks, huh," Tomas meekly responded. He knew he didn't have a voice in the decision.

"I'll tell the crew we made that decision and why, and that you agree with it," Nan continued. "Work for you?"

"I don't want people to think I had anything to do her disappearance," Tomas replied.

"Of course," Nan told him. "Are you okay?"

Tomas glared at her. "A woman I really wanted to get to know better is missing and I can't do a job I love. Of course I'm not okay."

Nan nodded with a sad expression on her face. "I know and I'm sorry, but this really is for the best."

As Tomas walked out of the station toward his sports car in the parking lot his mood changed from sadness to resolve. If the disappearances of Jason Young and Olivia Zhang were in any way connected he would spend his time away from reporting the news doing whatever he could to find those connections. He wanted answers. In a sense he was now free to do things he couldn't do before he was put on paid leave. There were no news stories to do, no pressing deadlines, no Executive Producers to answer to. He would put every investigative reporter bone in his body into solving these two mysteries.

As he drove home to his apartment he heard on the car radio the same song he and Olivia had heard by the band called Irving a couple of nights before. Suddenly he had an idea. "Call Lachlan," he asked his smartphone.

"Hello Boy Wonder!" Lachlan answered. Tomas still hated that moniker. "Are you okay? Everyone is talking about you. We are all worried about you."

"Tell them I've never been better," Tomas lied, but convincingly. "Hey are you still friends with that tabloid TV guy who does DNA tests on his guests to determine who is a child's father?"

The question clearly caught Lachlan off guard. "Ahhh, sure. Why do you ask?"

"I need his help. Would he do a favor for you if you asked?"

"I know he would. What are you up to?" Lachlan asked.

"I can't tell you right now, but I have a hunch and if I'm right, I'll have a blockbuster of a story."

"I'll have his DNA people reach out to you. What are you thinking?"

Tomas hesitated for a moment. "I'm thinking that I'm 99 percent wrong on something but just need to check it out to be sure. How much would that cost?"

"No need Boy Wonder. I can assure you they'll do it for free."

The next call for Tomas was to Prudence Young. She was surprised to hear from him. "Hey Ms. Young. Just so you know I'm flying out to Boise tomorrow. I would love to take you to lunch but I also need your help with something."

"Of course. Help with what Tom?" she asked.

"I can't explain now but I think you can help me find some answers regarding what happened to Jason."

That was all Prudence needed to hear. "Of course Tom. I look forward to seeing you again!"

Tomas watched as DC-3 took the police press conference live announcing the missing persons investigation into Olivia Zhang. MTB was there too. She walked up to the lectern at police headquarters and tearfully asked the public for help in providing information regarding Olivia's disappearance. "I've known Olivia since she was a young child. She is like a daughter to me and I beg anyone who has any information about what happened to her to come forward. I will also be suspending my campaign for a few days. We were supposed to fly to Iowa tonight with Olivia, but in light of what's happened, me and my campaign staff need some time to process what's happened."

The DC Chief of Police then took questions from reporters.

"Do you have any suspects at this time Chief?"

"We have interviewed the people who last saw Olivia before she disappeared but no suspects at this time. We really don't even have any evidence of foul play. This is a straight up missing persons case."

"I've been told a reporter with DC-3 named Tom Stein was interviewed by detectives. What's his connection to the case chief?"

The chief paused for a second. This was clearly a question he was not expecting. "Ah, Mr. Stein has been interviewed and has been fully cooperative with this investigation and that's all I'm really going to say about that."

"Is he a suspect?"

"As I said earlier there are no suspects at this time."

Tomas wasn't happy with the police chief's non-answer and didn't want to watch the news that night, but he did. And his name did come up. One station erroneously called him a "person of interest" in the investigation. Another report said he was the last person to see her alive, which of course was not true either. In the middle of one newscast he saw a promo for a tabloid TV show named *Inside Scoop*. The promo was to put it mildly 'ridiculous'.

"A young woman working for a candidate for president goes missing. Her reporter boyfriend questioned by police. What they are saying tonight about their relationship and whether he's a suspect in her disappearance on the next *Inside Scoop.*"

It was standard tabloid TV fare. The answers are unimportant. It is the lurid questions which will draw people in. Tomas knew that until Olivia's disappearance was solved there would be people including those in the media who might assume he had something to do with it. He resolved again to do everything he could to learn the truth.

It was good for Tomas to get out of DC and back to the relative normalcy of Boise the next day. Even the long plane ride with a stop in Chicago was a chance for him to just sit and gather his thoughts. He was convinced that Olivia was dead. But why? Who would have a motive to kill her?

He also wanted to get answers for the Young family about what happened to Jason. Now he could focus on that too. There was nothing else on his plate at the moment.

Prudence Young opened the door to him and gave him a big hug. He wanted to take her to lunch but she had insisted on making lunch. There on the dining room table was baked chicken on rice and a salad. Off to the side on the table was The Bloody Shoe sitting in its plastic case.

Prudence had seen the news about Olivia Zhang. "Were you two dating?" she asked.

Tomas didn't know how to respond to that. Prudence was deeply religious. How do you explain to her that you slept with a woman on their first real date? He and Olivia had even had sex in the first minutes of their first real date. Tomas leveled with her. "She disappeared the day after our first date."

"Some people say you may have been involved," Prudence offered.

"You know better."

Prudence smiled. She did know better. She just wanted some reassurance from Tomas.

"I'm going to find out what happened to her and Jason," Tomas reassured her. "I feel like the two disappearances must be related somehow." Tomas made a point of referring to Jason's case as a disappearance rather than a death because his body had not been found—only a trace of human remains. No one had an illusion that Jason Young was still alive. There just had not yet been definitive evidence like his body being discovered.

"You think Olivia is dead?" Prudence concluded in the form of a question.

"I'm afraid I do. Hopefully I'm wrong."

"Why do you want the shoe?" Prudence asked while looking at it.

"A hunch. I'm 99 percent sure I'm wrong, but the shoe will help me prove it."

"What's the hunch?"

Tomas thought for a second. "I don't want to speculate about something I'm almost certainly wrong about, but I have this feeling about one angle that I have to eliminate. I'll let you know once I do."

"That's good enough for me, Tom."

Tomas and Prudence had an engaging lunch. He told her about his new life in DC. She caught him up on notable events around Boise since he had left months earlier. She let on that she had been recruited to be a Republican delegate at the Idaho caucuses and she had many questions for Tomas about the Reverend Governor. "Between you and me, Tom, I think he can win."

Tomas thought about that for a moment. It really hadn't occurred to him that in his short stint in DC he had already interviewed the Republican and Democratic front-runners to be the next President of the United States. "Ms. Young, what do you know about MTB? I know you didn't find out about the affair until after Jason's wife filed for divorce."

"Not exactly true," Prudence offered. "His wife called me before she did it. We had become friends and she had confided to me that she was worried about Jason. I don't think she suspected he was having an affair with his boss but she was clearly worried about his well-being."

"Well-being. Why?"

"She thought Jason was in over his head. That he was both intimidated and scared of that woman, the Congresswoman. Jason told her that she had never seen a woman with a temper like hers. I don't think Jason's wife filed for divorce because she was trying to hurt Jason. She thought it would be a wake-up call to help save him and their marriage."

"Wow," Tomas replied. "And that's when she found out about the affair?"

"Jason confessed to her. He told her that if she would take him back then he would end the affair, and he would take her to Idaho and away from DC. But no doubt about it she said that Jason was scared."

"Scared of MTB?"

"Yes, scared of her. I cannot tell you why."

Tomas gave a lot of thought to the conversation he had with Prudence Young on the flight home. This was meant to be a long day trip primarily to retrieve The Bloody Shoe, which was in his backpack and had gotten him more than a little attention from the TSA Agents at the Boise airport. He landed at Dulles late that night. He would crash at his apartment over-night and then head to Richmond the next day. His parents were worried about him and wanted to see him and take him out to dinner. First though he would have to drop The Bloody Shoe and some bathroom towels at the lab. His hunch was a long shot, but if it paid off it would go a long way toward his connecting the disappearances of Jason Young and Olivia Zhang.

Tomas found it ironic that the restaurant his parents chose for dinner that night in Richmond was called The White House. It has been at one time the main home of part of an old southern plantation which had been converted into a five-star restaurant. The cheapest steak on the menu was forty dollars. The cheapest bottle of wine was even more than that. His parents liked to splurge for him on the rare occasion when Tomas was in town and he knew better than to object.

Over steak and Caesar salad his parents had so many questions for him. They asked about the new job, about Olivia, about covering people who wanted to be the next President of the United States. His father in particular seemed amazed that one of his sons at such a young age was a journalist covering some of the most important people in the nation. He spoke of going to a minor league baseball game with a client the past summer. There was a star player rehabbing in Richmond before being called back up to the big leagues and he was doing media interviews following the game. "I think that was the first time I really understood what you do for a living," he told Tomas.

Tomas smiled. That was not quite what he did for a living but he understood what his father was saying. The man who at one time himself was a commercial media personality was trying to comprehend how TV journalism and the media worked when dollars were not changing hands.

The meal was wrapping up. The Steins were not much for dessert. That's when a black man in a chef's white uniform approached their table. "Good evening. How was your meal tonight?" he asked. All agreed that it had been excellent and thanked the head chef for his culinary expertise. For Tomas, however, he could not shake the feeling of familiarity with the man. He had seen him before.

And then it hit Tomas. "Excuse me, Mr. Curtis? Mr. Shorty Curtis?"

The chef's demeanor changed from one of calm to a look of shocked surprise. Tomas knew at that moment that his instincts were correct.

CHAPTER 24

"No one has called me Curtis in a long time," the chef confided to Tomas. The pair had retreated to the chef's office in the back of the restaurant after Tomas had recognized him, leaving his parents at the dining room table bewildered as to what was happening.

"You changed your name?"

"Chef Tyree Barnes. Pleased to meet you," he said, reaching out his hand for a handshake.

"So how many other people out there know that Shorty Curtis has a twin brother?" Tomas asked the chef.

"Not too many," Barnes conceded. "Me and Shorty have been swimming in two very different ponds for a long time." He sat back in his chair and gave Tomas a once-over look. "How did you recognize me?"

"You look a lot like a photo I saw of Shorty at a sweet sixteen birthday party. A woman showed it to me. Did you know Olivia Zhang?"

Tyree laughed. "That photo was of me. I was filling in for Shorty that day."

"What?" Tomas asked surprised.

"Shorty gets this invite out of the blue to a birthday party from an old friend named Manuel Alvarez. Yeah, *that* Manuel Alvarez. As you know they had both served on the Capitol Police Force together. Shorty can't go for some reason and he calls me all upset about it because he needs

Alvarez's help with something. I tell him I'll fill in for him, and Shorty is like, 'Nah, that will never work.' And I'm like I'll bet you fifty bucks I can pull it off." Tyree had a big smile on his face as he told the story.

"Did you?"

Tyree shrugged. "I guess Olivia bought it. I got fifty bucks out of it. How is she by the way?"

"Missing. Presumed dead," Tomas responded almost too matter-of-factly.

"Oh wow," Tyree responded looking down. "Her and Shorty both gone."

"Are you going to Shorty's funeral?"

Tyree shook his head *no*. "I can't say that it is not safe for me in DC after so much time, but I've got a wife and two kids and I can't take that risk."

"Not safe for you?"

Tyree took a deep breath. "Shorty and me may have been twins, but we took very different paths early in life. He became a cop and I became the kid who was always running from the cops. In any case, one time I got into some big trouble with a neighborhood gang. Feared for my life man. One day Shorty pulls some of the gang-bangers over in his patrol car and they're all like shocked because they think he is me. He tells them he's my twin brother and that if they go after me they may just be shooting at a cop instead. It worked for that moment."

"That wasn't enough?"

"Shorty didn't think so," Tyree said. "He had some friends in Richmond who were willing to take me in. It was supposed to be temporary but it was down here where I found my love of cooking and the love of my life. Hardly ever been back to DC since."

"Because you could still be in danger?" Tomas asked, thinking to himself that after all this time the danger from gangs surely must have passed.

"Let's just say I wasn't taking any chances."

"Sounds like you two brothers were close," Tomas surmised.

"No. Barely talked. Hardly saw each other after I moved down here. It's crazy, but here he was a cop, and I was a thug, but after I moved to Richmond our lives moved in different directions. Here I am now one of the best chefs in the city making a good living with a nice house in the suburbs, nice cars, a fantastic family. Shorty was proud of me but he was also a little bit jealous."

"Jealous?"

"Yeah because it never worked out for him. Shorty was a heavy drinker and that addiction cost him pretty much everything. A career he loved, his only marriage." Tyree made an expression as if a profound thought had just occurred to him. "I'll bet you money that when they get the lab results back on his body, they will show that he was heavily intoxicated."

"The shooting started as a DUI stop," Tomas told him.

"Crazy thing is he was working as a tow truck driver. A couple of DUIs in his past and a history of alcoholism and someone hires him to drive a tow truck. Like I said, *Crazy!*"

Tomas saw a chance to ask Tyree about the man who shot and killed his brother just a week earlier. "He and Lt. Alvarez knew each other well?"

"Yeah, they went way back to the days when they served on the capitol police together. Strange relationship. Some days Shorty would say he loved him like a brother. At other times he would blame Alvarez for ruining his life!"

"Ruining his life. How?" Tomas asked intrigued.

Tyree got up and shut the door to his office; then he sat down in his office chair. "Look, I know that you're a reporter, but with Shorty dead I need to tell you about a secret that weighed on him most of his adult life."

"A secret?"

"A big secret that I know he would not want to die with him. But if I tell you and this gets out it could be *my* life in danger!"

Tomas nodded as if he understood. This would be off-the-record, and whatever the chef told him, he would have to treat it with kid gloves.

CHAPTER 25

TYREE BEGAN TO TELL TOMAS about the call he had gotten from his brother eighteen months earlier. "He was drunk. He was crying. Inconsolable really. I could barely make out his words. But one sentence stood out. Shorty told me, 'I really need your help!' Shorty had never before asked for my help like that. I drove up I-95 that night. I hadn't been in DC for a long time but I knew I needed to make this trip."

Tyree told Tomas about how he drove up to find Shorty passed out at a desk in the living room of his apartment. On his computer was a news story about a family in Idaho pleading for information about their missing son. It was the story Tomas had done in Boise on the Young family's plea for answers. Shorty was apparently struggling with the fact that he had some of the answers that they were pleading for.

Tyree stayed the night, and the next morning he found that Shorty was up and coherent. "I have to do something," he told his twin brother. "I need your help."

Shorty talked to his twin brother very little that day but did lay out for Tyree what he needed. "There's a storage facility I rent down near Groveton. I'll write down the address for you. I need you to meet me outside the facility tonight at midnight."

"Midnight?" What in the world was Shorty up to?

"No one will ever know you helped me. Please brother!"

Shorty left the apartment earlier in the evening and Tyree stayed inside. He read and watched TV until it was time to leave. He still suspected demons out there were looking for him in DC no matter how unrealistic that seemed. It was better if he was out and about as little as possible.

Tyree drove to the storage facility and parked his car on the street outside. He would see Shorty pull out in the flatbed tow truck he drove for work with a car draped in a cover on the back. "What's with the car?" he asked Shorty. "Get in," was his reply.

They drove to a remote area on the Potomac not far from where the District of Columbia met the Maryland state line. During the day the area would be bustling with walkers and runners and bikers, but it was completely empty at 1 a.m. on a Tuesday morning. Shorty then pulled onto a trail and drove the tow truck toward the river. He then backed up toward a wall at the water's edge while hoping the backup alarm on the truck would not alert anyone nearby.

"I need your help dumping this car here," Shorty told Tyree. "Once the car is in the water I want you to give the winch lots of slack." Shorty eased the car into the river and waded out. He then used the cord to pull the car out farther; then wrapped the winch cord around something and came back to shore. Whatever the cord was wrapped around, it acted like a pulley bringing the car out farther into the river. By the time he was done the car was completely submerged.

Tyree was lost in the story as if Tomas weren't even there. Tomas interrupted him. "So you saw the car?"

"Oh yeah, white Chevy Malibu with that crazy More-man plate on the back," Tyree responded.

So that was it! The car hadn't been in the water for twenty-five years. It had been parked at a storage facility for twenty-three and a half years. "Was Jason's body in the car?" Tomas asked.

"Yeah, Shorty put it there. He had retrieved an entire frozen body wrapped in something for more than twenty years."

"Wait! Frozen?" Tomas interjected.

"I'll get to that," Tyree assured him. "It must have been a gruesome thing to see. Shorty said he vomited three or four times in the process, but he managed to get the body into the car," Tyree confirmed. "He wanted everything about that body and that car gone from his life and he was determined to make it finally happen. Because that's the craziest thing about all this, man. That body tortured Shorty all those years."

"I don't understand," Tomas replied dumbfounded.

"That guy's dead body had been in the storage facility in a large freezer for all those years. It was speaking to him every day from beyond the grave!"

"He kept Jason's body in a freezer? How is that even possible?" Tomas wondered aloud. "A dead body in a freezer for all that time?"

"I wondered the same," Tyree confided. "After we dumped the car we headed back to the storage facility. It must have been three in the morning. Shorty was sober but said he needed a drink. I didn't want him driving drunk so I agreed to go drink with him at his apartment. Once the alcohol started to flow Shorty told me what happened and how he ended up with both a dead man's car and a dead man's body in his storage unit."

"What happened?" Tomas sat back in his chair fully aware that his parents were still sitting in the restaurant's dining room. He was also smart enough to know not to leave or even delay the conversation for a moment when someone was telling him an important secret.

"Shorty told me it all started one night when Alvarez called him in a state of panic. He urgently needed his help but would not say why. He asked him to come out to a remote area near the Potomac. Alvarez would meet him at the main road and guide him in. Once he got there Shorty saw the car. The More-man car."

"Was Jason's body there too?" Tomas asked.

"He told me that Alvarez had put it in the trunk. He told Shorty that they needed to dump the car and the body somewhere. That's when Shorty came up with the idea of putting it in his storage unit. It was big enough for the car and he had a freezer in there."

"Why did he have a freezer in there?"

"Shorty enjoyed hunting. He would store venison meat in a large freezer in the unit. He said putting the body in the freezer was only supposed to be a temporary solution. That was some *long* temporary solution."

"Why didn't he move it?" Tomas asked.

"I don't know. Where to? And how? I guess it was just easier to leave it in the freezer," Tyree concluded. "But it was an endless torture for him he told me. Can you imagine? Year after year he lived with the knowledge that a man's dead body was in a freezer in his storage garage. He told me that he would check on it at least once a week. He put a remote camera in there for a while. He said the one time that freezer stopped working he was able to fix it without opening it. He never looked inside it until that night when we dumped the car and the body into the Potomac. He had finally gotten rid of what had been a daily torture for him for a very long time. It drove him crazy and he coped with it by drinking." Tyree was looking down and shaking his head.

"What happened next?" Tomas asked,

"He told me to get back to Richmond and not to tell a soul what happened. We figured someone would find the car in a few days. We never imagined it would take eighteen months. It made Shorty even more depressed. He wanted that family in Idaho to have closure."

"Did you two talk much about it?"

"Only once," Tyree replied. "He told me on the phone that he knew he had made a terrible mistake and he just wanted it to be over. He seemed more concerned about me than himself, but I assured him that I was safe and that no one would ever know."

"I still don't get it," Tomas replied to all the jaw dropping information. "Alvarez and Shorty. They were both capitol cops at the time. Didn't Shorty realize he was committing a felony?"

"Didn't care," Tyree shrugged. "He owed Alvarez big time. He was Shorty's supervisor and he told me that Alvarez saved his butt more than once. And he knew Alvarez was connected. That if someone found out about what happened he was confident that things could be fixed."

"Did he think Alvarez killed Jason?"

"I don't think he wanted to know," Tyree responded. "I didn't ask him that though."

"Alvarez had to have killed Jason. It's the only logical explanation," Tomas concluded.

"Well I know that Alvarez killed Shorty. Maybe that's why I'm talking to you now. I know police will call it a 'clean shoot' … that Alvarez will be exonerated. Maybe you can find something which says otherwise. Just leave me out of it, okay?"

Tomas nodded. He thanked Tyree and headed back to his table where his parents had been waiting for some time. "I'm so sorry," he pleaded with them.

"Who was that?" his father asked.

"Possible source for a story," Tomas replied.

"A possible source for a story is the chef at this restaurant?"

"It's an odd coincidence to be sure," he replied.

"And what story? I thought you were on vacation?" his father pressed.

"Dad, jewelers go on vacation. Reporters, not so much!"

CHAPTER 26

TOMAS WATCHED THE RESULTS from the Iowa caucuses on television from his living room. The 'first-in-the-nation' vote to help determine the next President of the United States was a strange affair to him. Iowans would brave the bitter cold in the worst of what always seemed to be a tough winter to gather in small rooms across the state and participate in a bizarre process of candidate elimination which rarely ended in a definitive winner.

And this presidential election year was even stranger that most. One prominent national political columnist called it 'the rise of the no-names'.

There was no doubt America was in a political funk. The recession had been dragging on for some time now. So-called 'experts' would say the United States was not technically in a recession at times, but the mood of the electorate said otherwise. Inflation remained high and unemployment seemed to inch up every month. Gasoline prices were off their all-time highs but remained beyond affordable for many. The current administration kept assuring Americans that the nation was in 'transition' to cleaner, cheaper energy sources which had yet to magically appear.

Democrats controlled the White House and Republicans controlled Congress, but there was a palpable sense among the general public that each side was more interested in fighting each other than helping the American people. Many citizens were on their heels and no one really seemed to care.

And there was another factor shaping the presidential political landscape. No one could beat Father Time. In the past year no fewer than three U.S. Senators, all octogenarians, had died while still holding office. It seemed as if a whole generation of Baby Boomer political leaders, mostly Democrats, were dying off or fading away. That left a vacuum for a new generation of Democrats to fill the void.

Marilyn Taylor-Brown was perceived by many in the Democratic Party as a 'fresh face' even though she had been in Congress for decades. She was considered politically moderate at a time when the party had soured on the growing influence of the Democratic Party's left wing and the electoral defeats many blamed on them. She was an insider who could also be defiant. Technically she was the number three most powerful person in the House Democratic caucus and would use her platform at times to publicly criticize the two more powerful people ahead of her, not to mention those in the White House.

MTB had called the administration's energy policy 'shortsighted' and a risk to national security. "You can't implement a transition to greener energy," she would say on the stump, "if you keep losing elections over it."

MTB had been openly critical of how the previous Speaker of the House had handled the House committee investigating the January 6th rioting at the Capitol. The Speaker had refused to let Republicans staff the committee with the House members they wanted, choosing instead two Republican 'Never Trumpers' for the committee who would both leave office by the next election cycle. Taylor-Brown thought that was a big tactical mistake. "One half of the country thinks that this January 6th committee is a partisan political exercise," MTB said at the time, "and the other half *knows* it is."

The progressive wing of the party didn't like her and that seemed to only make MTB stronger—much like how the opposition of traditional conservatives to Trump only seemed to bolster him politically. Nominating

MTB would be a risky move. No sitting House member had won the presidency since the 1800s. And yet many rank-and-file Democrats seemed fed up enough to take that risk anyway.

On the Republican side the party's base seemed to be searching for a Trump-like candidate because Donald Trump himself wasn't on the ballot. Like with the Democrats, advanced age had taken a toll on Trump, and his health apparently was forcing him to withdraw from the spotlight. The speculation was that he didn't feel he had it in him to be king one more time, but maybe he could be the next king-maker. Rather than running for president he would work to cement the radical changes he made to the Republican Party for decades to come just as former President Ronald Reagan had done in the 1980s. There was no shortage of other Republican presidential candidates to choose from.

Gov. Ben Rivers was different than the rest. For one thing he emerged as a successful politician from a blue state, something none of his Republican rivals could boast. He was an African-American candidate at a time when Republicans were picking up a greater and greater share of minority voters and wanted even more. Rivers was also a preacher who could use his honed oratorical skills to captivate voters while on the campaign trail. Finally he just seemed more 'Trumpian' than anybody else. Why Trump hadn't endorsed him already was a mystery to many in the Republican party.

And yet many Republicans felt that Trump and 'Trump-ism' had for too long taken up too much air in the room. They wanted the Republican Party to move on to something more traditional and perhaps less polarizing. Iowa voters would give the first real clue as to whether that was possible.

It was in this environment that Iowans in both parties came to unusual consensuses. MTB easily took the caucus for Democrats, Rivers for Republicans. Each was now the clear, early front-runner for their party's nomination even though the process had a long way to go.

Tomas watched Rivers on television as he made his victory speech in Des Moines. "Tonight the people of Iowa have spoken," he told a crowd packed into a small hotel auditorium. "They spoke from the corn fields; they spoke from the bean fields; they spoke from industrial Cedar Rapids to the educational centers of Iowa City and from Ames to the beautiful streets of the capital right here in Des Moines and said with a convincing voice tonight that they choose Rivers!" The crowd erupted into cheers and applause at Big Ben's poorly executed attempt at a pun.

"I am so grateful to all the people I've met and who have supported me across this great state tonight. Whatever comes next, personally, I will never forget the grace you and God have shown me in this amazing campaign. And I also want to thank former President Donald J. Trump for …" The crowd burst into applause again. Had Trump finally endorsed him? "… for being the inspiration I needed to begin this long and difficult journey."

Seeing Rivers address the crowd at such a pivotal time in American history made Tomas want to get back to work even though he would not be covering the nomination process directly. That was when his phone rang. Tomas recognized the number even though he hadn't talked to this person for some time. It was Jerry Winston, the man who had helped recruit Tomas to DC-3 in the first place.

"How are you?" Winston asked.

"I'm holding up."

"Tom, I want to be straight with you right away. Marjorie Midas wanted me to reach out to you before you come back to work. She wants my input as to whether the timing is right."

"Well I'm certainly ready to come back." Detectives had not made any headway in the disappearance of Olivia Zhang but hadn't reached out to Tomas for more information either. She had apparently disappeared into thin air and as far as he was concerned, the heat was off him.

"I'm sure you are ready," Winston replied. "Can I meet you for lunch tomorrow. I'm in town. I know a great restaurant in Fairfax that I'm sure you'll enjoy."

Tomas realized he had never met Jerry Winston. The two had only talked on the phone. "Sure. But how will I recognize you?" Tomas asked.

He could hear Winston's smile on the other end of the line. "Oh, don't worry about that because I will certainly recognize you." It was a date.

CHAPTER 27

WINSTON HAD CHOSEN FOR LUNCH a Thai restaurant which had a reputation for having a gourmet twist to each dish it prepared. Tomas enjoyed Thai food but this restaurant had smells which he had never experienced. He couldn't wait to see if the tastes were just as interesting.

True to form Winston met him at the door. He was shorter than Tomas imagined with dark hair and dressed in an obviously somewhat cheap suit which nonetheless seemed to fit him well. "Great to finally meet you in person. I hope you like Thai food." Tomas nodded to Winston that he did.

They sat down and looked over the menu. Winston made a couple of suggestions but Tomas was focused on the curry. He loved curry. "What's your connection to Marjorie?" he asked Winston.

"I was her news director for fifteen years and built *The Industry Tonight* from scratch," he told him. Tomas had no idea. He had thought of Jerry Winston as a recruiter and consultant. He never mentioned being a former news director running the entire news operation at DC-3.

"But you left?" Tomas asked.

"I left," Jerry confirmed.

"Seems like a pretty good gig. Why did you leave?"

Jerry smiled. "Believe it or not Tom, I left because of a man elected president named Donald J. Trump."

"Really?" Tomas asked surprised.

"Yeah," Jerry sighed. "Trump really rocked this town. Some people felt as if his election forced them to take sides. I guess I took the wrong side."

"And what side was that?" Tomas asked genuinely curious.

"I wanted to tell the truth and be objective about Trump. He was after all the duly elected President of the United States. I felt that earned him both some deference and respect from the news media even if he didn't show much of that back to the news media. That wasn't a very popular stance to take in the DC journalism community at that time."

"The whole *fake news* thing," Tomas assumed.

"It was more than that," Jerry replied. "Many considered Trump a real threat. They would say he was a 'fascist' or a 'threat to Democracy' when in truth he was really just a threat to them—powerful people who were genuinely afraid of the havoc he could wreck from the White House. They would do everything they could to undermine his power to protect theirs. That's where 'Russia-gate' came in."

Tomas had never really thought much about the motivation behind the Washington establishment's attempts to falsely tie Trump to Russia during and after the 2016 presidential campaign. He knew it started as a Clinton campaign plot to deflect from her own scandal of sharing classified information through emails on a non-government and non-secure computer server in her basement.

"But you didn't want to be a part of that?" Tomas asked.

"No I did not. At first Marjorie seemed okay with it, but after our coverage of Trump's inauguration she clearly started feeling the heat."

"Like what?"

"She's true Washington elite, Marjorie is," Winston explained while taking a bite of food. "She hangs around in very posh and politically powerful social circles. People would come up to her and ask, 'What's up with DC-3?' and 'What's up with *The Industry Tonight*.' And 'You can't treat Trump like any normal president. He's a threat to our democracy. He's a threat to all of us.' She comes to me and says we have to find a way to get in line. Get in line with the networks. Get in line with the cable nets. Get in line with the mainstream media."

"Were you surprised?"

"I was. Marjorie had never interfered like that before. And I'm saying 'He's been duly elected by the American people. He deserves a chance.' She said 'no'. We had to be more 'anti-Trump'."

"She told you that!" Tomas replied somewhat astonished.

"Yes she did," Jerry replied. "What was crazy was that Trump was actually turning us into what he said we were. He was making us all become 'fake news'."

"So what happened next?"

"I resigned from my job but without any anger or resentment. The time had come to move on. I had achieved all I could at DC-3. Marjorie understood. I think she respected my position and my decision. That's when she retained me as a consultant. She also put in a good word with a couple of other station groups and before you knew it 'Winston and Associates Consulting Services' was born. Thank you Donald Trump!"

Tomas took a bite of his curry. "What did you think about Trump as a President?"

"I was glad I wasn't working in a newsroom anymore. That's for sure!" Winston said smiling.

"But what about the media coverage?" Tomas responded. "You got to see it from the outside."

"I read at one point that national mainstream news coverage of Trump was 95 percent negative," Winston told him while putting down his fork for a moment. "Ninety-five percent! There was no balance because love him or hate him, Trump also did some good things, right?"

"I think he certainly earned some of his bad press," Tomas observed.

"Me too, but *95 percent* negative?"

Tomas agreed. There were days he would watch the news and realize that Trump coverage by the news media was so negative that it wasn't hurting Trump so much as it was hurting journalism itself. Trust in the news media took a big nosedive as a result.

"Let's be objective for a moment and take out the name Trump. We'll call him 'President A' or as some of his detractors like to call him 'President A-hole'."

Jerry smiled and Tomas let out a small laugh.

"So President A is facing incredible headwinds. The news media is aligned against him. He's under investigation by a Special Counsel. And yet, here is a man who ..." Jerry stuck out his hand as if to count Trump's accomplishments on his fingers.

"Here is a man who ..."

"ONE: Maintained strong economic growth while keeping inflation low. His successor could not do that.

TWO: Turned America into a net exporter of energy for the first time in decades. His successor reversed that.

THREE: Created a sane and effective immigration strategy to curtail a humanitarian crisis at the southern border. His successor tried to eliminate that and look at the chaos we have down there now!

FOUR: Instituted Operation Warp Speed which helps bring COVID vaccinations to the free world in record time.

FIVE: Brought about an historic federal criminal justice reform.

SIX: Began a Middle East breakthrough that now has Israelis visiting many Arab countries which welcome them with open arms. Unthinkable before Trump.

SEVEN: Brought about the ending of NAFTA with his USMCA trade policy. Even Democrats don't complain about that one.

Which is related to EIGHT: Returned good-paying manufacturing jobs to the U.S., something Trump's predecessor said was impossible.

And then there is NINE which perhaps really should be number ONE: Eliminated ISIS. Remember ISIS?"

"Oh yeah, ISIS," Tomas responded.

"You know what one general told me about Trump and ISIS?" Jerry added. "Trump told the general that defeating ISIS would not be enough. They needed to annihilate them. And so that's what they did because he said Trump gave them the tools and the flexibility they needed to accomplish it. They would stop micro-managing the war on ISIS from the White House and let the military handle it. The president would just stay out of their way."

"Sounds like Trump grew on you," Tomas said smiling.

"Did I leave anything out? Oh yeah, TEN: He completely transformed the Republican Party from staid conservatism to populism, taking it from a party of elites to the party of the middle and working class. It's a completely different party now."

Jerry was out of fingers now but he thankfully did not pull out his toes.

"And ELEVEN: Altered the Supreme Court. Look, I'm pro-choice and definitely not pro-gun but you cannot say that the man did not deliver for his voters. That's an *honest* appraisal of some of his accomplishments in office. That is what we as journalists are supposed to do. Be honest and truthful no matter what our personal feelings or political leanings may be. And Trump's record in office is a consequential record if you can just forget for a moment that his name is Donald Trump."

Jerry was animated now, not because of what journalism had done to Trump but what Trump had done to journalism. "I don't care about the reporting of all the negative stuff on Trump. He's a big boy. He wanted the job. Have at him! But if you are going to call yourself a journalist you have to cover the consequential actions as well. Some of them were positive. Otherwise, you are just reporting half-truths and 'poof'; even if every negative thing you report about Trump is absolutely true no one with half a brain will believe you because they know you're not willing to give them the whole story."

Tomas thought about Jerry's point. He wondered if the country would be in this so-called 'malaise' if voters had gotten more balanced coverage of Trump and made a different decision in 2020 because of it.

"That does seem to be the media environment we are in today," Tomas agreed. "You know one thing about Russia-gate that was crazy to me?"

"There was a lot of crazy!" Jerry concurred.

"There was this Congressman who was on the House Intelligence Committee who would go on TV and say, 'We've got the goods on Trump and Russia. I'm learning all this new information. The FBI investigation on Trump is totally on the up and up.' They were all lies. I mean if a source lied to me like that then I would stop using him, and yet I see him still being interviewed all the time still. How can you possibly trust what he's saying is true now when he's lied to you to your face over and over again in the past?"

"You can't, and that's why I am on the lookout for reporters like you Tom. I know you want to give the news to the people straight. I know you want to tell the truth. You are committed to telling both sides of a story accurately no matter which side you may personally agree with. We need people like you in this town now more than ever. It's the only way the news media has a prayer of getting its credibility back with the American people."

Tomas didn't like the fact that the conversation had turned to him. As much as he liked being a news reporter on television he didn't like talking about himself. He changed the subject. "What do you think of Rivers and MTB winning in Iowa?"

"Iowa is very white. Rivers appeals to the Trump faction of Iowa. MTB appeals to the moderate white Democrat voters. We'll see how each holds up through more difficult political terrain."

Tomas looked down as his smartphone began to buzz. It was a call he had been expecting. "Can I take this?" Jerry nodded. Tomas picked up the phone and began speaking with the person at the other end of the line although Tomas said little. He was mostly listening. "Are you sure?" he asked the person on the other end of the line. "Well that was fast work, thank you!"

Tomas then hung up and looked over at Winston taking a sip of soda. "Anything important?" Winston asked him.

"Jerry, I may need your help with this."

"Help with what?" Jerry asked quizzically. What could Tomas possibly need his help with now?

"I've just discovered the first clear link between Jason Young and Olivia Zhang," Tomas told him. "It's something which may help explain why they both disappeared."

CHAPTER 28

"ARE YOU SURE ABOUT THIS?" Winston asked Tomas while leaning over the restaurant table toward him.

"Just confirmed it," Tomas replied nodding his head.

"You're saying that Jason Young and Olivia Zhang are related."

"No Jerry. I'm telling you that Jason Young is Olivia Zhang's biological father. There is no other plausible explanation."

"Wow! Tom!" Winston was in disbelief. "And how do you know this again?"

Tomas didn't want to get too deep into the dirty details but he figured Winston could handle the 30,000-foot overview of what he was doing. "After Olivia and I had sex there was a little bit of a mess to clean up. I used some towels that I threw into a hamper and hadn't had time to wash them."

"Usable DNA," Winston interjected.

"Yep," Tomas confirmed. "I flew to Boise last week to pick up a shoe that had Jason's blood on it from his days as a cross-country runner."

"They still have his shoe?"

"It's called The Legend of the Bloody Shoe and I won't get too deep into the details about that, but it had usable DNA from Jason Young. That was the DNA lab that just called me. They are a match."

Winston sat back in his chair. The wheels spun violently in his head as he attempted to process what he had heard. "So that means …"

Tomas cut him off. "Jerry, that has to mean that MTB is Olivia Zhang's biological mother. Again, it's the only plausible explanation. Olivia's birthday coincides with the time MTB left DC for Minnesota. It's too much to be a coincidence."

Winston stared at Tomas as if he had just witnessed a nuclear explosion of the political variety. "So let me game this out," he told Tomas. "Jason Young goes missing and a scandal ensues. Rep. Marilyn Taylor leaves office and returns to Minnesota only to find out that she's pregnant with Jason Young's child. She has the money, power and means to give birth in secret and so that's what she does."

Tomas interrupted him. "She may have known she was pregnant before the scandal broke. We don't know that."

"And there's no way to prove that," Jerry countered. "In any case, her seat in Congress unexpectedly comes open again and she wants back in."

"Yes!" Tomas interjected again. "But she can't come back to DC if people know about her love child with her missing and presumed dead former aide."

"Right," Winston confirmed while still thinking the scenario through. "She arranges for Olivia to be adopted by a wealthy Chinese family that her family is doing business with. Her daughter stays in her life without ever realizing that MTB is her biological mother."

"That's what I think happened," Tomas confirmed.

Jerry Winston looked at Tomas with amazement. "How did you figure out all of this?"

"Guess I'm just a genius," Tomas replied shrugging. "Actually it was because of a song."

"A song?"

"Jerry, I don't know why, but I've always had this thing for faces," Tomas began to explain. "I've only met MTB once but her face, especially her profile, has some very distinct features. When Olivia was over at my place a song was playing on my stereo and so these lyrics come up."

Tomas changed his voice into the same half-singing tone he had used on Olivia. *"Remember when we danced with your mother. She was so drunk in the living room. With her profile turned a certain way, she looks how you will look forty years from today."*

Tomas then switched back to his normal tone of voice. "Then I look over at Olivia and noticed she had some of the same facial features of MTB, especially around her nose and her forehead, and I told her about it."

"What did she say?"

"Blew it off. Frankly I did too," Tomas conceded. "But then Olivia goes missing and I'm thinking to myself that there must be some connection between her disappearance and Jason Young's disappearance. That's when it hit me. We know that Jason and MTB had a sexual relationship. What if he, she and Olivia are more than just connected; maybe they are *related*! It was just a hunch."

"A hunch from a song. It sure paid off!" Jerry was dumbfounded. The real truth was sitting under everyone's nose for decades but only Tomas was the one to figure it out. His facial expression turned from wonder to something dour. He looked around to see if anyone could hear them and when satisfied there was no one, he leaned even further toward Tomas. "Tom, look. You need to be very careful with this information. If this news gets out it is going to be met with a heavy backlash."

"What do you mean *if* this gets out?" Tomas responded. "I fully intend to report it when I get back to work."

"This will cause a big scandal Tom. I'm not sure you have enough to go with it yet."

Tomas read to Winston his own headline for the story. "Two missing persons connected to MTB are biologically father and daughter according to DNA evidence. How is that not a story?"

"Look, Tom, the bigger the story is the harder things fall," Jerry responded. "This news would have the potential to derail the presidential campaign of the Democratic front-runner. There are people in this town who if they get wind of what you are up to would do anything to stop you. And if they don't stop you, then they will do everything in their power to discredit you, dismiss you, hurt you. Not only does your story have to be air tight but you've got to be prepared for the backlash. I don't think we are there yet."

Tomas knew Jerry was trying to help him but his response was puzzling and not what he had expected. "I hear what you are saying but I still don't understand."

"Okay, first of all, Marjorie Midas wanted me to tell you directly that she wants you off the air a little bit longer," Jerry conceded. "That's a good thing. It buys us some time."

"Time for what?" Tomas asked almost incredulously.

"Time to develop your big story without having to worry about other newsroom assignments. But we also need more separation from your 'Chastity' scoop."

"What?" Tomas could not figure out Winston's logic at all.

Jerry smiled. "There's an old question sometimes asked in DC media circles about whether the Watergate scandal that brought down President Richard Nixon would have been exposed had he been a Democrat and not a Republican. I mean DC is 95 percent Democrat. Mainstream media journalists in this town are pretty close to 100 percent."

"I'm sorry Jerry. Where are you going with this?"

"Remember the Hunter Biden laptop scandal?" Winston asked.

"Lachlan and I were talking about it just the other day," Tomas confirmed.

"And remember how it was censored just about everywhere?"

Tomas nodded. Of course he did.

"Well one of the reasons was because the story broke in the *New York Post*, which everyone knew was a Trump-leaning newspaper. That not only raised suspicions in the liberal media but it gave many journalists an excuse to ignore it. I don't want that happening to you. When you break this story I want people to not only watch but also to have no excuses to *not* pay attention. If this comes out too closely after the Chastity story people might conclude that you are really just a lackey for Reverend Rivers with your own political agenda."

"I have no political agenda."

"I know that and you know that but they'll say you *do* in an effort to discredit you."

"Who is 'they'?"

Jerry pulled himself all the way back into his chair. He was no longer concerned about being overheard. "I have a friend. Retired Secret Service Agent. Likes to tell me stories about the workings of the 'shadow government' that he says he personally witnessed in this town."

"Shadow government?"

"Yeah, except I don't see it as a 'shadow government'. I see it more as a 'Praetorian Guard'."

The 'Praetorian Guard' was seen by many historians as the real power center of the Roman Empire. Un-elected and un-accountable to anyone but the emperor, the Praetorian Guard believed that their duty was to do anything to protect the emperor and in doing so to protect their own power as well, even if it was to the detriment of the Roman Republic and its people.

Jerry continued with his analogy. "DC is a strange town. We think people come here to help others, but many come here with motivations that are not pure. Power. Fame. Greed. Influence. People crave those things in this town. In fact they can't live without them. Why do you think they are so terrified of populist movements filled with people uttering phrases like 'term limits' and 'drain the swamp'. They like the swamp. They *need* the swamp. So many in power here stay in power until they are in their 80s or even 90s because if they leave and go back to a normal way of life, they fear they will die of political malnourishment."

"They'll die without DC. Seems a bit extreme, doesn't it?"

Jerry shrugged. "If your theory about MTB is right then it means that she had become so intoxicated by returning to power in DC that she was willing to lie to her only daughter about being her biological mother. She needed to be back here that badly."

"Never thought about it like that," Tomas said pondering the gravity of what Jerry just told him.

"Yes, but here is the thing with that. Many here are also determined to protect the status quo and to accomplish that they need help. They need others who will help protect them and protect *it* so that nothing ever changes—people who will make sure that their elected officials are safe from scrutiny no matter what Americans really want." Jerry then pointed at Tomas. "But someone like you who is willing to expose them—you are a threat. You won't believe the lengths they will go to silence you. You need to be prepared for that."

Tomas knew that Jerry knew DC and he probably did know what he was talking about. Tomas just didn't want to sit on the story any longer.

Jerry could sense his frustration. "Look! This is your story. You are the only one who knows this besides me and I'm not talking. We have the liberty here to break the right story at the right time. I can work behind the scenes in the meantime to help clear the way. If you're going to break this story, let's make it *big*!"

"Okay," Tomas reluctantly agreed. He didn't know what more information he could dig up but he would try. Tomas also wanted to tell Jerry in confidence about his meeting with the chef, but they were interrupted by another man.

"Tom! Tom Stein! I cannot believe I'm getting to see you again."

Approaching their table right out of the blue was Gay Jay.

CHAPTER 29

"I'M SORRY TO INTERRUPT but I so loved your story on me and saw you sitting there and just wanted to tell you that," Jay said with a big smile. He then pointed at Jerry. "Who is your friend?"

"Jerry Winston, meet Jay." Tomas then looked up at Jay. "You know I don't even know your last name?"

Jay shook Jerry's hand and then looked back over at Tomas. "It's Smith."

"Your last name is 'Smith'?" Tomas asked clearly surprised by the answer.

"Yeah, I get that a lot. Probably why I don't use it very often," Jay conceded. "Just call me 'Gay Jay'," he said looking back at Winston.

"Oh, you are that comedian!" Jerry responded perking up a bit. "I saw your cable special. Very funny stuff!" Jerry looked over at Tomas. "You did a story on this guy?"

"It was an "Industrial Art" piece. One of my first ones at DC-3."

"Wow, I'm going to have to look that one up online," Jerry responded enthusiastically.

"Tom did a great job on the story!" Jay confirmed. "I got *a ton* of compliments about it. May I sit down?" And then without giving anyone time to say yes or no, Jay sat down in a chair at the table and continued talking to Tomas. "You know a friend of mind told me you could have really hung me out to dry with that story, but you didn't Tom. I do appreciate that."

"How would your friend know that?" Tomas asked.

"Know what?" Jay responded surprised.

"That I could have hung you out to dry with the story?"

"He just knows me. I guess he was surprised I did the interview at all." Jay Smith, aka Gay Jay changed the topic. "Tell me about your friend. What does he do?"

"He's a consultant and he was the one who recruited me to DC."

Jay looked over at Winston with an excited look. "Did he?"

Winston nodded back at Jay. "Yes, and I can already tell it was a good decision."

"I'll say!" Jay added nodding in agreement. "I'm so happy you brought him here. He's great!"

"Look gentlemen, I have to go," Winston offered. "I'll pay the bill at the front. Tom, thank you for joining me for lunch. Nice to meet you Jay."

Tomas hadn't had the chance yet to tell Jerry about this conversation with the chef. That would have to wait. "What are you doing in town Jay?"

"Just got into town. Love the Thai food here. I have a crash pad here and I have a gig in New York tomorrow so I thought I would just take the train up."

"Aren't they supposed to have a major snowstorm up there tomorrow?"

Jay shrugged. "Haven't called the show off yet. Hope they do though. The person who helps take care of my cat is sick and there isn't anyone else available to check on her."

"You have a cat?"

"I do. She's a Himalayan and her name is Gaydar."

Tomas laughed. "Of course her name is Gaydar. Look, I'm off tomorrow. Would you like me to check in on your cat?"

"Would you? That would be great!" Jay pulled a handbag of sorts off of the floor. Tomas hadn't noticed that he had been carrying a handbag. Jay then shuffled through the bag until he produced a key. "Here's a spare key. I'll text you the address. I leave her food on a stand right by her bowl. You'll have no trouble finding it, and of course check her water bowl."

"Of course, but no litter cleaning, right?" Tomas asked.

Jay gave him a sly look and nodded *no*. "I have to go but I didn't want to leave without telling you 'thank you' for your story on me. I never knew I was so interesting!"

"Sure you did," Tomas replied with a smile.

Jay smiled back, picked up his bag, waved goodbye at Tomas and walked away.

Tomas sat at the table and then thought of Prudence Young. He had promised to tell her if he had any new developments on Jason's investigation but he wasn't ready to do that just yet. How do you tell someone that her son fathered a child she never knew about who is now herself missing and likely dead? How can you delicately break the news to her that her son's body sat in a freezer for more than two decades before being dumped in the Potomac River? Tomas went over 1,000 scripts he would use to tell Prudence about what happened to her son and none of them turned out right. He resolved to let her know before his news story broke, but not now. He simply could not find the words.

He then tried to fill Jerry Winston in on his conversation with the chef by phone but got his voicemail and did not leave a message.

As he drove home to his apartment Tomas was stuck. Jerry wanted more 'meat' to the story but how? Once home, as day drifted into night, Tomas could not come up with a practical way to push the story forward. He had what he had. He thought it was enough. He was like a writer staring at a blank piece of paper with no more words to type. He would have to sleep on it.

Winston would call him back the next morning. "I saw you called me yesterday. What's up?"

"Jerry, Gay Jay interrupted us before I had a chance to tell you about the chef."

"The chef?" Jerry responded perplexed.

Tomas told Jerry the story of his chance encounter with the twin brother of Shorty Curtis. Jerry was astounded.

"So let me get this straight," he told Tomas. "You somehow accidentally run into the twin brother of the man who helped conceal the body of Jason Young?"

"That's what happened."

"Incredible!" Jerry said. "How did you recognize him?"

"Olivia showed me a picture of him from years ago. She thought at the time that he was Shorty, but somehow I knew it wasn't. When I saw the chef at the restaurant I thought to myself *that's him!* I told you I had a thing for faces."

"Amazing!" Jerry concluded.

"Somehow I feel as if I was meant to tell this story Jerry."

"Well, I talked to Marjorie. She wanted you off another month. I convinced her to pare that down to two more weeks. See what more you can get before then. In the meantime I'm going to have to butter Marjorie up a bit."

"Butter her up?"

"Tom, you want to break a story on DC-3's *The Industry Tonight* that could end the campaign of the Democratic front-runner for the nomination for president. All signs now point to MTB winning the New Hampshire primary. If you bring her down then you will also boost Rivers up. Just like with Trump I suspect Marjorie will resist that at first. I need some time to convince her that breaking this story would be the right thing to do."

"So you are going to tell her what I have on MTB?" Tomas surmised.

"No, I'll be discreet. She won't want to know the details anyway. She only needs to know that something big involving MTB is about to break and we're the ones who need to break it. It would be helpful, however, if we had more."

"More like what?" Tomas asked looking for some direction from Winston that might assuage his growing frustration.

"Well for example, we both think Alvarez killed Jason Young, but we don't know that. We only know that he helped clean up the scene of the crime."

"Who else could have killed him then?" Tomas asked.

"I don't know. Maybe Jason actually did commit suicide? Or maybe it was a freak accident?"

"Alvarez is the only person alive we know of who could answer that question. Do you want me to reach out to him?"

"No!" Jerry replied in a slightly alarmed tone. "Too dangerous right now. Let me think about that and I'll get back to you."

Tomas realized that Jerry was right about Jason's death. He thought he knew what happened to Jason Young, but he really didn't know what happened to him. It was a Saturday and Tomas was restless. How could he find out the answer? There was only one way. He ignored Jerry's advice, pulled out the business card Alvarez had given him the day police found Jason's car, and texted it.

"This is Tom Stein. I know what happened to Jason Young."

Tom sent it and thought for a second about what he would text next. "I want to ..." That's when a reply came back. It was an address and nothing more, but Tomas knew that was the place he needed to be now. He grabbed his coat and keys and headed out to his car.

The address was a dive bar in northwest DC, and when Tomas arrived, Alvarez was one of only a few inside. It was apparent that he had been there a while and had already knocked back more than a few drinks. This was the first time Tomas had seen him since the riots and he looked different. He was dirtier and unshaven, and of course drunk. Tomas made a point to put his phone ringer on silent. He would have one shot at the truth with Alvarez and he did not want to be disturbed.

"Go ahead. What do you think happened to Jason Young?" Alvarez queried.

"I think you killed him."

CHAPTER 30

"THE ONLY PERSON I HAVE EVER KILLED in my entire life was Shorty," Alvarez responded looking down into his glass of whiskey on the rocks. "Saddest day of my life. Shorty had his issues but he was a good man. A tad weak at times perhaps, but he was a good man."

Tomas decided to focus on Shorty's death for now since he already had Alvarez talking about it. "Why did you kill him?"

"Bizarre, isn't it?" Alvarez said. "Pulled him over for a DUI traffic stop and all of a sudden he jumps out of his car and charges me. It was all I could do to get a shot off before he tackled me."

"You and I both know that's not exactly what happened," Tomas countered.

Alvarez looked up from his drink. "Off the record?"

The last thing Tomas wanted to do right now was go 'off the record' but Alvarez was an experienced media pro. He was the only person alive with direct knowledge of what happened to Jason Young, and Tomas wanted to know what Alvarez knew. "Off the record."

"I pulled Shorty over to warn him."

"Warn him about what?"

"Word on the street was that he had become mentally unstable, was drinking too much, and was hinting at some things which got the wrong people upset."

"Like what?" Tomas asked.

"Like he knew who had killed the guy whose car had just been fished out of the Potomac and it was a big deal," Alvarez said pounding his index finger into the table as if to accentuate his point. "People were getting nervous. He needed to stop for his own good. I needed to warn him about that."

Alvarez took another sip of his scotch. "He wasn't answering my calls or returning my texts and so I decided to drive over to his place. Then out of nowhere I see him driving the other way and he's driving so erratically that he almost hit my car! Damn! I'm thinking he's driving drunk so now I've got to get him off the road before he gets pulled over or kills somebody."

Another sip of whiskey. "I knew he was angry at me. Maybe he even thought I had ruined his life. But it never occurred to me that when he saw me he would charge at me like that. His eyes were crazy. I thought he was crazy. I knew he was angry at me but not like that. I pulled my gun and tried to shoot him in the leg but he ducked as if to try to tackle me and I shot him in the head. Oh man!"

Alvarez began to tear up. He was remarkably coherent for a drunk guy but he was clearly getting emotional. "Do you know that is the first time I have ever fired a weapon in the field as a police officer. First time. First time." Alvarez's voice softened as he took another sip of his whiskey.

"How could Shorty have known who killed Jason? He only helped you get rid of the body."

Alvarez straightened up quickly and peered at Tomas. "How do you know he helped me get rid of the body? Only Shorty and I knew that and he's dead."

"You're confirming that he did help you get rid of the body." Off the record or not, Tomas knew his questioning was getting Alvarez a bit rattled.

"How do you know that?"

"Like you said, Shorty was talking to some of the wrong people and it would appear that he said quite a bit."

"I hate reporters!" Alvarez blurted out dismissively while taking another sip of his drink.

"So how did Shorty know who killed Jason Young?"

Alvarez slumped a bit. Tomas was hoping this was information that Alvarez just wanted to get off of his chest and he would conclude that now was the time to do it off the record. Tomas pressed him again. "How did he know?"

"Because I told him!" Alvarez said in an almost angry tone.

"Told him what?"

"I told him that Marilyn killed Jason."

"What?" Tomas said, his mouth now gaping wide open. That was not the news he expected to hear at all.

Alvarez seemed annoyed in his drunken state but also a little relieved. It was a terrible secret he had been holding inside for a very, very long time. "It was an accident. She didn't mean to do it."

"Were you there when it happened?"

"No," Alvarez conceded. "She called me right after it happened. She could barely talk she was so overcome with emotion. There was no way it was intentional. She didn't have that in her."

"What happened?"

Alvarez sighed. "She and Jason would take his car down to an isolated spot near the Potomac to have sex. They were like teenagers doing it in the back of his car. One night she says Jason takes her down there and admits that he loves her but that he has to leave her and go back to his wife and leave town. I guess that infuriated her. I mean have you ever seen her temper?"

"I've heard about it," Tomas confirmed.

"In any case Marilyn told me that she became so furious that she picked up a sharp rock and threw it at him. Hit him right in the neck. Must have sliced an artery or something. By the time I got there he had pretty much bled out. He was dead."

"And that's when you called Shorty."

"I needed to pay attention to Marilyn. I mean she was a wreck! I was afraid she was suicidal. And she was also covered with Jason's blood from trying to stop his bleeding. I was going to take her home and clean her up and keep an eye on her while Shorty cleaned up the mess at the scene. I trusted Shorty. I knew he would help."

"And keep it all under wraps," Tomas added.

"Shorty never once let me down. I knew I could trust him. And to be completely honest with you I was kind of in love with Marilyn at the time. We had struck up a close relationship while I worked her security detail but she was in love with Jason. She didn't mean to kill him. I felt it was my job to protect her. She knew that too and that's probably why she called me. But to do that I needed Shorty's help."

"That's an awfully big secret to keep all this time about a very powerful person."

Alvarez shook his head. "She told me that the next day after she had calmed down a bit that she was leaving DC and going back to Minnesota. Never in a million years did I think she would come back to DC. But she did, and when she did she reached out to me right away. She knew I was the only one who really knew what happened. She had to know that she could trust me to keep our secret. I told her she could."

"But why did her daughter have to die?" Tomas of course didn't know for a fact that Olivia Zhang was MTB's daughter but he figured Alvarez might confirm it for him if Tomas pretended to know more about it than he actually did. Again, he did not get the answer from Alvarez that he expected.

"What do you mean?" Alvarez looked at Tomas quizzically. "Marilyn never had kids."

Tomas gave Alvarez a once over. Could he really not know that Olivia was MTB's daughter? Or was it even remotely possible that Olivia was not MTB's daughter? He decided to see if he could 'play' Alvarez hoping he would give up more information by using a bit of deception. "Olivia Zhang was MTB's and Jason Young's biological daughter."

It was Alvarez's turn to be shocked. "How do you know that!?"

"DNA testing."

Alvarez stared at Tomas as he thought to himself for a moment. He knew from watching the news that Tom and Olivia had a sexual relationship and that Tom had connections to the Young family. It made sense to Alvarez that Tom would have access to the DNA of Olivia Zhang and Jason Young. He further reasoned to himself that Marilyn had spent so much time out campaigning that Tom could have gotten her DNA from practically anywhere. "They had a love child; is that what you're saying?"

Tomas was stumped. As close as he was to MTB, Alvarez really did not know about that? "You seem surprised."

"I had no idea. She must have given birth in Minnesota. I had no idea she was even pregnant."

"Do you think she told Jason she was pregnant the night she killed him?"

"I honestly do not know. I wonder if she knew she was pregnant. You're absolutely sure about this?"

Tomas nodded his head. He wasn't of course absolutely sure, but it was still the only answer to him that made any sense. "That's the story I'm going with."

Alvarez perked up again. The nature of the conversation seemed to be sobering him up. "Wait, you can't report that. We're off the record!"

"I'm not reporting anything you said," Tomas assured him. "But the DNA evidence—that's rock solid."

"You can't report that! It will destroy her candidacy!" Alvarez said while growing increasingly alarmed.

"But it's the truth. That's what I do. I report the truth."

"Yeah right," Alvarez responded dismissively.

"It will be the first layer of the onion," Tomas continued.

"The what?"

"The first layer of the onion," Tomas repeated. "That's how investigative reporting works. You report what you know at first. That's the first layer of the onion. And then someone sees your story and feeds you more information, and so you do another story and peel off another layer." Tomas was moving his hands as if to imitate peeling an onion. "And then more people come forward. Another story, another layer peeled off, and then another and then another until you finally get to the stinking rotten core of the truth. I wonder where this onion will take me?"

"You'll destroy her if you do that. You will kill Marilyn's campaign and all she's ever wanted," Alvarez said pointing at Tomas.

"I'll report the truth," Tomas replied confidently.

"No you won't," Alvarez shot back. "They won't let you!"

"They?" Tomas repeated back. "'They'? And who exactly is that?

CHAPTER 31

IF ALVAREZ HAD ANY COBWEBS left over from the whiskey that he was still sipping he didn't show it. The nature of the conversation had focused him completely on Tomas and what he was telling him. "You work for Marjorie Midas, don't you?"

"I do."

"That is your first mistake," Alvarez said semi-chuckling to himself.

"Marjorie Midas is part of '*They*'?"

"I'm not saying that," Alvarez said while shaking his head. "Let me ask you a question. Did you ever ask yourself why all the people involved in politics in this town, the lawmakers, the lobbyists, the lawyers, the consultants and even the media personalities—did you ever ask yourself why every last one of them is rich? I mean you are sitting in one of the wealthiest areas in the country and that just so happens to also be our nation's capital, a place which produces virtually nothing. Ever wonder about that?"

"Not really," Tomas conceded, but he could see Alvarez's point.

"And if you were one of them. If you had all this wealth and power and prestige and influence for doing virtually nothing at all, what would it be worth to you to protect it?"

"I suppose a great deal."

"Right," Alvarez agreed. "So let me tell you a story. On election night

2016 I was at the Javits Center in New York doing security for Marilyn. I was working for DC police at the time but I was able to take some personal time to be there. It was going to be a historic night. The Democrats had chosen the building for their presidential election celebration in part because it had a glass ceiling, and everyone thought that night that Hillary Clinton would 'break through' it to become the first female President of the United States."

"Didn't quite work out that way," Tomas interjected.

"No it did not. *They* thought the election was in the bag." Alvarez made a point of using his fingers to form parenthesis signs every time he uttered the word *They*. "Trump winning was a complete shock to them. Suddenly everything *They* had counted on was in jeopardy. Something had to be done! Look what happened next. The FBI Director uses an interview with the President-Elect in an attempt to frame him. Audio is leaked of Trump's choice for National Security Agency Director having a perfectly legitimate conversation with his Russian adversary which brings a media firestorm nonetheless. *They* knew that if he got into that position that he would blow the lid off the NSA and that *They* might be exposed. Then *They* took an allegation of Russian collusion with the Trump campaign that *They* knew was completely bogus. *They* even managed to get a Special Counsel probe launched which was designed to keep Trump on his heels."

Alvarez took the last sip of his drink, got out of his chair and walked up to the bar. Tomas hadn't noticed before but the bartender had left the whole bottle of whiskey at the edge of the bar just for him. Alvarez raised the bottle as if to offer to pour one for Tomas. He shook his head no. Alvarez came back to the table with drink in hand and finished his story. "Remember what that Senator from New York said after Trump was elected—about how stupid Trump was to criticize the intelligence agencies?"

Tomas did. "He said, 'Let me tell you, if you take on the intelligence community, they have six ways from Sunday to get back at you.'"

"Ah, a rare moment of clarity from a political insider," Alvarez continued. "All the phony Trump scandals. All the worthless investigations. *They* were going to make things as difficult as *They* could for Trump. *They* also realized that *They* had miscalculated in 2016 and were going to make doubly sure Trump didn't win again in 2020. And then came COVID and *They* had their opportunity."

"You're saying *They* brought us COVID?" Tomas asked mimicking Alvarez's hand gestures.

"No," Alvarez shook his head smiling. "*They* aren't that good! But *They* did take full advantage. *They* convinced everyone that more mail-in voting was the right thing to do during the pandemic while planning to take full advantage of that to achieve their ends. *They* convinced their billionaire friends to help out by paying big money to send people to help out at the polls and do whatever they could to make sure there were no surprises this time. *They* even did everything they could to make sure *They* had their chosen candidate against Trump. Maybe not the best person for the job, but the one person *They* knew could beat him. And *They* pulled it off."

"You're not saying Trump actually won the 2020 election?" Tomas asked wondering if Alvarez really knew what he was talking about or was he just spinning some massive conspiracy theory.

"No I'm not, but I'll give Trump credit. *They* did all they could to stop him and he still almost pulled it off. Think about it. Not one single Republican member of the House lost re-election in 2020. Never happened before. The only reason Republicans lost the Senate was because of run-off elections where Trump wasn't on the ballot. He is also only the second incumbent president in history to get more votes in his re-election bid and still lose the election. The last president to do that ran again four years later and won! I think Trump lost, but I can certainly see why Trump thought he had really won."

"So this *They* ... they're Democrats?" Tomas asked.

"No, more like political agnostics. Sometimes *They* throw their muscle behind Democrats; sometimes Republicans. Whoever helps them most to achieve their goals."

"And how exactly do you know *They* exist?" Tomas asked.

"Because sometimes they ask for my help." Alvarez was done with the hands/quotation marks thing realizing it had become more annoying than illuminating. "And if they can thwart the President of the United States, just imagine what they can do to a piss-ant TV news reporter like you who works for a barely watched local TV station."

"Is that a threat?"

"No, Tom, it's a warning," Alvarez replied almost pleading. "Look, you are clearly smart and good at what you do. All you have to do is be like every other reporter in this town and go cover meaningless stories like the British Royals arguing with each other and you'll have a very bright and lucrative future here. But I'm telling you from first-hand knowledge that powerful people have too much invested right now in Marilyn to allow you to do your onion thing and destroy her politically. If Rivers is the Republican's guy then they are not going to let him win the White House. Way too risky. Marilyn is the safe choice and that makes her their girl. Whatever happened twenty-five years ago should be left in the past. Do the best thing for her and you."

"You know what Lieutenant," Tomas said while getting up from his chair. "I don't buy it. I think you still have a thing for MTB and want to help her get what she wants. I'm standing in her way. *They* Tomas said mimicking Alvarez's use of quotation marks, "… are really *You*. You can threaten me all you want but it won't work."

Tomas began to walk away from the table when Alvarez yelled after him, "I'm telling you Marjorie Midas won't let you run your story."

Tomas turned around, looked at Alvarez and shrugged. "Then I guess I'll peel my onion somewhere else."

As Tomas walked outside and approached his car he noticed what seemed like an unmarked police car pulling away from his. It was one of those Dodge Chargers that no actual Dodge Charger enthusiast would buy for himself.

Tomas got into his car and called Jerry using his car's hands-free system. He got his voicemail. "Jerry, it's Tom. I know you told me to stay away from Alvarez but he confessed to me that MTB killed Jason accidentally in a fit of rage. Give me a call. Let's talk next steps."

As he began to drive off Tomas realized that he had completely forgotten something, and that something was Gay Jay's cat.

Jay's crash pad was not very far from the DC-3 Broadcast Plaza. Jay was staying in a hotel where the suites were known to be pretty nice including having full kitchens. Tomas took the elevator up to Jay's room and began to put the key in the door when he heard a commotion inside. What was up with the cat? He turned the key quickly fearing the cat was destroying the room and Gay Jay would blame him for it. He then he hurriedly opened the door.

A look of utter shock and disbelief came over his face. "What in the world?"

CHAPTER 32

"YOU'RE GAY!" TOMAS EXCLAIMED in utter shock as the Reverend Governor attempted to put his underwear back on. Jay did the same.

"You're gay?" Tomas asked, again stunned. "You, the Reverend Governor Rivers is gay?" Tomas realized Rivers was having a hard time getting his underwear on because of being watched, so Tomas turned around and faced the door. "This is absolutely 100 percent crazy. The Reverend Governor, the front-runner for the Republican nomination for the President of the United States, is gay."

"You can turn around now Tom," Rivers told him. Tomas turned around to see him putting on a shirt as well. Jay seemed content to just hang out in his underpants. "Are you okay Tom?"

"Is what I'm seeing what I think I'm seeing?"

"Yes sir," Rivers replied with a subtle smile.

"You're gay?" Tomas repeated still not quite processing the scene in front of him.

"Yes, Tom. I'm gay," the Reverend Governor confirmed. "You don't seem too comfortable with that though."

"It's not that I'm uncomfortable," Tomas responded exasperated and not wanting to sound homophobic. "It's just that you're a black minister; you're a Republican; and you were a college football lineman for God's sake. Not a lot of those types of people tend to also check the gay box."

"Tom," Rivers said trying to calm Tomas down.

Tomas cut him off. "You were in the military!"

That's when Jay decided to pipe in. "They didn't ask and he didn't tell!"

"I mean I had absolutely no idea that there was even the possibility you were gay." Tomas pointed over at Jay. "Him I get, but *you*? Did this relationship all start at my interview with Jay?"

"No," Jay interjected again. "We've been seeing each other for a couple of years now. It's why I moved to Chicago from LA and now have this place here." Gay Jay then broke into a song lyric of sorts, "Because I think we're going to be here a while!" He then broke into a wry smile. "Like four more years?"

"Stop measuring the White House drapes," Big Ben admonished him.

"Wait!" Tomas said suddenly looking at Jay. "Aren't you supposed to be in New York?"

"They canceled my show due to the snowstorm. I texted you not to come over."

Tomas pulled his phone from his pocket. There was Jay's text. He had sent it while Tomas was talking with Alvarez. "How does no one know about you two?" Tomas asked shrugging.

Jay answered again. "Because we're discreet about it. We don't see each other that often but we make time, like the night you interviewed me."

"So that was planned?"

"Oh no!" Jay insisted. "Ben had no idea you were coming to interview me. I hadn't had a chance to tell him about it. But when you told him about it in the bathroom he wanted to see the interview in person. Ben told me afterward that he thought me doing the interview was a bad idea because I said some things I probably shouldn't have and the story would not be received well. But you used discretion. It came out great!"

Rivers chimed in. "That's why I interviewed with you for the Chastity story. I saw what you did with Jay. I knew I could trust you to tell it straight without trying to be sensational."

Tomas thought about that. It all made sense now as to why Rivers gave the Chastity story to him. "You have to admit this is all a bit strange. I mean look at you two," he said pointing at Rivers and then Jay. "You're like twice his age and twice his size."

"… with about ten times the melanin!" Jay interjected smiling.

"I didn't mean it that way," Tomas responded, now trying to sound like he was neither homophobic or racist.

Rivers had sat down on the couch and Jay was now sitting on the bed, so Tomas sat in a nearby chair. "Why have you kept your sexuality a secret?" he asked Rivers.

"I didn't want anyone to know. None of their business."

"And it's a potential political liability?" Tomas asked.

"That's occurred to me but that's really not it. I just didn't want people to use my sexuality to define me, because it doesn't define me."

"What do you mean?"

Rivers sighed. "I admit I struggled with being attracted to men when I was young. It didn't seem right to me. Why would a loving God make me this way? Why couldn't I just be straight like all my friends? One day a minister catches me praying about it in church. He comes up and sees I'm clearly troubled and asks me what's wrong. I was afraid to tell him about it but I did. And you know what he told me?"

Tomas shook his head no.

"He told me that none of us can know God's plan for us. That each of us is created by him from a sort of mold-able clay. The material is his but the shape and substance are ours. That we may be born black or white, straight or gay, but that the greatest gift God has given us is free will. He gives us the clay and we get to mold it. We get to choose. I choose not to let things that are truly insignificant about me determine who I am."

"And that extends to your conservative politics?"

"Sure. I mean for years I wasn't political at all until I saw firsthand how politicians can really hurt people. I wanted to help them instead. Conservatism spoke to me because it frees people to be what they truly want to be. Do you know what white liberals like to call blacks?" Rivers asked.

Tomas had no idea where the Reverend Governor was going with this so he just shrugged.

"They call us 'marginalized'," Rivers said looking over at Gay Jay. "Do you know what white liberals like to call gay people?"

"Don't you dare use the 'LG' word," Jay cautioned him.

"They like to call us 'marginalized'. Let me ask you a question Tom. In the short time you have known me is there anything 'marginalized' about me?"

"No sir." Tomas was starting to get his point.

"No sir!" Rivers repeated emphatically. "That's because 'marginalized' is code for a type of pitiful inferiority. I am 'marginalized' by a repressive American society which of course means I deserve their liberal pity and of course I need their liberal help. It is white, liberal, paternalistic hubris. Well I say 'No thank you' because as long as God gives me free will to choose my own path in the greatest and free-ist nation in the world, that means that I have the opportunity and ability to help myself. That's why I'm a conservative."

"You've clearly made some different choices," Tomas concurred.

"I have. And maybe I've made some bad choices along the way. But what's most important is that they were my choices, not the opinion of someone else about what my choices *should* be."

"So do you ever plan on 'coming out'?" Tomas asked Rivers.

"Maybe one day but not today. And I know what you learned tonight will remain our secret."

"I'm not going to out you Reverend. That's your call."

"And I assure Tom that if I win this, I am not going be a black president and I'm not going to be a gay president. I am going to be 'The' President of the United States."

Tomas understood. "By the way," he asked looking around. "Where is Gaydar?"

After petting the cat Tomas left and drove by the DC-3 Broadcast Plaza on his way home. He missed being in the newsroom. He had always been a creature of habit and drove home his usual way from the station. The drive involved passing through an industrial area just off the Beltway where Tomas noticed flashing lights in his rear-view mirror. "My God what now?" he thought to himself as he pulled over. Tomas reached for his registration in his glove compartment when he saw the officer in an otherwise unmarked car get out of the driver's side door with a gun drawn.

"Driver, get out of the car *now!*" he commanded.

"What is going on?" Tomas said to himself startled.

"Driver, out of the car *now* with your hands in the air!"

Tomas slowly exited the car with his hands in the air. He had no idea what was happening but he wasn't about to get shot for not complying with the officer's commands.

"Driver, get on your knees. Hands behind your head!" The officer yelled at him with his gun pointed straight at him. Tomas complied. At that moment someone else caught his eye. He jumped up from in front of his car and grabbed Tomas from behind, and then placed a cloth over his mouth and nose. The smell was sweet and intensely overwhelming. Suddenly his muscles felt weak, and he began to lose consciousness. The next thing he knew someone was throwing water in his face.

CHAPTER 33

JERRY WINSTON WAS IN HIS HOTEL ROOM when a sobbing Nan called him the next morning with the news. Jerry had known Nan for a long time and could never remember her being so upset.

Tom Stein had been found dead in a warehouse not far from the DC-3 studios. Someone had discovered his body early that morning after noticing his abandoned car parked outside with a door open. They called police after finding his body on the ground in a pool of blood with a gunshot wound to the head. The gun was a few inches from his outstretched hand.

Police had initially ruled it a suicide even though two shots had been fired. They speculated that the first shot was a practice shot so that Tomas could fire the second one with certainty. Gun residue had been found on his hand. There was no suicide note but also no sign of a struggle.

Jerry shook with a combination of deep sadness and incredible rage. He had gotten Tom's voicemail the night before and tried to call him but hung up when his call went straight to Tom's voicemail. He knew that Tom had not committed suicide and that his death had to have been connected in some way to whatever he had told Alvarez, and also what Alvarez had told him.

Winston was conflicted. He was so angry that he wanted to do something to make things right. More than that, he wanted outright revenge against whoever did this.

But he also knew that at the moment he could not do anything. If someone was willing to kill Tom Stein to keep him silent there was no telling what else they were willing to do. Jerry had a wife and son in college and daughter about to go to college. They needed him and Jerry wasn't about to put him or them in mortal danger either. He would retreat back to Philadelphia for now and stream DC-3's newscasts from his home while he tried to think of something; *anything* he could do.

Far from assuaging his anger, time only seemed to intensify it as he watched the headlines on DC-3's newscasts unfold over the days and weeks and months on his computer.

"Good evening, I'm Ron Stone from your election night headquarters where DC-3 can now project that Marilyn Taylor-Brown will be the next President of the United States and the first woman to hold the office. The key state in her victory ironically was her opponent's home state of Illinois, which went to Taylor-Brown by a small margin."

Sometimes those headlines would leave Jerry distraught not knowing what events were connected to Tom's death and which may not be.

"Good evening. I'm Ron Stone. We have breaking news on this December morning from DC's north side. That's where police say the body of a woman who they believe to be Olivia Zhang has been recovered from a shallow grave. Police were led to the scene by Bobby Ray Gibbons, also known as the Sunrise Strangler, a serial killer who would target young women joggers early in the morning. Zhang is believed to be the first of his four victims in all."

Sometimes a headline would make Jerry shake into a deep rage he had never really felt before.

"Welcome back. I'm Ron Stone. A surprise announcement this morning from the office of President-Elect Marilyn Taylor-Brown. Her new press secretary will be Manuel Alvarez, the former police lieutenant who shot and killed a man after a traffic stop last year. Taylor-Brown's office said that she understood how some in the African-American community would object to the appointment, but that Alvarez had been cleared in the shooting and she was confident about his innocence and his ability to do the job."

Sometimes a headline would make Jerry question whether the dark forces he had at times been warned about were manipulating the process.

"Good evening. I'm Ron Stone. The head of the Elections Office in Cook County Illinois now admits there were voting irregularities with both mail-in and absentee ballots. Cook County Clerk Helen Burns concedes that mistakes were made in both admitting and tabulating the ballots. She insisted the mistakes would not be enough to change the outcome of any race including the race for President. Illinois was a critical state in Democrat Marilyn Taylor-Brown's electoral win over Republican Benjamin Rivers. Video from a conservative-leaning news website showed unmarked boxes with ballots inside being unloaded from a van into an area near a room where votes were being tabulated on election night. However, election officials say there is no evidence those boxes were ever opened or counted."

Sometimes the headline would shock Jerry right out of the blue.

"Good evening. I'm Ron Stone. In a political shocker former Illinois Governor Ben Rivers has come out as being gay. The surprising news came when the former Republican candidate for President announced that he's leaving politics to focus on his ministry, and that he also plans to marry Jay Smith, the comedian better known as Gay Jay. The news came as a big surprise to many in the Republican party. Republican Senator Owen Evans, himself an ordained minister who in the past opposed gay marriage, told reporters he would preside over the marriage ceremony if Rivers would consider running for President again."

Sometimes a headline would make Jerry suspect how far some would go to hide the truth.

"Welcome back, I'm Ron Stone. Police are investigating a shooting in Richmond that left a well-known jeweler dead. Issac Stein was shot to death at his store on Hull Street Road in Richmond. Police say two armed robbers shot and killed him when he surprised them during the robbery. Stein was the father of former DC-3 reporter Tom Stein who committed suicide last year. Stein has said publicly that he did not believe his son committed suicide and had recently committed millions of his own dollars to find answers about what happened to his son."

Jerry Winston saw it all unfolding before his eyes and knew that those responsible would get away with everything they had done unless something was done. He felt like a coward hiding out in Philadelphia. He did not know how, but some way and somehow he was going to make sure that the truth was told. He would find a way to expose the corruption surrounding MTB and her election.

He felt he owed that much to Tom. And in his state of incredible rage, he also felt a higher purpose toward his own country. Something had to be done and he was the only one who could do it because he was the only one who knew the truth! The country needed to know it too.

He had to do something, but what could he possibly do? How could he alone overcome this overwhelming tidal wave of Fake News'?

www.ingramcontent.com/pod-product-compliance
Lightning Source LLC
Chambersburg PA
CBHW051105030726
47504CB00006B/1799